The Verdict

C. J. Cooper

CONSTABLE

CONSTABLE

First published in Great Britain in 2021 by Constable

1 3 5 7 9 10 8 6 4 2

Copyright © C. J. Cooper 2021

The moral right of the author has been asserted.

A CIP catalogue record for this book is
available from the British Library.

ISBN 978-4721-2969-7

Typeset in Minion by SX Composing DTP, Rayleigh, Essex
Printed and bound in Great Britain by Clays Ltd, Elcograf S.p.A.

Papers used by Constable are from well-managed forests
and other responsible sources.

C. J. Cooper grew up in a small village in South Wales before moving to London as a student. She graduated with a degree in Ancient History and Egyptology and spent seven months as a development worker in Nepal. On her return to Britain she joined the civil service, where she worked for 17 years on topics ranging from housing support to flooding. She hung up her bowler hat when she discovered that she much preferred writing about psychotic killers to ministerial speeches. She lives in London with her husband and two cats.

Follow C. J. Cooper on Twitter @CJCooper_author.

Praise for C. J. Cooper:

'I loved this book – tightly plotted, edge-of-seat gripping'
Sophie Hannah

'I raced through it – edgy, tense and wry'
Harriet Tyce

'I for one am terrified of the woman next door!'
Louise Candlish

'A dark, twisty, claustrophobic read'
Jo Spain

'Intricately plotted, this gripping thriller is written with great style'
Lisa Ballantyne

'Immensely entertaining, the growing sense of menace – of "where have I seen you before?" – grips and chills in equal measures'
Cath Weeks

'Intuitive and addictive'
Alison Bruce

'A fabulous, page-turning read!'
Caroline England

'An irresistible slow descent into darkness, with twist upon twist upon twist'
Catriona McPherson

By C. J. Cooper

The Book Club
The Verdict

For my sister, Lisa, with love

Prologue

I could feel him there, on the periphery of my vision. He must have been looking at me. Everyone was looking at me. But I didn't look back.

I kept my eyes on the clerk, corvid and Dickensian in his cloak and wig. From my perch in the jury box I towered above him, above all of them. It was borrowed power, the authority of office – I understood that. For all the theatre, I knew it wasn't a performance. That was why it had to be me standing there. Why it was always going to be me.

He said, 'Answer yes or no to the first question only,' and I felt a ripple of annoyance. I didn't need to be reminded how it went. I knew not to rush my lines.

'Have you reached a verdict on which you are all agreed?'

They knew the answer already. That was why we were all here. Just four days together, and this would be our last. I said, for the sake of the occasion, 'Yes.'

'And do you find the defendant, Ian Craig Nash, guilty or not guilty?'

I knew it wasn't fair to prolong the moment. I didn't hesitate. I said, 'Not guilty.'

Around me I felt the tension leave the bodies of the other jurors. The woman next to me gave a quiet sob.

And then the scream rang out across the courtroom.

Chapter 1

It landed on my doorstep on Valentine's Day, one of two envelopes among the pizza flyers and minicab cards. It looked official, so I opened the other envelope first: a letter from an estate agent, promising that properties in my road were in high demand. I wasn't disappointed, truly I wasn't. I had no expectations of Aidan any more. No doubt *she'd* be getting something, propped on a breakfast tray with croissants and a rosebud. She looked like the type who'd expect it.

I tore at the brown envelope carefully, and there it was, bulky text in Valentine's pink: *Jury Summons*. I wasn't sure whether I was daunted or excited. It was my first summons, and at thirty-six I supposed I'd got off lightly. I'd have to take time off work. Get Alan to cover. I checked the dates – two months away. If Easter fell then, he wouldn't be happy. I felt a shiver of *Schadenfreude*. Tough.

I misted the leaves of the dragon tree with a mixture of water and plant food – low dose for the winter months, just enough to keep them green and shiny – picked up my bag and left for the office.

One thing I've always liked about civil servants: they don't do Valentine's Day. I worked briefly in a magazine office when I was younger, and there would have been at least one ostentatious flower delivery, a minimum of three cards left on keyboards and hushed giggling in the kitchen. At Her Majesty's Revenue and Customs, no one seemed to see any significance in the date. Or perhaps they were being sensitive. I suppose that's possible, even for people who work on VAT policy.

Alan was at his desk already. He always gets in before me, though not nearly as early as he claims. Once or twice I've arrived before my usual time and he's turned up ten minutes before I'd normally be there, looking shocked and muttering some nonsense about delayed trains. He thinks, you see, that if he arrives before me, he's justified in sloping off at five on the dot, regardless of whatever shit is hitting the fan. It annoys me but I don't say anything. It's not like I have a lot to get home for myself.

I logged into my computer and went straight to my diary, clicking through to April. There was bound to be some post-end-of-financial-year stuff to deal with, but nothing had been scheduled so far except the usual team meetings and staff one-to-ones. I ticked the box next to Alan's diary and viewed his schedule: nothing there that wasn't in mine. I blocked out the week then wondered if it would be enough. The letter had only given me a date to turn up at the court. How long did jury service take?

'Alan?'

He swivelled his chair in my direction. After the office re-organisation he'd somehow got the seat at the window, the one next to mine. I was flanked on either side by desks. So much for seniority.

'Morning, Natalie. Good weekend?'

'Fine, thanks. You?' He started to reply, but it wasn't like I was interested. 'Have you ever done jury service?'

He leaned back in his chair, pleased to be able to dispense his wisdom. Alan's older than me, in his pre-retirement phase, and he likes to instruct me when he gets the chance. It doesn't happen often.

He said, 'Twice, actually. I got a murder the first time.'

I was impressed in spite of myself. 'How long did it take?'

'About a month.' He read the dismay on my face. 'The other one was arson, though. We were in and out in a week. They were going to give us another case, but it was coming up to Christmas and they didn't bother in the end.'

Beyond the partition behind my desk, Malcolm, another of my team, raised his head like a meerkat. 'Have you been summoned then, Natalie?'

I nodded. 'How are you supposed to plan how long you'll be away for?'

'They say to assume two weeks, but it depends. Look on gov uk.' Alan again. He had that look he gets when he's thinking, like he's constipated. I could guess why: he wasn't sure whether to be pleased I wouldn't be around to keep tabs on him or dismayed that he might actually have to cover my work.

'Right, you'll be holding the fort for the second half of April then.' Might as well strike while the iron was hot. I'd better tell Fiona, my boss, too; let her know I wouldn't be contactable and to keep an eye on Alan. The idea was faintly thrilling. It had been a long time since I'd been able to forget about the BlackBerry while I was on leave.

Malcolm was talking again, saying something about fraud cases going on and on. Would I want that? I wondered. The complexity could be enjoyable. And it might be good to have some proper time away from the office, interesting to lose myself in something other than work. And better fraud than something horrific – child abuse, say, or rape.

'I was the foreman both times I was on a jury.' Alan's lips had a self-satisfied curl. 'You probably will be too, Natalie.'

I didn't like him knowing things I didn't. 'Why?'

'Oh, you see all of human life on a jury.' He laughed. 'You forget that not everyone . . . Well, this kind of job is good training in a way.' I stared at him. VAT policy? 'I mean, we're used to looking at evidence, formulating conclusions. Even just chairing a discussion. Most people don't have that kind of experience.'

God, he was full of it. But he had a point. After all, what was a trial but a process? I understood process. I trusted it. I'm a bureaucrat, that's what we do.

And sitting there then, I thought: he's right. I am well qualified for this. Whatever case I get, I'm going to do my best to do a good job.

That was what I thought. Exactly that. Pay attention, because this bit's important. Back then, that was all I wanted: to do a good job; by which I suppose I meant that I'd play my part in making sure all the evidence was scrutinised, that I wouldn't allow myself to be blinded by prejudice or carried away on flights of fancy. That I'd do what I could to make sure the jury reached a conclusion on the basis of whatever facts were presented to us.

What I didn't aim for then, before I'd set foot in that courtroom, before the witness statements and the diagrams and the photos and the video, was to find the truth.

That came later. After the scream. And I think now it might have been better if it had never come at all.

Chapter 2

I'd brought two books. Everyone said there was a lot of hanging around. Someone told me they'd waited three days even to be assigned to a case. It sounded like a monumental waste of time, though I'm not knocking my colleagues at Her Majesty's Courts and Tribunals Service. All those private-sector idiots who claim that if they ran their businesses the same way as the DVLA or the NHS or the courts or whatever bit of the public sector they're whinging about at the time, they'd go bust . . . Well, how many businesses have to serve everyone, whether they can pay or not? How many of them are led by people who have to get re-elected by their customers every five years? How many have a few hundred other people who see it as their job to take a pop at them every week at Prime Minister's Questions?

So I'm not going to complain about the waiting. I'm not.

I'd started out with some book on change management – *Reaching for the Stars*, or some such rubbish, which a colleague had pressed earnestly into my hands on learning I'd be out of the office for a couple of weeks. I'd just volunteered to run a staff group on the topic, hoping to tick off the required corporate contribution for that year's performance appraisal, doing your actual job no longer being sufficient for the top of the office. I'd stuck with it for a couple of chapters, but my eyes were glazing over and I'd switched to P. D. James in the interests of being awake if and when I was called. The woman opposite glared at me when she saw the cover – perhaps she considered reading something called *The Murder Room* poor taste in the circumstances – but I ignored her.

A slight woman with short grey hair and an east London accent had already talked us through the housekeeping arrangements: the passcode for the door into the jury corridor, the evidence needed for travel and expense claims, the location of the canteen and the loos. She'd taken a register, and we'd watched the video on how it all worked, shown on a TV that got wheeled into the room on a stand. It was like being back at school, and I found that oddly reassuring; for once, it was someone else's responsibility to make sure everything went according to plan.

There were two other TV screens in the room, mounted on the walls at either end. They showed a table with a list of cases – the name of the defendant and the judge, the number of the courtroom, a reference number and a column headed 'Status', which was mostly empty. The court served south-east London, and the defendants sounded as cosmopolitan a bunch as you could hope for: a David and a Mark, Jayden and Tyrone, a Sayid, and Aaliyah and Lisa for the girls.

All of human life.

I wondered who I'd get. Just before lunchtime, I found out.

The grey-haired woman reappeared and read out a list of names. *Isabelle Fernandez, Brian Clifton, Natalie Wright . . .* I got to my feet, and around the room others stood too, exchanging nervous smiles. We trooped out trailing scarves and bags and lined up against the wall of the waiting room as if about to face a firing squad. An usher, a motherly woman in spite of her voluminous black cape, introduced herself as Janet and led the way down a corridor and up a flight of stairs, turning to put her finger to her lips before opening the door to a second corridor, off which the courtrooms apparently lay.

Portraits lined the walls, stern-looking photographs of judges past. All of them white, all but a couple men. About halfway down, Janet stopped and pushed open another door, standing to one side and gesturing to us to pass. The court opened up before us, all dark wood panelling, the judge in scarlet robes and others – the barristers, I presumed – in black, just like I'd seen on TV. Janet guided us to the jury box, squeezing us onto the wooden benches, hips and elbows touching. But the crush was temporary: more names were read out and a handful of jurors were escorted from the room. I didn't understand why. Had it been random, or had those of us who remained passed some kind of test? But there was no time to ponder, because now we were twelve. The Twelve. And there was an oath to be taken.

We spoke in turn, Janet whispering to each of us to check which version we wanted – Christian, Muslim, the affirmation of the atheist. We were a mixed bunch, Spanish, Chinese and Scottish accents among the London and Estuary English, some stumbling over the words, one man confounded by the task of holding the Bible in one hand and the laminated card with the words of the oath in the other. I gave my affirmation flawlessly, if I say so myself. *Foreperson material*, I imagined the others thinking.

When we were finished, the judge leaned forward and peered at us over her spectacles. The Honourable Victoria Something – her name sounded Nigerian, but I didn't catch it properly – was a kindly looking soul, though I imagined her atypical background meant there was steel there somewhere. She told the usher to hand a folder to each of us. She was still talking, her accent pure

RP, as I followed her instructions to open it and lift out the first sheet of paper; then for a moment her voice faded away as I read the words of the indictment.

Intentionally penetrated . . . did not consent . . .

Oh God, no.

. . . did not reasonably believe . . . consented . . .

Rape. It was a rape case.

I swallowed, and my hands were cold as I replaced the folder on the ledge in front of me. I tried to stop the thoughts that were already running through my head: the statistics on conviction rates; the difficulty of proof . . . I breathed deep.

The clerk was speaking now, addressing someone on the right-hand side of the room. The defendant. 'Are you Ian Craig Nash of 236A Mountford Road, Lewisham?'

Lewisham. Like me. I raised my eyes and looked at him. Short brown hair, unremarkable face. He was wearing a dark-blue T-shirt, lightly muscled arms sticking out of the sleeves. Why didn't he have a jacket? The courtroom was so cold. I pulled my own coat more closely around me.

'Yes,' he replied, his voice quiet. The clerk read out the charge and asked for his plea, and then one of the lawyers was on her feet – they were all women, I saw now. Of course: only a rape case would have bucked the norm like that. She was calling a witness. It was all too quick – shouldn't there be some kind of interlude, a chance to catch our breath? The woman on my right coughed, then cleared her throat and coughed again. A police officer was stepping into the witness box. I picked up my pencil and held it poised over one of the scrappy sheets of notepaper I'd taken from my folder.

I can do this, I told myself. I just had to watch, and listen, and think. I would focus on the evidence, the stories they told. There had to be proof, evidence beyond a reasonable doubt. I'd watched enough courtroom dramas to know that was how it went. That was the bar: no more, no less. All I had to do was to test what I heard, assess whether the standard had been reached. I could keep a cool head – it was what I did every day. And I'd make sure the eleven other people on the jury did the same.

The police officer was holding up his hand, swearing his oath in the voice of someone who had done this before but still didn't like it. I wrote the date at the top of the paper, then *PC Alex Watson*.

It had begun.

We heard only two witnesses that day: the first, PC Watson, twenty-something, awkward but seemingly diligent; then a young detective, DS Emma Willis-Jones. I didn't like her, her pointy nose and her tanned face – a drop of winter sun somewhere – shiny hair tied back in a ponytail, just the way I bet it was when she played netball with the other popular girls at school. Unlike the constable, she wasn't wearing uniform, and her blue and white striped shirt was unbuttoned at the neck to show a silver pendant. She gave her evidence in a clear voice, not needing to check her notebook. She was capable, composed. I suppose in that way she was a bit like me.

They were easy to listen to – dry facts delivered without emotion. I scribbled away as they spoke, my pencil hardly pausing: the arrival at the neighbour's flat, a woman in tears, the allegation, knocking at another door in the small block where they both lived, the arrest. He had seemed calm, PC Watson said; there hadn't been any trouble getting him to the station. I noted it all down, my pencil growing blunt, a soft crackle as I finished one sheet of paper and started on the next.

I sat in the second row of the jury box and from time to time I looked at my fellow jurors, the four in front and the three beside me. They seemed alert enough, but they scarcely picked up a pencil between them.

At one point we were asked to leave the court; it wasn't clear why. Janet led us back up the stairs between the rows of benches and through a door in the panelling at the back. This was the jury room, and from then on, we would enter and exit the court that way. It was small and windowless, with grubby cream walls and a large table in the middle with just enough room on each side to squeeze into the seats around it. A door at the end opened into a tiny loo with a sink, and in one corner a smaller table held an aged television, a bottle of water and a stack of plastic cups.

We shuffled into seats, excusing ourselves as we went, unsure of each other. A tall woman with blonde hair took the seat opposite me. I'd seen her in the waiting room – she'd been knitting. I liked that, that she'd come prepared to wait, to fill her time doing something useful. She said, 'I saw you taking lots of notes.'

I shrugged self-deprecatingly, though I suppose it might not have been a compliment. 'It's the way I listen. I find I concentrate better if I write things down.' It was half true. The other half being that I thought it might be helpful to have a record of what people had said, given that we were supposed to be using that to decide whether or not a man was a rapist.

She said, 'I'm no good at taking notes. Can't read my own writing.' She laughed raucously and I wondered whether the sound would carry into the court. I wanted to tell her to shush, but it seemed a bit much given we'd only just met. Maybe when I was foreperson . . .

I wondered whether I should suggest some introductions, treat it like a meeting. Perhaps the others would be relieved if someone took charge. I sat up a little straighter in preparation, looked around the table. A few seats down, a stuffy-looking kid in a jumper adjusted his glasses on his nose and said, 'Shall we do introductions?'

Oh shut up, *foetus.*

But before anyone had the chance to respond, the door opened and Janet was ushering us back in. The judge watched us as we took our seats. We'd been able to leave our bags in the jury room, and there was less shuffling and arranging of arms and legs than there had been on our first arrival. I picked up my pencil, poised for action, but there was no need. Quarter to four and apparently we were done for the day. I looked up at the dock as we trooped back out. He was staring straight ahead, the skin on his arms a bluish pallor. I hoped he'd wear something with long sleeves the next day.

Out in the spring sunshine I found myself shaking off the air of the courtroom, grateful to be able to go home. I was already wondering about her – Chantelle, that was the name of the woman who said she'd been raped. Not 'the victim', I reminded myself; it wouldn't be right to think of her that way. We hadn't seen her yet, and I let my imagination wander to what she'd be doing this evening, whether there'd been people in the public gallery who'd tell her what had happened today. Whether she wanted to hear every detail or couldn't bear to talk about it. Whether she'd be able to eat, or later, to close her eyes and sleep. I imagined how I'd feel standing in that witness box: was there anything she could do to ready herself for that?

And I thought about him, the accused. Ian. Would they let him go home, or would he be spending the night in a cell? I had no idea how it worked. We'd been told the trial would last three to four days. It didn't seem long. Three to four days and he'd be either walking out under the same sky as the rest of us, or taken away to locked doors and iron gates, to a world without choices. I wondered if he suspected which way it would go. I wondered if he hoped for justice or feared it.

As I crossed the car park I heard footsteps quickening behind me.

'Natalie?'

I turned to see one of the other jurors, a woman with a tired smile and sensible eyes. 'It is Natalie, isn't it?'

'Hi, yes. Sorry, I don't think . . .'

'Helen, Helen Owens.' I saw her wondering whether the surname had been a good idea. Then, 'Don't worry, I know we're not supposed to talk about the case.'

I smiled as if the thought hadn't occurred to me. 'It's nice to be out so early. I hadn't realised court days were so short.'

She nodded. 'I know. Someone at work told me to make the most of it. I think we're all in the wrong jobs.'

'What do you do?'

'Social worker. I'm based in Hackney.' That explained the tired eyes, I thought; she must have seen it all. 'You?'

'Civil servant.' I added my standard dinner-party line in case she thought I was a spook. 'I work for the taxman.'

She was quiet for a moment. It usually has that effect. Then, 'Are you heading back to London Bridge?'

She chatted for the ten minutes or so it took to reach the station, not seeming to require much in the way of a response. She was a few years older than me, a couple of daughters in school, no mention of her husband but she wore a ring. As we parted, she said, 'I don't see how we're going to reach a verdict.'

I shrugged, knowing what she meant and trying not to worry about it. 'It's only the first day. They might have more.'

'Yes. I just hope . . . You know, one person's word . . .'

It was what I feared too. I said, 'It's innocent until proven guilty. If there's no real evidence, I suppose there can only be one verdict.'

And even as I said the words I thought: can it really be that simple? But Helen was nodding. It *was* that simple. There was no other way for it to be.

At home, I picked up my BlackBerry and tapped in the password. I hadn't taken it to court, unsure whether I'd be allowed to keep it with me, and as far as Alan was concerned I was out of commission for all but the direst emergency. He'd been given strict instructions to leave me a voicemail if there was anything that needed my attention; I was pleased to see there were no messages. I scrolled quickly through the day's emails – as quickly as it's possible to scroll through 186 items, anyway – but resisted the temptation to respond to any of them. If I gave Alan the opening, he'd assume I'd pick up anything difficult.

When I'd finished, I went to the sitting room and pressed a finger into the soil in the pot holding my dragon tree. *Dracaena marginata* is one of the easiest house plants to keep, but nevertheless it's important to water it at appropriate intervals. Too much is as bad as too little: it starves the roots of oxygen. The soil was on the edge of crispness, so I added a moderate amount and gave the leaves a spray of plant food.

Later I settled in front of the TV with my dinner on a tray. Maybe I'd watch a film, enjoy the luxury of the extra time; but flicking through the channels, a nature programme caught my attention. A squirrel was burying some nuts, watched from a distance by another one. I thought I recognised the voice providing the commentary – an actor, Scottish. Who was it?

'*The would-be thief is in for a surprise.*' Shot of the nut-burying squirrel peering suspiciously over his shoulder. '*He's been spotted, and this squirrel has a trick up his sleeve . . .*'

Was Chantelle watching television now? Or reading a book or a magazine, trying to take her mind off things? Or was she lying in bed, staring up at the ceiling, imagining how it would be to stand there in that courtroom, the things she would have to say? And what about Ian? Was he desperate for his chance to tell his side of the story? Or terrified that when the moment came, he'd be caught out, his lies exposed in the harsh glare of the fluorescent lights?

'*The squirrel has only pretended to bury the nuts, and now he's off to find another hiding place.*' Squirrel number two had come out of hiding and was pawing at the spot recently vacated by squirrel number one. After a while, he stopped, empty-handed, realising he'd been duped.

Such deceitfulness, even in the animal kingdom. Why expect people to be any different? We're hard-wired for it. We're the worst of the lot.

I thought of Aidan. He'd thought he was going to get away with it. He'd thought he was the cunning one, but he was squirrel number two. It had taken me a while, but I'd got wise to him in the end. I found myself smiling as I reached for my glass of wine. Yes, I'd seen through him eventually. And then Aidan found out he was dealing with squirrel number one.

Chapter 3

The woman on the stand was in her early fifties, auburn hair well cut and streaked with grey. Her voice when she spoke carried a tremble of anxiety. She fixed her eyes on the prosecution lawyer as if she were a life raft on a tumultuous sea.

'Ms Havilland, can you explain to the court how you know Chantelle Patterson?'

'I live next door to her. I mean, I live in the flat next door to her.'

The barrister nodded. She was employing her best coaching voice, soft but still clear, warmer than when she'd addressed the police. 'And you were both living there in July 2018, is that right?'

'Yes, that's right.'

'And at that time, last July, the defendant, Ian Nash, also lived in those flats, didn't he?'

Eloise Havilland's eyes flickered towards the dock and then fastened back on the lawyer. 'He did.'

'Is it a large block of flats?'

I paused in my writing, unclear how this was relevant; but Eloise knew where it was going. The tremble in her voice was fading away. 'No, it's just a two-storey building. There are three flats on the ground floor and three on the first.'

A pause as the barrister looked down at her papers. Eloise started talking again – apparently she was one of those people who, like nature, abhorred a vacuum. 'There are another two blocks on either side of ours. They're a bit bigger, and there's a garden—'

'Yes, thank you, Ms Havilland.'

She shut up, chastened, and bit her bottom lip.

'So do you live on the same floor as Chantelle?'

Eloise nodded. 'Yes, we both live on the first floor.'

'And when the incident took place, where was Ian Nash living in relation to you?'

'He lived on that floor too.'

'So you, Chantelle Patterson and Ian Nash were all living on the first floor. And there were no other flats on that floor.'

'That's right.'

The barrister held up a photograph. 'Your Honour, may I invite the jury to examine the item marked 2a in their bundles.' Papers rustled as we obeyed. 'Can you tell me what we're looking at, Ms Havilland?'

She leaned forward in her seat, though it could hardly have been necessary. Perhaps she wanted to show how seriously she was taking her task. She said, 'It's the outside of our block.'

The photograph showed a squat 1980s building, orange bricks with white render over the first floor, a mock-Tudor gable in the middle. The sides of two other buildings adjoining it at right angles were just visible at the edges of the photo. Not smart, but not desperate either. The kind of place I imagined might have been called 'respectable' thirty years ago.

'And could I ask the jury to look at item 2b in their bundles. Ms Havilland, could you explain to us what this is?'

'It's the doors to our flats. Mine and Chantelle's and . . .' a momentary pause, 'his. Ian Nash's.'

It was a photograph of a small landing, two plain brown doors on one side and a third in the middle of the wall opposite them. A triangular window threw beams of light onto cheap blue carpet. The door on its own had a small mat in front of it. I found myself thinking it looked quite pleasant.

'And in this photograph we can see the numbers of the flats, numbers 10, 11 and 12. Can you remind the court which is your flat, Ms Havilland?'

'Mine is number 10.'

'So that's the one on its own on the left-hand side of the landing as you come up the stairs.'

'That's right.'

I thought: just get on with it. We get the point. They all lived close to each other.

'And Chantelle was in which flat?'

'Number 11.'

'So Ian Nash was in flat 12.'

'Yes.' The faintest of grimaces and that flicker again, eyes darting to the dock.

'As you said, it's not a big block. Do you see much of your neighbours?'

'Well, we're all out at work during the day . . .'

'But you see each other coming and going? In the stairwell or the car park?'

'Yes. That's right. And Chantelle comes over every so often for a cup of tea.'

'But not Ian Nash? He didn't drop by like that?'

Of course he didn't. Why would a thirty-something guy call on a fifty-year-old woman for tea and shortbread? The judge shifted in her chair. I wondered if she was thinking the same thing.

'No, but I saw him now and again. You know, like you said, going in and out.'

The barrister let the silence grow once more as she inspected her papers. It was a signal: we were getting to the important bit.

'Ms Havilland, can I ask you now to cast your mind back to Saturday the twenty-first of July last year.' Another pause. 'Did you see Chantelle Patterson that day?'

Something tightened in Eloise Havilland's neck and her lips pressed together. She nodded, then remembered she had to speak aloud. 'Yes.'

'Can you tell the court what time that was?'

'About ten past five in the afternoon.'

'And where did you see her?'

'She was sat at the top of the stairs outside our flats. I was just coming back from work.'

'I see. And did you notice anything unusual about Chantelle that day?'

The tremor was back in her voice. 'She was crying.'

'Crying?'

'Sobbing. Her face was red and there were tears streaming down her cheeks.'

'Had you seen her cry before?'

'Never.'

'So this was very unusual?'

Oh come on.

'Yes.'

'What happened then?'

'I asked her if she was all right.'

'And what did she say?'

'She . . . she didn't say anything at first. So I asked her again, and she said "Ian".'

'Just "Ian"?'

'She said it several times. "Ian, Ian . . ." She was crying so much I couldn't make out anything else.'

I looked across at the table where the defence lawyer sat. She had her head down, taking notes.

'So what happened then?'

'I said she should come into my flat, I'd make her a cup of tea.'

'And did she do that?'

'Yes. I helped her up and—'

'You helped her up? Why was that?'

'She looked shaky. I didn't want her to fall.'

'You thought she looked "shaky".' The barrister turned towards the jury box and let the word hang in the air before us. I wrote it down dutifully, complete with quote marks. 'And so you went into your flat. Did Chantelle say anything else then to explain why she was so upset?'

Eloise swallowed. I could hear the saliva in her throat.

'She told me that Ian Nash had raped her.'

I forget the names of the lawyers now. I'm not sure I could have told you what they were even at the time. They weren't part of the story. They were just the directors, editing together their own features from the same raw materials, a different angle here, the lighting adjusted there to emphasise this part of the scene or that.

But I remember what they looked like, the sound of their voices. The lead for the prosecution was slender, attractive in a patrician sort of way, blonde hair in a neat little bun sticking out below her wig. She was self-contained, barely moved from the spot as she directed her questions, only turning now and then to the jury, the slightest elevation of an eyebrow sending us the silent message: *Did you hear that? We know what that means, don't we?*

The defence lawyer was her polar opposite, a rotund black woman with trendy thick-framed glasses. She waved her hands as she spoke, picked up papers and put them down again, patted at her robe, paced before the witness box. There was something of the Columbo about her, as if all that nervous energy were somehow essential to uncovering the truth. Every so often, in the middle of examining a witness, she'd pause so long I'd begin to worry she'd lost her train of thought; but I think it was all part of the act. It was as if she were saying: *I'm not smooth like the other one. I haven't had to rehearse all this. I'm just here to tell it to you like it is.*

They seemed evenly matched but for one thing, hinted at on the first day and becoming ever clearer as the days went on: the prosecution had no evidence.

Yes, the neighbour, Eloise, said she'd seen Chantelle crying, but we had to be careful about that. All it told us for sure was that Chantelle had been upset. When Eloise had first asked her what was wrong, all she'd said was 'Ian'. It wasn't until they were in Eloise's flat that she'd said he'd raped her. The defence lawyer had prodded and poked at that, asking how long they'd been talking, what Eloise had said, hinting that she'd put the words in Chantelle's mouth.

I saw the moment Eloise realised what she was suggesting. She went quite still in the witness box, two spots of colour high on her cheeks, and for a moment words failed her; but she didn't look to the prosecution bench. She steadied herself and then she said, 'I knew what had happened. It was obvious. But I told her, "You have to tell me. You have to say the words." And she said, "He raped me."'

She spoke with all the conviction of someone with right on her side; but being sure of yourself doesn't mean you really know what happened – you can take that from me. I knew we had to look at what she said from all sides, consider why she might have drawn the conclusions she had.

Eloise seemed protective of Chantelle. I wondered – *speculated*, it's true – whether she'd seen her as some kind of surrogate daughter. There she was, an older woman living on her own, lonely perhaps, inviting her young neighbour round for a cup of tea, encouraging her to call by if she ever needed anything. Ian had moved in in March that year, just four months before she'd found Chantelle crying in the stairwell. Had Chantelle started to drop by less often? Had Eloise seen them flirting? Had she been jealous?

Or had it all been quite different? Had Eloise seen something else, something predatory in Ian's behaviour? Some subtle sign she hadn't even consciously noticed until the day she discovered Chantelle sobbing his name and knew in her gut what had happened?

I looked up at him, at Ian, as Eloise left the stand. He watched her go, his face blank. That day he was wearing a decent enough suit, with a shirt and tie. It was the kind of thing Aidan might have worn, and I guessed it was supposed to make him appear smart, trustworthy. But it didn't work that way with me. The faded T-shirt he'd worn before had made him look vulnerable, and I was glad it had gone. Glad I didn't feel sorry for him any more.

The next witness was taking the stand. He was a forensic physician, we were told. A doctor, in other words. He'd examined Chantelle at some kind of medical suite. I was surprised it was a man; Dr Marcus Hall. He had gentle eyes and a sombre air – but still.

We were shown a diagram, a line drawing. At first I didn't understand what I was seeing, but when he told us that the two curves at the bottom of the picture represented Chantelle's buttocks, I realised with a jolt what we were all looking at, all of us in that room focused on those A4 sheets of paper. It was a schematic of her genitalia. I was suddenly profoundly grateful that she wasn't there.

Dr Hall had a soothing voice; I wondered whether it had always been like that or whether it was something he'd developed in his line of work. There was evidence of recent sexual intercourse, he said, semen inside the vagina. He had found no scratches or bruising, but there was a small tear to the fourchette, as marked (pointing to the paper) with an arrow on the diagram. At first I wondered if I'd heard him correctly, but then he explained that the fourchette was the name for a fold of skin at the rear of the vulva. I swallowed back the bitter taste that rose in my mouth.

Those were the words we had to deal with, sitting there listening to the professional tones, pretending to be calm, analytical. *Vagina. Fourchette. Vulva.*

'And could you explain to us, Dr Hall, what could have caused such an injury?'

'It is not possible to be certain. A tear to the fourchette can result from forced penetration, but can also be sustained during normal sexual intercourse.'

I wrote down: *Medical evidence inconclusive.* I didn't have it in me to write anything more.

We broke for lunch after that, but that diagram had hollowed me out; the thought of food turned my stomach.

I went to the canteen anyway, having nowhere else to go. It was for jurors only, tucked away at the top of a flight of stairs from the jury corridor to avoid contact between us and anyone involved in the cases. I queued up for a cup of tea and made my way to a table where the Chinese woman on the same jury was already sitting. We'd finally made our introductions that morning – by mutual consent, undirected by the stuffy kid in the jumper, who, it turned out, was called Sheridan – and I knew her name was

24

Chen, though an accountant called Brian had misheard and kept calling her Jen instead. I knew too that her spoken English wasn't great – I assumed her inclusion on the jury meant that her comprehension was better – and had hoped that by sitting next to her I'd avoid looking stand-offish whilst not having to talk to anyone. But we'd barely exchanged tentative smiles when chair legs scraped against tiles and Sheridan was sitting down next to us, slopping his Coke over the table.

My annoyance must have shown on my face because he said, 'Sorry – is it OK if I join you?' Chen was nodding and smiling and then another chair scraped and there was Accountant Brian and Can't-Read-My-Own-Writing Lorraine, both with trays of steaming lasagne and chips. Clearly not everyone had been put off their food.

'All right?' said Lorraine, pointlessly. 'Anyone want a chip?'

We met Chantelle that afternoon.

They showed us the video of her interview with the police first, so by the time she stepped into the witness box, I knew that she had dark hair, that she was slim, with the fragile kind of prettiness that owed most to the fresh skin and bright eyes of youth, that her voice was high and carried an Essex accent. In the video she had been quiet, still, huddled in a plastic chair with her hair over her face, her statement prised from her with gentle questions, a female officer telling her she could use whatever words she felt comfortable with. As if anyone could feel comfortable in that position.

In the courtroom, she gave her evidence with a screen shielding her from the dock and the public gallery, but she faced the jury box. I thought about that as I watched her settle, her eyes on the judge as she was told she could sit down if she wished. It seemed wrong to have her displayed to us like that, an exhibit in her own defence, when – in theory, at least – she wasn't the one accused. But I didn't look away from her as she spoke. I watched her so I'd see what the others saw.

She said she'd been renting her flat for two years when Ian had moved into the block. They'd chatted a few times. He was sometimes a bit noisy with his music, but when she'd mentioned it he'd apologised straight away. After she'd split up with her boyfriend, he'd got a bit flirty, telling her it was his loss, that if it were him, he'd never have let a girl like her get away, that kind of thing. She hadn't taken it seriously. He'd turned up on her doorstep one afternoon with a CD, told her he thought she'd like it. She'd thought it was sweet, had liked that he'd remembered her telling him about the old player she'd brought to her flat from her parents' house, about how she used it to play the CDs her dad had introduced her to when she was a kid, the eighties rock from bands with big hair and jangling guitar solos. Ian had said it was the first album he'd ever bought; but when he spoke, she'd smelled the drink on his breath. She'd thought – a pause here, a trembling breath – he looked upset, and she'd felt sorry for him. She'd invited him in.

Her lawyer prompted her gently. 'What happened then?'

'He told me I should put the CD on.'

'And what did you say?'

'I told him my CD player was in the bedroom.'

'Not in the living room?'

'No, I've got speakers in the lounge. I plug them into my phone if I want to listen to music. I don't really listen to CDs, just my dad's now and again.'

'So what happened then?'

'He said, "Come on then," and started walking down the hallway.'

A question formed in my mind, but the lawyer had anticipated it. 'Had he been to your flat before?'

'No. But it's only small. You go down the hall to get to all of the rooms.'

'I see. So Ian started walking down the hallway. What did you do?'

'I followed him. I wasn't worried then. I thought he just wanted to listen to some music and talk. I thought maybe whatever was bothering him, he wanted to talk about it.'

The lawyer nodded, her blonde bun bobbing up and down. 'So you got to the bedroom, is that right?'

'Yes.'

'And then what happened?'

Chantelle looked down. 'I sat on the bed and he went to the CD player and put the CD on.'

'And then what did he do?'

She didn't lift her eyes. 'He came and sat next to me.'

For once, the shuffling and the throat-clearing, the squeaking of the benches – all of it had stopped. I could hear my pencil sliding across the paper, noting down every word.

'What happened then?'

'I asked him if he was all right and he said he was a bit stressed. He said it was work stuff. He said . . .'

'Take your time, Ms Patterson.'

She nodded, her eyes on the floor. 'He said he needed to unwind.'

'To unwind.' Something in the lawyer's tone made the words ominous. Or maybe it was just that we all knew what came next.

'Yes. And then he leaned over and kissed me.'

'Did you kiss him back?'

Chantelle looked up, straight at her lawyer, and I suspected she'd been told to do that. She said, 'I was too shocked to do anything.'

'Did you ask him to stop?'

'Not then, no. Because I was so shocked. I didn't know what to do.'

The lawyer nodded again, understanding, encouraging. 'What happened after that?'

'He . . .' Chantelle's words disappeared in another trembling breath.

'Please take your time.'

She reached out and took a sip of water from a glass on the stand. 'He pushed me back on the bed.' There was a crack at the edge of her voice. 'And then he put his hand under my top.'

A tear spilled from her right eye and I watched it roll down her cheek. Something pulled inside me, and I felt my fingers tighten around my pencil.

The lawyer kept her eyes on Chantelle. 'So he pushed you backwards. At that point, were you lying down?'

'Yes, but I tried to get up. I tried to push his hand away.'

'So you resisted?'

'Yes, I told him to stop.'

'You told him to stop.' The lawyer drew out the words, dropped them heavily into the silent courtroom. Later, when we are deliberating, I will read out my notes from this part of the evidence. We will consider them alongside the indictment: *did not reasonably believe that she had consented*. They are important, you see. They could be the difference between guilty and not guilty.

'And did Mr Nash listen to you? Did he stop what he was doing?'

'No.' And there it was. There in the set of her jaw and the hardness in her eyes. Finally, I saw the anger.

'So what did he do?'

'He rolled on top of me and he put his knee between my legs. He held my hands over my head and he told me to stay still.'

The lawyer waited for us to absorb this. Then, 'Please go on, Ms Patterson.'

'He was pushing down my jogging bottoms, and then . . .' A tear ran down her other cheek. She was wearing foundation, and two pale lines tracked the contours of her face. 'He took out his penis and he put it in my vagina.'

The words rang around the courtroom, stark and appalling. And even as my stomach turned, I registered the phraseology, the necessity of it to Chantelle's case. Because there's a very specific definition of rape in English law: penetration by a penis. If you're penetrated by anything else without your consent it counts as 'sexual assault by penetration'. That's the phallo-centric world we live in.

Chantelle continued, her voice shaking. 'I went still. I was so frightened. I just lay there and cried and waited for him to finish.' She was sobbing now.

'Thank you, Ms Patterson. We're nearly done.' There was a tightness to the lawyer's voice that made me think she wanted it over with too. 'Can you tell me what happened after that? When did Mr Nash leave?'

Chantelle pressed a tissue to her eyes. Her hand was shaking. 'He came – he ejaculated – on my stomach. Then he just rolled away and lay there on the bed next to me. He didn't say anything at first.'

'At first?'

'After a minute he got up and – you know – he put himself away. Then he took the CD out of the CD player and said something about having to go because he was expecting a phone call.'

'And what did you do?'

'I didn't say anything. I just wanted him to leave. I didn't move. I lay on the bed and then he walked out and I heard the door to my flat close.' Her eyes were squeezed shut. 'I wanted to take a shower but I didn't because I knew . . . I knew I shouldn't. I knew there'd be . . . there'd be . . .'

The judge leaned forward in her chair. 'I think we should take a break there.'

It was as if a spell had been broken. I blinked and took a breath, filling my lungs with the stale courtroom air. Then I got to my feet and followed the others to the jury room.

It must have been half an hour before we went back in. Chantelle was still on the stand, a fresh glass of water in front of her. I looked up at Ian as we filed back to our seats. He was looking straight ahead, giving nothing away.

The defence lawyer was on her feet now. It was a fine line she had to tread, pushing the witness, making it clear that she didn't believe a word she said whilst avoiding being seen to bully her. I thought she did it well.

She asked Chantelle how well she knew Ian; had they flirted? She'd broken up with her boyfriend – how recently had that happened? Had she been trying to make him jealous with a new relationship? (I wondered whether the ex might be called to the stand, not knowing then how little either side would bother with extraneous detail; presumably they had too many other cases to worry about, or maybe there were rules about such things.) Why had she not called the police straight away? If she was so afraid of Mr Nash, why was she sitting outside his flat when her neighbour came home?

At first Chantelle stayed calm, but as the questions went on, her voice began to rise and a red flush spread across her neck. Her eyes darted first to the prosecution and then to the judge. But the questions continued.

The bed was in a corner of the room; which way had they been facing? Had Mr Nash put his leg between her knees or her thighs? How had he forced her legs apart without bruising them? How had he held her wrists while undoing his flies at the same time?

The lawyer didn't fixate on why Chantelle hadn't struggled. She knew the judge would remind us in her summing-up that people responded to fear in different ways, that we couldn't draw any inferences from a reaction that wasn't the same as the one we thought we'd have ourselves. Instead, she pounded relentlessly at the logistics of the act, finding inconsistencies in Chantelle's descriptions, pinpointing anything that didn't make perfect sense and homing in on it, amplifying it.

Chantelle grew more brittle with every answer, her eyes bright and her voice hard-edged. I could see the tears gathering – anger this time, I thought – but now there was no reprieve. The judge told her to take a sip of water, to try to compose herself, that the defence had the right to ask her questions and that she must answer them.

I saw them then, the way the defence had intended us to see them: gaps in the chain. Tiny little chinks that opened up the space for doubt.

Was it possible that she was lying?

I watched Chantelle, her wet cheeks, her lips thinned to a line. What reason did she have to be here, to put herself through this? What reason if she wasn't telling the truth?

I felt drained by the time she left the stand, and when the judge told us that court was adjourned for the day, I was relieved. There was little conversation as Janet led us out of the jury room, and I set off for the station at a brisk pace. I didn't want to talk about what we'd heard.

It hadn't happened, the moment I'd been waiting for. There'd been no golden nugget of evidence, nothing to make me put down my pencil in relief, no need any longer for notes, no more arguments or questions.

There's still time, I reminded myself. The prosecution might have concluded, but that didn't mean it was the end. Perhaps tomorrow there'd be something certain, something firm to hold on to.

Tomorrow – when Ian took the stand.

Chapter 4

The third day of evidence was the last. We started late, Brian the accountant having got himself stuck in traffic. He should have taken the Tube.

We sat in the jury room, making small talk. Someone called Simeon was bragging about being a concert flautist, telling us how he'd played at the Royal Albert Hall. The others looked impressed but I wasn't biting. Everyone at work seemed to have a kid who'd done something at the Royal Albert Hall. It had been some London school thing, I'd have put money on it, and I bet he hadn't been more than twelve at the time.

Every so often someone made an oblique remark about the case – it had been upsetting to listen to Chantelle, they hadn't been able to get it out of their heads – but no one said what they thought had happened. We'd taken the judge's warning seriously: no discussing the evidence until we'd been sent out to deliberate.

Eventually Brian turned up, an hour and a half late, flustered and carrying the cold spring air on his clothes. Another delay, no one sure what for, and then we were trailing back into the courtroom.

I'd wondered whether the case would overrun: the judge had said the evidence would be heard over three days, but the prosecution had rested after Chantelle had left the stand, a full two days in. Surely the defence would take longer than a single day? But when the barrister got to her feet, she told us that she would be calling only one witness: the defendant, Ian Craig Nash.

I felt the hope begin to trickle away then. Did the defence really have nothing else to offer? No one to corroborate any part of Ian's story? Not so much as a single character witness to tell us he wouldn't hurt a fly, that he was very respectful of women, he paid his electricity bill on time and gave money to animal charities? Was this all we were going to get?

I studied him as he walked to the stand. He kept his head up and his back straight, and when he was told there was a seat behind him if he wanted to take it, he chose to remain standing. He was wearing the same suit as the previous day, another white shirt – it looked newly pressed, so I assumed it was fresh – and a blue tie, nylon masquerading as silk.

He confirmed his name and address, looking at the jury as he spoke, presumably following the instructions of his lawyer; but his eyes didn't travel beyond the first row of seats. He didn't look at me.

His lawyer adjusted her glasses and patted at the sides of her gown, as if checking for her car keys. 'Mr Nash, can you explain to the court the nature of your relationship with Chantelle Patterson?'

For a moment he looked thrown, leaning towards her with a wrinkled brow. Yet surely this was the easiest of things to answer? Surely he would have known it was coming?

She glanced down at a sheet of paper on her table, pretending there had always been an adjunct to the question. 'By which I mean, can you explain how you came to know her?'

A little nod then. He'd been thrown by the wording of the question. Perhaps he wasn't the sharpest of tools; or then again, perhaps it was just the stress.

'She was my neighbour.'

'We've heard that her flat was in the same building as yours, on the same floor in fact. Is that right?'

'Yes.' His right hand reached across to his left. A tug at his cuff.

'And that you also lived on the same floor as a Ms Eloise Havilland, whom the court has also heard give evidence.' Silence. 'Is that correct, Mr Nash?'

'Yes, that's correct.'

'Were you friends with Ms Patterson?'

'I wouldn't say friends.' His voice was fading and he stopped to clear his throat. 'I was getting to know her, I suppose. We'd say hello if we saw each other, stop to chat sometimes.'

'You were becoming friends. Would that be a reasonable way to put it?'

'Yes.'

'Ms Patterson has said that you were sometimes "flirty" with her.' She somehow managed to make the quote marks audible. 'Would you agree with that description?'

'It was more the other way around. She flirted with me.'

How fucking typical. God, was it really going to be this banal? *She wanted* me, *Your Honour*. My eyes flicked to the right, where Lorraine sat next to me. Her expression gave no clue to what she was thinking. Maybe she wasn't thinking at all.

The lawyer had picked up the thread. 'So you thought Ms Patterson was flirting with you? Could you explain what made you think that?'

A shrug. 'She was giggly, you know? She'd ask me sometimes if I liked what she was wearing. And then she told me she'd split up with her boyfriend. I got the impression she was waiting for me to ask her out.'

35

'And did you?'

'No. I didn't think it was a good idea. Living next door and that.'

I wondered how many people were filling in the blanks for him. *Shitting on your own doorstep.*

'And what about Ms Havilland? Were you and she friends?'

'No, I didn't know her well. I don't think she liked me much.'

'Why do you think that?'

A humourless laugh. 'Well, all this for a start.'

The lawyer looked up at him sharply. He'd gone off script. 'Did she do or say anything before you were arrested that gave you the impression she didn't like you?'

His lips tightened. He knew he'd been reprimanded and didn't like it. But he was back on track. 'She came and knocked on my door a couple of times. Told me my music was too loud. And if I saw her, I was always the one who said hello.'

The lawyer returned to her table, picked up a piece of paper and put it down again, flicked through a few pages in a lever-arch file. 'I'd like to talk to you now about what happened on the twenty-first of July last year. It was a Saturday, the day you were arrested. Can you tell me how you spent that morning?'

'I was at work. I'm an estate agent. Was an estate agent.' It was a subtle appeal to our sympathy: whether guilty or not, he'd already been punished.

'I see. And did anything particular happen at work that day? Anything out of the ordinary?'

'I had an argument with a colleague. He'd taken a viewing around one of my properties and they'd made an offer. He was trying to get the commission.'

'And you thought the commission should have been yours. Was that worth a lot of money?'

'Yes. A couple of grand.'

'So what happened?'

'We had a row. I walked out. I was only doing a half-day anyway, so I just went home.'

'You told the police that you arrived back at your flat at about one p.m. How would you say you were feeling then?'

'I was fed up. Stressed.'

'Angry?'

'No, not by the time I got back. I was feeling bad about the row. It wasn't the first time it had happened, that guy trying to steal my commission. I shouldn't have bothered arguing about it. I should just have spoken to the manager and got her to sort it out. I knew I'd get it in the neck from her on Monday.'

'So you were back in your flat, fed up, worried about what was going to happen when you went back to work on Monday. What did you do then?'

'Got changed. Got myself a beer. Stuck the TV on for a bit, but there was nothing on.' A hesitation, so slight I could almost have missed it. 'After a while I thought I'd go next door.'

And there was that hush again. You could almost see the thought bubbles forming in the air, little balloons above the heads of the jury.

'When you say next door, there were two flats on your floor. Chantelle Patterson lived in one, Eloise Havilland in the other. Who were you going to visit?'

'Chantelle.'

'And why did you decide to do that?'

He cleared his throat again. 'I wanted to talk to someone. To take my mind off things.'

'And why Chantelle? Why not phone someone else?'

'I suppose she was close, so it was easy to just go and knock on her door. I'd seen her the day before and she'd asked what music I'd been listening to. Asked to borrow the CD. I thought I'd take it round.'

37

The lawyer looked up suddenly, fake-surprised. 'So Ms Patterson had asked to borrow one of your CDs?'

'Yes.'

'Can you explain how she came to do that?'

'It was the day before – the Friday. I was going to the pub with some mates and I'd had some music on as I was getting ready. Chantelle came out into the hallway as I was locking my door and asked me what I'd been listening to. She said she liked it.'

'So you said you'd lend her the CD?'

'I asked her which song she meant. I thought I'd just tell her the artist and she could download it – it was a compilation CD, you know? I'd had it for years, loads of stuff I liked from back in the day. But she said she liked all of it, so I told her it was a CD and she asked to borrow it.'

'But you didn't go and get it then?'

'No. I was on my way out. I said I'd drop it over to her one evening.'

Something nudged at the corner of my mind. I took a new sheet of paper and wrote, *Invited over? CP knew music was on CD = bedroom.*

'So on that Saturday, the day after that conversation, you thought you'd take your mind off things by chatting to Ms Patterson, and at the same time you could lend her the CD she'd asked for.'

'That's right.'

The lawyer half turned as he replied and looked over at the jury box. It was a look that said, *All sounds reasonable enough, doesn't it?* Then she was back to the table, another piece of paper lifted up and examined, another pat at the sides of her gown.

'So did you go then to Ms Patterson's flat?'

'Yes.'

'What time was that?'

38

'I'd got home about one-ish. I suppose by the time I went over there it would have been half past two. Something like that.'

'Please describe to the court what happened then.'

'I knocked at the door. Chantelle answered straight away. I told her I'd brought the CD she wanted to borrow and she asked me to come in.'

'So you went into Ms Patterson's flat at her invitation?' She turned to the jury again, trying to score a point; but I wasn't falling for that. Chantelle had never claimed he'd been there uninvited.

'Yes. I went in, and I gave her the CD.'

'You gave her the CD? Ms Patterson says that you took the CD to her bedroom.'

'No, that's wrong.' It was the first time one of the witnesses had directly contradicted another. I stared at him, looking for his tell. I'd read once that people wrinkle their foreheads, grimace, avert their eyes when they're not telling the truth. I didn't see any of that. But then I'd also read that they only do those things about twenty per cent of the time. So where did that leave us?

'So you gave her the CD. Then what happened?'

'She said the CD player was in the bedroom and she just started walking down the hallway. I thought maybe she was going to leave the CD there and come back, so I stayed where I was.'

'And where was that?'

'Just inside the front door. At the end of the hallway. But then she told me to come with her.'

'She told you to come into the bedroom with her.' Another look to the jury. I thought: so what? She could have said she was desperate for a shag and then changed her mind. It didn't matter. It wouldn't have meant it wasn't rape.

'Yes. I didn't move at first. I wasn't sure it was a good idea.'

'Why was that?'

'Going into the bedroom together . . . I thought maybe she wanted to have sex.'

'And you didn't want that?'

'Like I said, I didn't think it was a good idea to get involved when we lived next door to each other.' *Yeah, right*. Men are always thinking about the long-term implications of sex; they're well known for it. And his face hadn't flickered then either.

'But you did go into the bedroom, didn't you? Why did you do that if you didn't think it was a good idea?'

He looked down then. 'She laughed. She asked me if I thought she was going to bite. I was embarrassed, I suppose. So I laughed too and I followed her to the bedroom.'

'So you both went into the bedroom. What happened then?'

'Chantelle put the CD on. I sat on the bed. She came and sat next to me. We listened to the music for a bit. We talked. Then we started kissing.'

'Who kissed who?'

Whom. I can't help noticing stuff like that – it's the civil servant in me. And this was a lawyer, after all. I'd expected better.

'It was mutual. She'd been talking about splitting up with her boyfriend. I said it was his loss – something like that – and then we were kissing. I'm not sure who started it.'

'Did Ms Patterson ask you to stop?'

'No.'

'Did she push you away?'

'No, she was kissing me too.'

There was less pacing going on then, and I wondered if this part made the lawyer uncomfortable. Really, how could it not?

'Did you have sex?'

'Yes.'

'Who instigated it?' Then, perhaps worried that he wouldn't understand, 'Who made the first move?'

'I'm not sure. I suppose we both did.' He was tugging at his cuff again, aware of the logic problem; they couldn't both have been first. 'We were lying on the bed—'

'Let me stop you there, Mr Nash. Earlier on, you said you were sitting down. How had you come to be lying on the bed?'

'We'd sort of overbalanced when we were kissing.'

'So would it be right to say that you had been kissing *enthusiastically* in order for that to happen?'

'Yes.'

'Ms Patterson has said that you put your hand inside her top and she pushed you away. Is that right?'

'No. I mean, yes, I had my hand in her top, but she didn't tell me to stop. She didn't push me away.'

'Did she do anything at all to make you think she wanted you to stop?'

He gave a short laugh, and my stomach clenched: how unattractive, how *inappropriate* it was to laugh at such a moment. His smile turned into a grimace. 'No. She unzipped my jeans, so she seemed pretty happy about it to me.'

The lawyer didn't like his tone either. She couldn't prevent the disapproval edging into her voice. 'Did Ms Patterson remove your jeans?'

'No, I did.'

'How did you do that when you were lying down?'

'I didn't. I got off the bed to take them off.'

'So you were standing, taking off your jeans, while Ms Patterson was lying on the bed. Is that right?'

'Yes.'

'And while you were doing this, Ms Patterson didn't attempt to get up?'

He shook his head. 'No.'

'She didn't attempt to leave the bedroom?'

'No.'

'Ms Patterson has told this court that she was crying.'

'That's not true.'

'She has said that you held her hands above her head.'

'That's not true.'

'She said that you pushed down her jogging bottoms and forced yourself on her.'

'No, that's not what happened.' He shook his head again, and I could see a vein standing out in his temple. 'We had sex, but I didn't force anything. She seemed to enjoy it at the time.' That grimace again.

'What made you think she enjoyed it?'

God, the questions she asked. But I understood why she had to do it – she had to cover the 'reasonable belief' point. She had to make him explain why he thought Chantelle had consented.

He had the grace to look embarrassed. 'She was – er – moaning. She dug her fingernails into my back. And she said . . .'

'Go on, Mr Nash. What did she say?'

He swallowed, as if he needed help to get the words out. 'She said, "Fuck me hard."'

I flinched; I couldn't help it. But before I could process what he'd said, a noise echoed around the court. It had come from above me and to the right, from the place where the public sat. Not a shout, not words – just a short exclamation. The judge's eyes flickered upwards, her lips pursed; but there was silence. I tried to follow her gaze but couldn't see anyone. Whoever it was must have been sitting in the corner, out of my line of sight.

The lawyer had retrieved another piece of paper from the table and was looking at it, perhaps trying to decide whether the sound had mattered, whether we'd think it signified disbelief; whether it was better to make her witness say the words again, or let it go. After a moment, she raised her head.

'So you're saying that from Ms Patterson's behaviour, from what she said, it was absolutely clear to you that she was a willing participant in sexual intercourse.'

'Yes.'

There wasn't much for my pencil to do after that. The lawyer asked Ian whether he'd been aware of Chantelle crying in the hallway: he claimed he'd been on the phone and then gone to the gym. He hadn't seen her when he left the building, but she'd been fine when he'd left the flat. If there were records of the call or the visit to the gym, we didn't hear about them. Presumably they were considered irrelevant, but I could imagine a lawyer in an American drama saying, 'Goes to credibility, Your Honour.' Who knows what difference it might have made if someone, anyone, had bothered to dig a little deeper that day; but no one did.

The cross-examination was surprisingly brisk. What was there, after all, to be said? The accounts were so different that the prosecution had little else to do but repeat what Chantelle had said, each statement concluded with a rhetorical 'You're lying, are you not, Mr Nash?'

He said, she said. If the burden of proof had been the other way around, Ian's evidence wouldn't have been enough to save him. But the burden lay with the prosecution, and as I watched him that afternoon, there wasn't a doubt in my mind: they had proved nothing.

The summing-up left little impression on me. There was a distastefulness about the proceedings, the evidence of the three days distilled to the essence of what had brought us all to that room: either a man had raped a woman, or a woman had lied about being raped. Neither lawyer expended much passion in their closing arguments, and for that I was grateful. It would have seemed out of place when there was no good to be hoped for, nothing to be gained but justice. Justice was everything and nothing.

Afterwards, the judge summarised the evidence, such as it was. 'In this case,' she said, 'you may feel that the medical evidence does not help you reach a conclusion one way or the other.' I'd known it, but still it was a relief to hear it from someone who must have seen these things before. A voice of experience – another woman – giving us permission to disregard that ugly line drawing. To never have to think of it again.

Then she warned us against drawing conclusions from what Chantelle had described as her reaction. I listened, faintly offended, wanting to retort that I would never have been so stupid as to imagine that in such circumstances a person couldn't shut down, couldn't distance themselves from what was happening instead of kicking and screaming. But then it occurred to me that there were another eleven people on the jury; perhaps some of them needed it spelling out.

Finally she took us through the indictment, the three elements we had to consider in reaching a verdict: the penetration, the lack of consent, that there had been no reasonable belief that consent had been given. And I remember what she said next. I remember every word.

She leaned forward in her chair and seemed to focus on all of us at the same time. 'You need to be sure. We used to talk about reasonable doubt, but now we just ask you to be sure. It is a simple word. It is not enough to think that the defendant *may* have done it. It is not enough even if you think he *probably* did it. In order to return a verdict of guilty, you must be *sure* that he committed the act of which he is accused.'

And as I stood and followed the usher to the jury room, I felt the lead return to the pit of my stomach. Because I knew what the process demanded. I respected it. I understood that was the way it had to be.

But I remembered that first tear rolling down Chantelle's cheek. And part of me wanted to cry with her.

Chapter 5

Have you ever sat on a jury? I wonder. You wouldn't talk about it, of course; I imagine you as an upright person, an upholder of the law. The kind to take the judge's admonition seriously: never to discuss the case or your deliberations, not even after the verdict has been given. It's hard, though, you must agree? To sit there, day after day, watching other people talk about probably the most difficult thing that has ever happened to them, to have opinions about what they are saying, to take a decision that will alter their lives for ever for good or ill; and never to be able to talk about it afterwards?

I wonder now whether it bred in me a kind of madness. Whether turning in on myself, revisiting time after time the things the witnesses had said, the expressions on their faces – Chantelle red-faced, furious with the defence lawyer, Ian's vile little smirk as he claimed she enjoyed it at the time – whether it was that which made me question what had once seemed so clear: whether obeying the rules of the process was what was important after all. Whether my real duty was to something less prosaic and infinitely more difficult; whether my real duty was to find the truth.

Night after night as I lay in bed, or sat wondering through the early-morning train rides to work, still half shrouded in the fog of sleep, I sifted through the words I'd heard in Court 9. I asked myself whether 'not guilty' was the same as 'innocent', whether not being sure, knowing that I could never have been sure on the basis of the evidence put in front of us, was enough to let me sleep at night.

We were back in the jury room and Janet was bustling about us like a mother hen, checking there was a fresh supply of cups, a spare bottle of water, that we all had enough paper. I was on edge: I knew we had to elect a foreperson. I knew it had to be me.

I don't want to come off as condescending. Aidan would like that: he once called me, in the midst of the last of our face-to-face encounters, a 'patronising bitch'. I assume he found the intellectual capacity of the twenty-five-year-old bimbo he was fucking at the time less threatening to his ego.

But I digress. As I say, I don't mean to disparage my fellow jurors. They were a reasonable enough cross-section of society. Some of them – and I think here particularly of Lorraine of the illegible handwriting – were perhaps not the sharpest; but Helen was a sensible woman and Accountant Brian was bright enough. Even Stuffy Jumper Kid – sorry, *Sheridan* – had enough about him to be useful. Nevertheless, I knew – without being arrogant, purely as a statement of fact – that in all probability I was quite a lot cleverer than any of them; if, that is, you're prepared to take IQ as a proxy for intelligence, and for all its flaws no one seems to have yet come up with anything better. Mine is 149, which puts me in the top one twentieth of one per cent of the population. So like I say, the odds were in favour of my being the brightest in a group that size. It was simple statistics.

So when Janet clucked at us about not having yet elected a foreperson (she said 'foreman', but I don't like that kind of shorthand; it's insidious) and told us to let her know when she returned whom we'd picked, I was already considering my tactics. Should I volunteer, as if it were a burden I assumed no one else would want to take on? Should I set out my credentials? Should I wait and hope someone else had already identified me as the prime candidate?

I was mulling it over when Lorraine, bless her simple heart, turned to me and said, 'Do you want to do it? I've seen you taking loads of notes.'

I shrugged, smiled, prepared to take on the mantle of authority. *Some have greatness thrust upon them . . .*

'I don't mind doing it.' The voice was male, confident. Fucking Simeon. I turned to him, hoping my expression stayed neutral. 'After all, I'm a musician . . .'

Yes, we know. And you've played at the Royal Albert Hall.

' . . . and I've played at the Royal Albert Hall. I'm used to performing in front of an audience.'

I hoped someone else would say it for me, and happily Helen did. 'That's very impressive. I'm not sure, though, that it's quite the same thing . . .'

I said, 'I'm happy to do it. I have to chair a lot of meetings in my job.' *Which is clearly far more useful experience than blowing down a tube. Even at the Royal Albert Hall.*

But Simeon wasn't backing down. 'I'm happy to do it too.'

Helen had torn a strip of paper in two and was writing something on the scraps. 'OK, we'll draw straws. I mean, each of you pick a piece of paper.'

Accountant Brian murmured, 'I'm not sure we should do it that way . . .' but no one paid any attention. Suddenly I wasn't sure I cared after all; let the flautist do it if he wanted to that much. I'd direct from the sidelines while he relived his glory days in the school orchestra.

I said, 'It's fine. I'm happy for Simeon—'

But Helen cut me off. 'No, here you go.' She was already holding out her hand, two scrunched-up pieces of paper in her palm. Simeon reached across and chose one before I could say anything more, so I picked up the second one. By the time I'd unscrewed it, Simeon had already read his out: 'Not foreperson.' He looked up and gave a tight smile. 'That's OK.'

I put my paper face-up on the table so the others could see. *Foreperson*.

'OK then,' I said. 'So shall we set some ground rules?'

Have you ever seen that 1950s film about a jury, *Twelve Angry Men*? I hadn't then, but I watched it afterwards. The way they handled that discussion: anyone could see from the outset that it was a recipe for disaster. It might have turned out all right in the end, but it was touch-and-go for most of the film. And everyone hated each other by the time they'd finished.

There was none of that on my jury.

For a start, I got everyone to agree that we wouldn't talk over one another. They forgot, of course, when the discussion got going, but it meant that nobody objected when I interrupted and asked them to wait their turn. They'd all signed up to the rules, you see, so they had to obey them. And we agreed we'd work through all the evidence in chronological order, to make sure everyone had noticed everything there was to notice, before we took a vote on the verdict. There was none of that straw-poll business at the start; I didn't want people to feel defensive if they were in the minority, thinking they had to stand their ground as a matter of principle. I was sure that if we went through it all together, looked dispassionately at every piece of evidence, challenged any bit of speculation, by the time we got to the end we'd all agree on the verdict. We'd decide together, and we'd be confident our decision was right.

It was three o'clock by the time the judge had finished summing up, and I'd half expected her to send us home. I was tired – how quickly I'd adjusted to the short days! – and I almost groaned when she said she would give us an hour to deliberate. I wondered later whether she thought it was so open-and-shut that we might reach a verdict in time to spare Chantelle and Ian a night of anxious waiting. But I was sure of how it needed to be, and everyone agreed: we'd go through all the evidence before we voted.

Everything was straightforward enough to begin with. We started with their relationship before the incident – Ian and Chantelle's, I mean. Ian's description had suggested more warmth between them than Chantelle's, but it was a matter of degree, nothing that couldn't be ascribed to two people interpreting their interaction differently. Perhaps, ventured Chen, Ian was lonely and more keen to establish a friendship; but Stuffy Jumper Kid said, 'Yes, maybe, but we can't know that,' and we all agreed we shouldn't speculate. Helen and I ran through our notes of Eloise Havilland's evidence, and everyone agreed she seemed protective of Chantelle.

I scribbled more notes as we talked, replayed the main points that had been made, tried to bring the more reticent jurors into the discussion. There was an even split between the sexes but, with the exception of Simeon and Stuffy Jumper Kid, the men, generally, were quieter. I wondered if they were worried about saying the wrong thing, concerned that suggesting any positive response to Ian would be taken as gender bias by those of us with two X chromosomes. Occasionally my attempts to elicit a comment from one of them paid off, but for the most part they simply confirmed that they didn't have anything to add, that they agreed with what the others were saying.

We'd just finished running through the pre-incident evidence when Janet returned; we were to go back into the courtroom to be dismissed for the day. She asked which of us was foreman ('fore*person*', I wanted to correct her, but didn't) and I felt a frisson of borrowed power as I took my place immediately behind her, first among equals now, directed to what had become a special seat since we'd retired to deliberate, in the front row of the jury box, closest to the judge.

I looked up at Ian as I took my place, wondering if he would ask his lawyer about me, about whether she thought it made any difference to his chances that the jury had elected a woman to lead their discussions. If he did, she'd probably tell him it didn't matter. Why worry him for no good reason?

And yet as I watched him standing there, his hands clasped together in a way I imagined was designed to stop them trembling, I was determined to be fair to him – to both of them. To weigh the evidence dispassionately. To do what the law required. My feelings weren't important here; it didn't matter what I wanted to believe. My job now was to look at what could be weighed and measured. To look at what could be proved.

The process, I reminded myself. It's all about the process.

I just hoped that at the end of it, we'd be making the right decision.

Chapter 6

Everyone was there on time the next morning, and the relief as we followed Janet to the jury room was palpable – we were on the final stretch, and no one wanted more delays.

By now, the table was scattered with notepaper and pencils, and we danced around each other to get to the seats we'd occupied the previous day. Everyone looked at me and I felt like a conductor about to raise her baton.

I followed the plan I'd prepared to manage the discussion, and heads nodded along, responding to my stage directions. I thought: *it's all going well. I'm doing this well.* But when I'd restated the ground rules and summarised our discussion of the previous day, when everyone had agreed that we should now focus on the events of 21 July, there was a pause.

I looked around the table. 'So where shall we start?'

The silence grew, but I didn't fill it. I wanted to make someone else take the lead. It was important they didn't think I was taking over, that it didn't breed resentment. Eventually, Helen spoke. 'Perhaps we should go back to Ian's evidence. He talked about what happened that morning, didn't he? I mean, as we said we'd go through everything in order.'

More nodding, a few fingers turning pages of notepaper.

We talked about the argument in the office, what it might have meant for Ian's mood; we cross-referred to what Chantelle had said about thinking he was upset, that he'd smelled of drink (Siobhan, a pale-faced juror with a nose ring, recalling, 'He admitted he'd had a beer,' then Lorraine, 'Yes, but just one. And Chantelle didn't say she thought he was drunk'). We moved on to the CD, the different accounts of how they'd come to be in the bedroom. We all agreed there was no way of knowing who was telling the truth, who had led the way and who had followed.

And then we were on to the incident. Such a loaded word, but it's the one I used then too. I couldn't think of anything better. 'Alleged' would have sounded as if I were doubting Chantelle, and any other word without that prefix would have been as good as saying 'guilty'. So it was 'the incident' or 'the events of that afternoon'.

It was hard not to be squeamish. Yet I had to say the words, to lead the twelve of us through what had been said by Chantelle and by Ian, to test its logic, its believability. And that was when things got unpleasant.

I said, 'So there's no dispute over the fact that they had sex. What we need to consider is whether Chantelle consented or, even if she didn't, whether Ian might have reasonably believed she had.'

Stuffy Jumper Kid tapped the paper in front of him with the end of his pencil. Evidently he had made notes too. 'She said she froze.'

'Yes, and she also said she was crying.' There was suppressed anger in Siobhan's voice.

'Do we think it's possible in those circumstances' – I meant, of course, having sex, but I'd already had to talk about penises and vaginas and penetration, and I was trying to ration the direct terms where I could – 'for someone not to see that the other person is crying?'

My voice was doubtful – as it should have been. If Chantelle was crying, Ian must have seen it.

Lorraine frowned. 'I can't believe it myself.'

'No, either she was crying or she was not. He would have known.' It was Isabella. She was Portuguese and not, as I had first assumed, Spanish. Her accent was like sunshine. It didn't fit here in this dingy room.

The man sitting on my right stirred to life. So far he had barely spoken, but the little diagram I'd scribbled as people introduced themselves – their names in position around the table – reminded me that his name was Neil. I turned to him and he was smiling. There was something unbecoming about that smile.

He sighed, loudly, wanting to be noticed, but didn't speak. For a moment I was tempted to ignore him – but no. I had to be better than that. I was the foreperson. It was up to me to ensure everyone's voice was heard.

I smiled back at him. 'Was there something you wanted to say about that, Neil?' He sighed again, but my smile didn't slip. I wouldn't ask again. I would sit there until he felt foolish and decided to communicate like a normal human being.

He laughed. 'It's just – come *on*.' He looked around the table as if it must be obvious what he was thinking. His gaze lingered on the men and I knew I wasn't going to like what was coming. 'I mean, do you know what the dictionary definition of consent is?'

I felt myself stiffen and wondered how this was going down with the others. 'I think we all understand what is meant by—'

'I looked it up last night.' I wondered if that counted as researching the case but dismissed the idea. 'It's "permission or agreement".'

'I don't think that takes us any further forward . . .'

Helen said, 'Yes, I think we need to concentrate on the evidence.' I nodded, appreciating the backup.

But Neil wasn't about to give up. 'What I mean is, if a man and a woman are together in a bedroom . . .' He was grinning, as if this was some kind of joke and he was about to deliver the punchline. 'If *I'm* with *you*,' he swivelled to face me, and my stomach turned, 'and I put my hand on your knee, say . . .'

I thought, *he's not going to do it*, but he did. He placed the palm of his hand on my knee, his fingers spread out like a thick-legged spider. I looked down at it, this alien thing resting on my jeans, and for a second I froze. I froze, just like Chantelle said she did.

But then he lifted his hand again, waving it around as he talked. 'If you don't say anything, you don't ask me to stop – that's consent.'

I couldn't have been the only one to want to slap him then, to wonder how much of a responsibility we had to any woman he ever met to leave him in no doubt he was an arsehole. I snapped, 'If I have tears running down my face, I think it's pretty clear I'm not consenting.'

It was unmistakably a rebuke, and for a second the room was silent. I hadn't wanted to do that, to contradict anyone so sharply, but what was the alternative? I couldn't allow the others to think his point was reasonable. I was the foreperson. I had to set the boundaries.

Neil shrugged, pretending he wasn't bothered. Accountant Brian was talking, trying to move us on, but for a moment I couldn't concentrate. I was remembering how it felt to have that uninvited hand on my knee. I'd felt the shock of it like ice against my skin, but how much worse might it have been for Chantelle? That first unwanted touch, no one else in the room, no way to stop the second or the third . . . With an effort, I pushed the thought away.

Later, we talked about the logistics: the position of arms and legs, the pulling-down of jogging bottoms, wrists held together, the knee between thighs, then between knees, then over legs, holding them down, the wall, the edge of the bed. Chantelle's evidence was unclear, the defence lawyer's questions prising away at gaps, opening up uncertainties. How could we say there weren't doubts? I felt the consensus building: we would never know what had really taken place in that room.

We went through the accounts of what happened afterwards, when Chantelle was sitting on the stairs, after Ian had gone out. We agreed they added nothing. I recapped on the discussion, checking that we had considered everything: the statements from the police, the medical report, the transcript of the interview Ian had given when he was arrested. There was an imbalance there, I remember: we'd been refused permission to replay the video of Chantelle's statement to the police, but we had Ian's words in black and white in front of us. It didn't seem fair, though I'm still not sure which side it favoured.

When we'd all agreed that we'd looked thoroughly at everything that had been presented to us, I brought out the paper with the charge and read it aloud. I reminded everyone of the three elements, and there was no escaping the words then: Ian Nash penetrated the vagina of Chantelle Patterson with his penis, he did so without her consent, and he did so without reasonable belief of her consent. My voice sounded calm, steady, and again I thought how bizarre it was to be sitting here saying those words to a roomful of adults in precisely the tone of voice I'd use to ask about the incidence of VAT repayment fraud.

And then the moment arrived: we were going to vote. I was about to turn to my left – where Chen was sitting; there was no

way on God's green earth I was going to ask Neil to vote first –
when Helen interrupted.

'I think we should write down our verdicts. So no one is
influenced by what people have said before them.'

It was a good idea; I was annoyed I hadn't thought of it myself.
When we'd all scribbled on our bits of paper and crumpled them
into a ball – no one hesitated, I was pleased to see that – Helen
collected them in a plastic cup and handed it to me.

I tipped out the white balls and reached for the first one.
Everyone was silent, the air thick with anticipation. The paper
had been scrunched tight and I fumbled to straighten it out,
wishing my nails were longer. I smoothed the wrinkled surface
and read aloud what was written there.

'Not guilty.'

My throat tightened on the words. I swallowed, took a breath.
It has to be this way, I told myself. There's no evidence and we all
know it.

I picked up the next ball of paper, unscrewed it, read out the
same words. The next was the same, and the next.

I noticed the differences in the handwriting – sloping to the
left or the right, one with loops on the 'g' and the 'y' (a woman,
surely), another with broad, masculine slashes across the 't's, tiny
letters crouched in the centre of the paper as if embarrassed to be
seen.

I reached for another ball of paper, relieved now that the end
was in sight. I unrolled it and stared at the letters, the handwriting
neat and even. For a second my lips refused to form the word, but
I had to see this through.

'Guilty.'

Chapter 7

The piles of paper sat on the table, ten in one and two – defiant, incomprehensible two – in the other.

I glanced at my watch: five past eleven. We'd deliberated for over three hours. Over three hours of looking at every piece of evidence, of focusing on the facts, of reminding ourselves that we needed to be *sure* in order to return a guilty verdict. All that time, and we'd failed to reach a unanimous conclusion.

I had failed.

Simeon said, 'So where do we go from here?' I bet he was pleased, then, that it wasn't up to him to keep the show on the road. I fought the urge to hide my face in my hands.

'It seems to me we have two options.' There, that sounded as if I knew what I was talking about. 'If the two people who've indicated they consider the defendant to be guilty are prepared to say who they are and explain their thinking, we can focus on those points.' I looked around the table, but no one stirred. 'Alternatively, we can work through all the evidence again and take another vote.'

To their credit, no one groaned, but I can't have been the only one praying for option one. Another three hours of revisiting everything we'd already discussed? Please God, no.

There was a creak as Siobhan straightened in her plastic seat. 'I don't mind saying I was one of the people who wrote down guilty.'

'Yes, I did too.' Chen. I hadn't seen that coming.

I shuffled my papers as if they were important. 'OK. Siobhan, do you want to go first? Was there any particular part of the evidence that made you draw that conclusion?'

For a moment I allowed myself to hope we'd missed something. That Siobhan would get to her feet and, Columbo-like, pace around the room as she highlighted some overlooked fact. That we'd turn to one another in horror, appalled that we'd almost failed to notice a vital piece of evidence, certain, finally, of our verdict.

But instead she looked across the table at me, anger in the set of her jaw. 'No, but that's just it. I can't see how you'd ever be able to find evidence in a case like this.' She frowned. 'I just don't believe that anyone would make up something like that. I believe Chantelle.'

What could I say to that? *I know, and I want to believe her too*?

I turned away. 'And what about you, Chen?'

'What he said, about his penis. How it go inside her.'

I hoped the shock didn't show on my face. Chen had seemed so reserved; I wouldn't have expected the straightforward explanation. But I still didn't understand what she meant.

I said again, 'OK,' as if this was all part of the script. 'So it sounds like you have very different reasons for your decisions. For you, Siobhan, it's almost a matter of principle . . .' Siobhan nodded. 'And for you, Chen, it's about a specific piece of evidence.'

'Yes.'

'So perhaps we could start with that piece of evidence and see why other people haven't drawn the same conclusion.'

Around the table heads were nodding and I felt everyone relax a notch; they thought I had things under control. I hoped they were right.

Chen picked up her pencil, tapped it against the table. 'What Ian said, he stand to take off jeans. But then he said put penis inside her. I can't see how. How he reach.'

I was bemused, and looking around the table I saw I wasn't alone. I was about to ask her to say more – my standard trick in cases where I didn't have a clue what one of my staff was talking about but didn't want to admit it – but Isabella came to my rescue.

'No, that is not what he meant.' She leaned across the table, painted fingernails waggling. 'They were lying down when he did it. So he just took his penis and put it in. Like this.' She made a movement with her hand. I wasn't any the wiser, but Chen seemed to be getting it; perhaps you had to have English as your second language. 'You understand what I am saying?'

There was more mime and then Chen was nodding. 'I see. OK. Then I think not guilty.'

Was that really all it took for her to change her mind? I asked, 'Are you sure, Chen?'

'Yes, yes. I not understand before. I understand now.'

I wasn't sure of the logic, but Chen seemed satisfied. What more was there to do? I turned to Siobhan. 'So, Siobhan, you said that you believed Chantelle was telling the truth.'

'Yes.'

She was on her own now, and I felt for her. But she couldn't just pick a side – that wasn't what we were there for. I tried to formulate a way of saying there was no evidence that wouldn't sound dismissive.

'But there's no evidence.' Lorraine, of course, tactful as ever. 'I know what you mean. I want to believe Chantelle too. But we have to be sure. I don't see how we can be sure without evidence.'

The others murmured in agreement. Siobhan folded her arms. 'I just can't believe that anyone would make up a story like that. A woman wouldn't do that.'

I opened my mouth to reply, unsure of what I was going to say, but Helen got there first. 'Unfortunately, that's not true.' She was quiet but firm, just the kind of voice you'd want for a social worker. 'I've come across young girls who lie about all kinds of things you wouldn't imagine anyone lying about. There are things in their lives, you see . . .'

'Really?' It wasn't a challenge. Siobhan sounded like she wanted to believe her. It's such a strong thing, the herd instinct. Even when you don't want to think of yourself as part of the crowd. I could see it in her eyes: already she wanted to change her mind.

Accountant Brian said, 'I just don't see how we can reach a guilty verdict when there's no real evidence.'

Siobhan puffed out her cheeks and for a moment I wondered whether she was going to cry. Instead she said, 'But there were two of them in a room. How is anyone ever going to be convicted if we insist the victim has to prove it happened?'

It was something I'd thought about myself. I wondered how many of the others had been worrying about the same thing. But there were only two choices available to us: guilty or not guilty. We weren't in Scotland, with the safety net of 'not proven'. We couldn't hedge our bets.

I said, 'I know exactly how you feel. You hear those statistics on conviction rates and here we are, another jury about to acquit a man of rape.' I corrected myself. 'I mean, *looking* as if we're about to acquit him. But the truth is, however hard it is to find evidence, there *are* things the police could have done.'

It was what I'd been telling myself. I didn't want to believe the process wouldn't work; that everyone on the side of right could have done all they should have and a guilty man could still go unpunished. We jurors couldn't know what had happened for sure, but that wasn't our fault. There were others to blame. The police who'd investigated, who hadn't given us the evidence we needed. I would serve them up on a platter for Siobhan, for all of us, so we wouldn't have to lie awake at night worrying that we had failed a woman who'd been raped.

I said, 'They could have checked the CD player for prints. Ian said Chantelle had led the way to the bedroom and put the CD in the player, didn't he? Chantelle said he'd done it.'

I could see Siobhan's resistance beginning to falter. She nodded slowly.

'They focused too much on the incident itself, but the medical evidence didn't tell us anything. If they'd looked more widely, tried to corroborate other aspects of Chantelle's statement, things might be different.' I shook my head. 'But we can only work with what they've given us.'

Siobhan sighed again. She said, 'I suppose you're right. I just feel terrible that Chantelle is going to think we didn't believe her.'

Helen, sitting next to her, placed a hand on her arm. 'There's support out there for people in her position.'

'All we can do is know that we've fulfilled our responsibility as jurors,' I said, trying to convince myself as much as Siobhan. 'That we've examined all the evidence thoroughly and used our judgement to reach a fair verdict.' I looked around the table again. 'I think we can say in all good conscience that we've done that.'

Siobhan bit her lip. For a moment she was silent – then she nodded, one small, swift dip of her head, as if ashamed. 'Then I suppose it has to be "not guilty",' she said.

There was a sigh, a lightening in the room. I felt something loosen in my spine. Lorraine picked up the phone to tell Janet we'd reached a verdict, and I heard the relief in her voice.

Later, I would wonder how many of us really believed Ian was innocent; how many of us were torn between knowing what the rule of law demanded and fear that we were letting a rapist onto the streets. He would leave the court straight away, a free man. There was no transition, no waiting in a cell while things were finalised, no paperwork. He would step out of that courtroom, walk down the corridor, across the shiny-floored lobby and through the heavy doors with their glass panels, down the steps into the car park and an April day. Perhaps we would even see him as we left ourselves. How would we feel if he recognised us, wanted to thank us?

The rules ended in the courtroom. There was no etiquette that I knew of for meeting someone you'd sat in judgement over, someone whose freedom was your responsibility.

But at that moment, as I sat waiting for Janet to return and take us back in, I refused to think about that. I could feel it all coming to an end, and I was glad.

I didn't look at him as I stepped into the jury box and took my seat. I remembered reading somewhere, or perhaps I'd seen it on TV, that jurors won't look at a defendant when they've decided on a guilty verdict. I wondered if Ian had heard that too. I didn't want him to think I was on his side.

The clerk, a stern-looking man with a beaky nose, said, 'Madam Forewoman, please rise,' and I got to my feet, my hands folded together in front of me.

He said, 'Answer yes or no to the first question only.' A pause to make sure I'd absorbed the instruction. 'Have you reached a verdict on which you are all agreed?'

'Yes.' My voice was clear.

'And do you find the defendant, Ian Craig Nash, guilty or not guilty?'

I wouldn't pause, I wouldn't draw out the moment. I said, 'Not guilty.'

There was a collective breath, as if the room itself had exhaled. And then a woman screamed.

I was looking at the clerk and I saw the horror flash across his face. The scream had come from above me and to my right. The public gallery.

I stood there, afraid to turn my head, afraid the scream would turn into words, to abuse. Chen was sitting beside me and I could feel her trembling. There was movement up in the gallery; I could see the shadows in my peripheral vision, hear feet on floorboards, a sob. I couldn't help it then. I looked across at the dock.

And then the judge was calling us to order, thanking us for considering the evidence so thoroughly, and Janet was leading us from the jury box, up some steps next to the judge and out through a door we'd never used before.

We stood in a corridor. A few people had tears in their eyes. Helen was white-faced. For a moment no one spoke; but then it was as if a button had been pressed, and words were tumbling out from all directions: *who screamed, saw her, perhaps her mother, see his face, guard had to repeat the verdict, think they were his parents . . .*

I didn't speak. I didn't tell anyone what I'd seen when I'd looked at Ian standing in the dock. I felt like I'd used up all my words in those few seconds on my feet.

We were taken to another room to hand in expenses claims. I wasn't going to bother submitting any, but for some reason I found I didn't want to leave the others just yet. I stood at the back of the room, waiting while two efficient-looking women checked that people had correctly completed their forms. When Siobhan got to the front of the queue, I heard her say, 'Is there any way we can give feedback to the police?'

Helen was standing next to her and she added, 'I just think they should know the kinds of things juries consider. If they'd only looked for other evidence . . .'

A grey-haired woman with glasses glanced up from the form in her hands. 'No, the verdict is the verdict. They'll look at all of that themselves.'

'It's just that if they hadn't focused so much on one part of the story . . .' Helen again. *She thought he was guilty.* My hands went cold.

The grey-haired woman put down the form. 'Perhaps they didn't. Perhaps the reason they didn't present any other evidence was that there wasn't any.' She looked at Helen over the rim of her glasses. 'Hmm?'

People started to leave once they'd dropped off their forms, pausing to say goodbye to me as they passed. A few said thank you. I saw Helen rearranging her bag on her shoulder and fell into step beside her.

'I'm so glad that's over.'

'Yes.'

'Are you going back to London Bridge?'

A short pause before she nodded; perhaps she didn't want to walk with me. I said, 'I found that really hard.' I swallowed. Why did I want her reassurance? But suddenly my eyes were swimming with tears.

She looked at me then. 'You had it harder than any of us, I think. I wouldn't have liked to be in your shoes.' She touched her fingers to my arm, like she had with Siobhan. 'I thought you handled it very well.'

'Thanks.' We'd reached the lobby and the heels of Helen's sensible court shoes clicked across the tiles. One of the security guards on the X-ray machines tipped an imaginary cap at us and I smiled back at him. *People can be friendly. They can be kind.*

Out in the weak April sunshine I scanned the courtyard, but there was no sign of Ian. I stole a glance at Helen; her eyes were fixed straight ahead. She didn't want to risk seeing him. I checked my watch – the business with the claim forms had taken longer than I'd thought. I said, 'He'll be long gone by now.'

She didn't answer. We passed alongside the barrier that prevented cars driving up to the front of the court building, and onto the street. The pavements were as busy as the road and Helen kept up a swift pace, the two of us ducking and weaving around the other pedestrians. We'd barely spoken by the time we reached the station, and I was about to wave goodbye when she stopped me.

'Look, I hope you don't think this is weird.' She was reaching into her shoulder bag, rummaging in its depths. 'Would you mind if we exchanged numbers?'

I looked at her blankly. I'm not the kind of person people normally make an effort to keep in touch with. 'Sure, if you like.'

'It's just – all this . . . I mean, it'll pass, I'm sure . . .' I nodded, as if I knew what she meant. Actually, for once I thought I might. 'But at the moment it's like it's filling my head. And I know we're not allowed to talk about it . . . I just thought it would be nice to be able to speak to someone, you know, one of us . . .'

I smiled. 'I think so too. Feel free to call, any time.' I was surprised as I spoke to realise I meant it. I read out my number and she programmed it into her phone.

'There. I've sent you a text so you'll have my number too. Right then.' For a moment we stood looking at each other, and then Helen reached out and we hugged, brief and awkward. I looked back at her once as she was swallowed up in the crowd of commuters at the ticket barriers, and wondered if we'd ever speak to each other again.

Chapter 8

The weekend after the case had finished, it was all I could think about. It wasn't just that I'd lie in bed turning it over in my mind, trying to distract myself with thoughts about work, or the forthcoming christening of my niece, or whether I should try one of those holidays where single people go around in a group, anything to stop my brain replaying that scream. It was the same during the daytime. It would creep up on me as I was cleaning my teeth or watering the dragon tree or piercing the cellophane on a microwave lasagne. I'd find myself standing there, the images flashing in front of my eyes: Chantelle in tears; Eloise Havilland, her mouth set in a grim line, *I knew what had happened*; Ian's smirk. *She seemed to enjoy it at the time.*

Details I hadn't fully registered during the trial clawed their way to the surface of my brain. Why had Ian followed Chantelle to the bedroom if he hadn't wanted to get involved with someone living next door? Why had he left so abruptly afterwards – what phone call on a Saturday afternoon would have sent him scurrying from the bed of a willing woman? He'd admitted he'd been angry after that argument at work. Had he felt powerless?

Had he decided to go over to Chantelle's and make himself feel better by taking what he wanted?

And the other thing, the thing I told myself meant nothing, but which returned to me time and again: the look on his face when I glanced back at the dock. He was grinning.

On the Monday I went back to work, a week earlier than I'd told them to expect me. Janet had told us we might be assigned to a second trial, but that hadn't happened. I assumed they had enough jurors and I was relieved; I didn't know how I could have concentrated on a new case when my brain was still full of Chantelle and Ian. Back at the office people asked what had happened, but when I told them it was a rape case they went quiet and didn't ask anything more.

I'd looked at my BlackBerry on the train and it was already clear that a week off had been enough to leave my email inbox overflowing. Alan, predictably enough, had done the bare minimum to keep things ticking over, responding to requests for advice with the sort of on-the-one-hand, on-the-other-hand briefing that drove the minister's office mad. Sat at my desk, I'd barely pressed send on my first email to Ciara, his private secretary, when my phone rang. I glanced down at the name on the screen and took a deep breath.

'Hi, Ciara.'

'Thank God you're back! Have you seen the letter from Marsden?' Elliot Marsden was the Secretary of State for the Environment, Food and Rural Affairs, a portly chap with ruddy cheeks who looked every inch the country farmer he was. On his appointment, he'd declared the role his dream job, and he and his civil servants, flushed with excitement at having a minister who wasn't secretly smarting at having been overlooked for a proper role, had been in a state of hyperactivity ever since. I'd read his latest missive on the way into the office, a letter to the Chancellor proposing increasing VAT on food imports from countries where farmers used nuronics, pesticides that were apparently causing incalculable damage to the bee population. More to the point, UK farmers weren't allowed to use them, an asymmetry I imagined went down like a bucket of cold sick with Marsden's wax-jacketed chums. I'd assumed his pleas would get the usual polite Treasury brush-off, but apparently I was wrong.

'HMT have asked for implementation costs.'

'Right . . .'

'And they want something by two.'

'Today?'

'I'm afraid so. The Chancellor has a visit to Kent next week.'

'They're not seriously considering an announcement?'

Ciara sighed. 'Number Ten are keen . . .'

I supposed I should have been pleased we'd been asked; it wouldn't have been the first time we'd found out about a policy change from Sky News. I hung up and got to my feet. 'Everyone, I'm going to need you to drop what you're doing. We need implementation costs for a VAT hike. I'll email around in a minute with the commission.' I braced myself for the complaints. 'Private office want it by two.'

I sat back down and started to type, letting the background grumbling wash over me. It was typical craziness, announcement-driven policy-making of the kind I most detested; but at least it would take my mind off the trial.

There was no let-up over the following days. Treasury had lost interest in defending the bees after seeing the upfront costs, but DEFRA weren't giving up. There were more requests for calculations, questions about the assumptions, and increasingly sarcastic emails from one of the DEFRA spads – special advisers

– that had got up our own minister's nose to the extent that he'd asked for a letter to go to Marsden 'to tell him to get his tanks off my fucking lawn' – or, as Ciara's email put it, 'to clarify that our position is based on long experience of implementing VAT policy, and is intended to ensure policy objectives are achievable at proportionate cost to the Exchequer'. By the time the Chancellor had returned from Kent and I'd checked the transcript of his speech – oh happy day! A week and a half of running around like headless chickens and the end result was no mention of bloody bees – thoughts of the trial had been driven almost entirely from my head.

Almost. I still wondered whether we'd done the right thing. I worried that I'd missed something, misread a vital detail. But I told myself it was in the past. There was nothing now that I could do to change it, no way of finding out what had really happened. I reminded myself what I'd told Siobhan during the trial: all we could do was consider the evidence in front of us. We had done that – even the judge had thanked us for taking the time to consider it carefully. We had nothing to reproach ourselves for.

When the next Saturday rolled around, I indulged in a lie-in. It's not something I do often – I work long hours during the week and I don't like to waste my weekends in bed, at least not now I'm single again.

But no, let me stop there; that's a rather misleading comment. You've picked up on the suggestion, I imagine, that when Aidan and I were together, we'd laze around wrapped in creased bed sheets, sleepy and sexy, too absorbed in each other to make it out of the bedroom. That wasn't us. We just weren't that kind of couple. We preferred to get up and do something – visit a museum or an art gallery, stroll round a market. He even insisted we go mudlarking once, wandering along the Thames foreshore under leaden skies picking up bits and pieces given up by the river.

To Aidan's disgust, I emptied my pockets before we climbed back to street level, leaving a pile of clay pipe fragments and pot shards next to the steps. He took his home and put them in a shoebox.

I suppose I should have known then we were never going to last.

But like I said, that Saturday morning I was alone. It was grey outside and I had no reason to drag myself from my bed. I had to be up early again the next day; it was Evie's christening – Evie being the daughter of my sister Stella and her tedious husband Michael – and I'd have to find my way to a damp church somewhere in Ealing and be sociable until I could leave without causing offence. One lazy day before that ordeal didn't seem too much to ask.

I sat there cocooned in my duvet, reading a thriller on my Kindle. I was sure I'd worked out who the murderer was – it was usually the same with this author; you just had to identify the guy who seemed a bit wet, the one the heroine regarded with tolerant amusement until thirty pages from the end, when she started to get the uneasy feeling that he wasn't quite what he seemed. I enjoyed them all the same – recognising the formula was part of the fun, knowing that you were clever enough to spot the pattern.

It was a rumbling stomach that eventually had me heading to the kitchen. I opened a cupboard, then shut it again, stared at the contents of the fridge. It was no good. I would have to go shopping. So much for a lazy day.

Out on the street, the traffic crawled along, the roads heaving even at the weekend. The blast of exhaust fumes hit me in the face and I kept to the far edge of the pavement. The air quality in London was dreadful; maybe Elliot Marsden should have been worrying about *that*.

The supermarket was crowded with people taking advantage of a day off work to stock up on household necessities. I squeezed past old women with a bit of cheese or a packet of sausages in their baskets, people who spread out their shopping through the week so they'd have some human interaction, and younger ones apparently there for the express purpose of shouting at their children. There were fewer men, a handful of them on their own but most in supporting roles to their wives or girlfriends, carrying baskets or adding a DVD to the pile of groceries; anyone who thinks there's sexual equality in this country should take a look around their nearest supermarket.

'Oh Christ, sorry!' A woman with a trolley had banged into my legs. 'Sorry, sorry. Tarquin, put that down!'

I squeezed out a smile and rubbed at my shins. 'It's fine . . .' But she'd already turned away and was clutching the arm of a chubby-faced toddler who'd managed to find the one box of Coco Pops with a hole in the side. Sticky brown grains of puffed rice were cascading onto the floor at his feet. *Tarquin*. In Lewisham. I shook my head and made for the checkout.

I could still hear her as I stood in the queue. 'No, we don't need any of that . . . Put it back, please . . . Put. It. BACK, Tarquin!'

I watched the man in front of me load the contents of his basket onto the conveyer belt. A carton of milk, six bottles of Peroni in a cardboard cradle, a packet of scones and a clear plastic tray with a perplexing combination of samosas, mini Scotch eggs and cocktail sausages. Maybe it counted as fusion cuisine. He was taller than me, in a dark wool coat with a hoodie sticking out at the neck.

From behind me the woman's voice carried over the clatter of trolleys. 'Do you want to go on the naughty step? Is that what you want?'

The conveyor belt was moving but the man in front hadn't put the plastic divider in place behind his shopping. I tutted as I stretched across to get it, but he didn't seem to notice. Honestly,

71

some people were oblivious. And then he was reaching for his wallet and taking out a card, and as he pressed it to the reader he turned a fraction and I saw the side of his face.

I felt the breath leave my body.

Because I knew that face. I'd spent a week watching it for a reaction as he stood in the dock. It was him. It was Ian Nash.

Chapter 9

'Look, if you're upset, just say you're upset. I can't cope with your passive aggression. Not today.'

This was wishful thinking on Stella's part. My sister wanted me to be miserable because she hadn't asked me to be godmother to the squirming little beetroot who had just been christened Evie Adele Olivia. Three names, just to prove how important she was. Stella claimed the Adele was homage to a dear departed aunt of Michael's, but I knew better: she'd played 'Chasing Pavements' non-stop through most of 2008. In any case, I wasn't upset. I don't like children and I don't believe in God; anyone would agree those were poor qualifications for godmother-hood. I couldn't have cared less that she hadn't asked me – which was, of course, why it was really Stella who was upset.

'Any reason for all the vowels?'

'What?' She was dressed top to toe in Boden. That's the kind of woman my sister is. She picks things out of the catalogue imagining herself wearing them as she drinks coffee with 'the girls' or takes Evie to baby yoga. And the amazing thing is, those things will actually happen.

'Evie Adele Olivia. E, A, O. All vowels.'

She took a breath and I could tell she was trying not to raise her voice. 'Look, Natalie, Saskia and I have really bonded since the children were born . . .'

I wasn't going to respond to that. Stella had met Saskia at antenatal classes and had taken an immediate liking to her on the basis that she lived in a Victorian house in Kew that wouldn't give you much change from five million. I knew this because Stella's Saskia-related conversation was all bifold doors and light wells and *five minutes' walk from the botanical gardens*. She wanted to live in Saskia's house, and the next best thing was the chance of her daughter doing so in the vanishingly unlikely event that Stella and Michael ever did anything so remotely interesting as to die young.

'Evie Adele Olivia Wainwright.'

'Look.' It was the third time she'd said that. *Look. Look at me. Look at me with my wonderful life.* 'I just wanted you to know it wasn't that we didn't think of you . . .'

'E, A, O, W. You wouldn't want to put her initials on things, would you? EAOW. It's like a noise a cat might make if you pulled its tail.'

Stella's nostrils flared like a horse. 'Oh, just fuck off.' She turned and walked away, swinging that blonde hair over her shoulder, off to find Michael to complain about how awful I was. Well, good. I wrapped some canapés in a paper napkin and shoved them in my bag for later. Evie was near the door, swaddled in the arms of Michael's mother, the sole grandmother since both our parents are dead. That's right, I'm Evie's closest relative on her mother's side. And I still didn't get to be fucking godmother.

I stuck my tongue out at her, and her silver-penny gaze rested on me as I left the room.

* * *

74

The traffic on the South Circular was the usual horror story, and by the time I got home, my stomach was rumbling. I poured a glass of wine and retrieved the napkin-wrapped canapés from my bag, tipping them onto a plate and taking them through to the living room. I switched on the TV and let the voices wash over me as I ate.

A little light sparring with my sister usually made me feel better about myself, but today it hadn't worked. My thoughts kept returning to the supermarket, to Ian, his hands on his wallet, his broad back in that dark coat, the line of his jaw as he turned towards me. I'd kept my eyes down after I'd realised who he was, and he hadn't seen me; or if he had, he must have been as keen as I was to avoid acknowledgements, because he collected his carrier bags and was gone without a word. The moment he'd left, I was angry with myself. I paid for my shopping as quickly as I could, hopping from one foot to the other as the woman on the till rang up the items. I stuffed them in my bag and rushed into the street, scanning the crowd in both directions, but there was no sign of him. I have no idea what I'd have said if I'd caught up with him. I didn't have a plan. But in that moment, I'd been sure that if I spoke to him, *I would know.* I would somehow know whether he was innocent or guilty.

I reasoned that he would have gone home, but when I tried to drag the address from my memory, it slid through my grasp like quicksilver. The street name had started with an M, I was sure. Or perhaps it was an N? The harder I focused, the further it slipped away.

I'd wasted my chance to speak to him, and now I could only try to find clues in the circumstances of our meeting.

He'd been shopping. In a supermarket. That was a normal thing to do, right? Surely people who were racked with guilt didn't pop into Sainsbury's for milk and samosas? Or then again, perhaps he didn't feel guilty. He'd denied it, after all. Perhaps that was the meaning of that final smile: he was congratulating himself on having got away with it, on having pulled the wool over our eyes. Perhaps he was going to pop open one of those bottles of beer and toast himself, give three cheers for how clever he'd been. Maybe he thought that if he could get away with it once, he could do it again. Maybe he was now more dangerous than ever.

Maybe we'd made him that way.

I put down the plate and took a swig of wine, screwing up my eyes as it went down. I tried to resist the idea, but it was no good: I'd been the foreperson. I was responsible for that verdict.

OK, I hadn't done it on my own. The others had agreed the evidence wasn't there. But what if I'd taken a different approach? What if I'd entertained the question Siobhan had asked, if I'd given us more space to consider something other than playing by the rules? The odds were stacked against Chantelle – asking her to relive what had happened, to give a clear-cut account, no hesitation, repetition or deviation. No space for any emotion, to recognise that trauma would have clouded her recollection. Looked at now, it seemed so unfair. Maybe I'd colluded with a system designed to avoid giving women the justice they deserved.

As for the case for the defence, that solitary testimony from Ian: I'd taken it all at face value. I hadn't asked the others what it said about a man that not a single character witness could be found to testify on his behalf. I'd decided the evidence against him wasn't watertight, that was enough.

And as I sat there in the cold light of the television screen, it was suddenly clear to me: I couldn't carry on like this. I couldn't live with the suspicion that another lying man thought he'd got away with it – not again. It wouldn't be easy, but that didn't matter.

I was going to find the truth.

* * *

I went back to the supermarket every night that week. This was my routine: leave the office by 7 p.m., walk to Westminster Tube station, check through my downloaded emails on the way to London Bridge, reply to anything either important or quick to deal with when the signal returned on the train to Lewisham, go to the flat, boil the kettle, change my clothes, drink tea, check the dragon tree didn't need watering, go to the supermarket.

There I would patrol the aisles with a basket, searching for a man almost a foot taller than me with short dark hair and strong hands.

That first day I spent just half an hour in the store, anxious, believing people were watching me. I ended up buying a lettuce, a bottle of fish sauce, six finger rolls, a wedge of Brie, a pack of kitchen roll, a bottle of wine and a photography magazine.

After that, I refined my technique. I'd walk straight in, not pausing to pick up a basket. First stop was the fresh fruit aisle, where I'd collect some strawberries or a bag of salad. Then I'd go on to the bakery, standing at the end where the special offers were to get a good look down the length and breadth of the store. After that, it was cheese, then a tin of something, then – a wry smile to myself: I hadn't realised how much I needed! – back to the entrance to pick up a basket. On my way there, I'd jettison some of the items, pause at the bottom of household goods, scan to the back and sides again, let my eyes wander over the queues at the checkouts. Then it was the freezer section, surrounded by the hum of the chiller cabinets, then meat and poultry, confectionery and finally beer and wine. I'd do a return circuit to put things back, perhaps picking up a ready meal to stick in the microwave when I got home, and then finally – the bit that always made the breath catch in my throat – head for the tills, waiting to catch sight of the dark coat with a hood sticking out at the neck.

My feet ached from walking the hard floors, and after the first day I wore trainers. I didn't own a hoodie myself, but I wrapped a scarf around my neck ready to bury my face in it if I needed to. I wanted to see Ian, yes, but that didn't mean I was ready for him to see me. I knew I was hurting my chances by going at the same time each day, but work meant that evenings were the only option. On the third day I'd told myself I'd get there later; but I was too restless to wait. It wasn't until I was pacing the aisles, my heartbeat increasing every time I saw a tall man in a dark coat, that the nervous energy started to dissipate; and as the minutes ticked by and every face was a false alarm, I'd start to remember that I was hungry and tired, and there was less than eleven hours before I'd have to be back in the office again. Then I'd pay for my ready meal and make my way home, not sure whether I was disappointed or relieved.

When Saturday came around again, I was in the supermarket half an hour earlier than the day I'd seen Ian, and I stayed half an hour later too. The aisles were crowded with weekend shoppers and I felt less self-conscious, but it was hard to check all those faces, hard to stay alert for that one figure in the midst of all the others. In the end, I bought a pack of croissants and headed into the din of the street market outside, telling myself it was time to let it go. I couldn't keep haunting a supermarket.

It was warm for May and people had got overexcited in the way they do when they've started to believe that summer is on its way. Coats were draped over arms, and here and there a hardy soul sported short sleeves. I scanned their faces – it was automatic by then – but there was no one I recognised.

Some people claim they like the street market; they use words like 'vibrant' and 'community'. Funny how no one ever uses words like that for places with money. It doesn't do anything for me. It's smelly and crowded and everywhere you look there are rails of grubby polyester blouses and plastic bowls of apples and bananas soaking up the pollution. All the same, that day I found myself lingering, trying to ignore the feeling of anticlimax. The trial is over, I tried to tell myself; there's nothing more you can do.

I wandered the stalls, stopping to browse at one selling second-hand books. I bought a copy of the *Bhagavad Gita*, 'a masterpiece of Sanskrit poetry', which felt like the kind of thing a thinking person should have read. A few steps further on I stopped again and contemplated some hand-knitted booties. I was thinking of Evie, of course, and was on the point of getting out my purse again when I realised there'd be no way of giving them to her that Stella wouldn't choose to interpret as an apology. I put them back and continued on my way.

By the time I reached the end of the market it was nearly lunch-time, and my rumbling stomach reminded me of the croissants. I considered getting a bus home, but there was a clutch of shouty teenagers at the bus stop; I'd walk instead. If Aidan were with me he'd have suggested keeping going into Brockley or Blackheath, having brunch at some overpriced café or gastropub. Maybe even now he was tucking into eggs Benedict, the bimbo sitting doe-eyed across the table as he checked his watch and reminded her that Fulham had a three o'clock kick-off. I pulled out my phone and tapped out a short text, just to remind him I was there.

When I reached the main road, the traffic was a solid metal cord, barely moving as it stank and growled in a cloud of exhausts. I would have risked crossing, but I'd been caught out before by nippy motorcycles hidden by the cars and vans, and I stopped at the traffic lights and pressed the button. On my right, a young mother fussed with the buttons on her toddler's coat. I caught the kid's eye and she started to raise a chubby finger in my direction. I turned away.

Turned to where a dark-haired man stood with his hands in the pockets of a navy wool coat.

For a moment, I simply stared, hearing the blood pounding in my ears. The man hadn't shaved – his stubble was beginning to turn into a beard – and beneath his eyes the skin was puffy and bruised, as if he hadn't slept. There was no hoodie that day, just a blue T-shirt with something printed on it that was mostly hidden by the front of his coat. But there was no question about it: it was Ian.

He was staring straight ahead, waiting for the lights to change. I made myself look away before he noticed me watching him. I'd rehearsed this, I knew what I was going to say. *It's Ian, isn't it? I don't know if you remember me* . . . And he'd say yes, of course he did, and I'd say . . . Well, I hadn't got that far. I think that's because I'd never really believed it would happen.

A movement at my side and he'd started to cross: the lights had turned amber for the traffic and the woman next to me was telling her daughter to wait for the green man. I saw Ian reach the other side, striding down the pavement in the opposite direction to the one I'd been planning to take.

I shook myself out of my trance and followed.

Chapter 10

I had to hurry to keep up with him, my eyes fixed on the back of his head, his shoulders in the navy coat. He was taller than most of the other pedestrians, but I didn't let my gaze drop for a moment. I wasn't about to lose him a second time.

I'd closed the gap between us to a few metres when he turned abruptly and disappeared into a doorway on the left. It was a newsagent, the kind of place that promises to do your dry-cleaning and send money abroad in addition to supplying bread and milk. I took my phone from my pocket and pretended to study it as I stood on the pavement outside.

I thought: I'll wait for him to come out and I'll say something. I'll tell him who I am, and I'll ask to meet him for coffee.

Another voice in my head wondered what I'd say when he asked why I wanted to meet, but I didn't have an answer to that so I ignored it. One thing at a time.

The seconds dragged past. There was an envelope at the top of my phone screen; Aidan probably, but for once, he didn't seem important. A rumbling sound made me look up; it was an old lady with one of those shopping trolleys on wheels. She was heading in my direction, determination etched into the lines of her face. The pavement wasn't wide enough for both of us, but she showed no sign of slowing down. I stepped back to let her pass and my back hit something solid, the edge of my heel pressing down with a crunch.

'For fuck's sake!'

I swung around to see a tall man in a navy coat glowering at me. *Oh Christ.*

'Watch where you're going, love. You nearly broke my fucking toe.'

It was his tone that did it, the tone and that word. I felt the blood rush to my head and in a second all my nervousness was gone.

'Well, if you'd been looking where *you* were going, perhaps you'd have seen I was trying to avoid the old lady with the shopping trolley. *Love.*'

We glared at each other and he muttered something under his breath and pushed past me onto the pavement. 'Wait!' He didn't stop and I hurried after him. 'Please wait. I wanted to talk to you.'

He turned then, his brow furrowed. He really was a lot taller than I was; I stayed a few steps away so I could look at him without craning my neck.

'What do you want?' There was suspicion in his voice. 'Do I know you?'

He was looking at me more closely now, trying to place me. I said, 'Yes, you do. Well, we've seen each other before.'

He shrugged, but when he spoke again some of his confidence was gone. 'Right. So are you going to tell me where, or am I supposed to stand here and guess?'

'In Southwark.' I waited for the penny to drop. 'Last month.'

He blinked and took a half-step backwards. I could see him trying to find something to say. At least I'd had a chance to prepare for this meeting, even if I hadn't done it very well. I still had him at a disadvantage.

He said, 'You were . . .'

'On the jury, yes.' A couple holding hands walked past and I lowered my voice. 'I was the foreperson.'

He swallowed, looked around as if at any moment someone was going to jump out from behind a lamp post and push a microphone in his face. He opened his mouth and then shut it again.

I said, 'Can we talk? I just wanted to . . .' *Ask you a few questions.* But no, that sounded like something the police would say. 'I just wanted to explain.'

He looked confused, but I didn't give him a chance to ask what I meant. I reached into my pocket for my phone. 'I promise I won't take much of your time. What's your number?'

'What?'

'I need to go now, but we can meet later. There's a pub not far from here – the Phoenix. Do you know it?'

'Yes, but—'

'Let's say four o'clock. Give me your number and I'll text you if I'm delayed.'

I thought he was going to argue, but he didn't. It was the shock, I suppose. I tapped the number he recited into my phone, then held up my hand. 'Wait a sec, I'll just make sure I've put it in right.' We both knew I was checking if he'd lied.

I pressed the dial button and his phone jangled in his pocket – some rock song I didn't recognise. He said, 'I'm not sure this is a good idea. Aren't we supposed to—'

I cut him off. 'I've got to go. We'll talk later, OK? The Phoenix, four o'clock.' I turned and walked away. I didn't look back, but I ducked down the first side street I came to, walking in the opposite direction to my flat. I didn't want him knowing where I lived.

It took another fifteen minutes of random junctions and wide circuits to get home, and when I turned into my own road, I risked a glance over my shoulder. There was no sign of him. I let myself in, left the croissants on the kitchen counter and went to my desk. By four o'clock, I would be ready.

I got to the Phoenix early, wanting to choose the table. I'd only ever been there after work, meeting Aidan for a drink and sometimes a bite to eat before he came back to mine. It was a different place in the afternoon, empty except for a couple of student types at the bar and a man with a pint and a spaniel snoozing under the table in a corner. They hadn't bothered to put the music on, and the daylight showed the scuffs on the floorboards, the rings left by glasses on the tables.

It had been drizzling, and I folded my umbrella and stowed it under a seat at the side of the room before going to the bar and ordering a glass of wine. I took it back to the table, positioning myself facing the door so I'd see Ian before he saw me. If he turned up.

I pulled out my phone, trying to find something to do with my hands. I wondered how many other people did the same thing. Before the smoking ban, it would have been a cigarette. Perhaps that was the real reason people were obsessed with their phones; it wasn't the text messages or the kitten videos. They just needed a social prop.

At the bar, the students were laughing with the barmaid, an Australian woman with dyed black hair. I was too far away to hear what they were saying, and that was good; they wouldn't be able to overhear anything either.

The door swung open and my stomach lurched. It was Ian; he'd actually come, and he was early too. He stood in the doorway, silhouetted against the light from outside, almost filling the space. I watched him scan the room and raised my arm. He froze for a second, and even from across the pub I could tell he'd hoped I wouldn't be there; but the next moment he was approaching the table. I stood – I didn't want him towering over me – and then wished I hadn't because it felt like I should greet him in some way, perhaps offer to shake his hand. Instead I looked down at my glass. 'Can I get you something to drink?'

He shook his head. 'I'll get these. It's the least I can do in the circumstances. Same again?'

I nodded, though my glass was still nearly full, and he went to the bar without asking which wine I was drinking. He was nervous too. I watched as he ordered, trying to calm my breathing. When he came back, he sat down without taking off his jacket; he didn't expect to be there long.

I said, 'I told you I wanted to explain.'

He held up his hand to stop me. 'What's your name? You know who I am. You know all kinds of stuff about me, but you haven't even told me your name.' His tone was sharp; he might be nervous, but he was angry too.

I squared my shoulders and smiled to let him know he didn't intimidate me. 'It's Natalie. Natalie Wright.'

He nodded, scowled down at his pint. 'OK. So how did you find me?'

The shock must have shown on my face. 'What do you mean? I didn't find you.'

'So it was a coincidence? You just happened to see me in the street?' His lips curled and I remembered that smirk on the witness stand; it wasn't supposed to go like this. I drew myself up and looked him in the eye.

'That's right. You may recall I wasn't even looking when I bumped into you. As you pointed out at the time.'

He didn't say anything, just kept glowering at his pint glass. I'd had enough of this. I wasn't the one who had to justify myself. I said, 'Frankly, I don't care whether you believe me or not. I thought you'd want an explanation, but if you're not interested, I'll just leave now.'

I got to my feet, reaching for the strap of the handbag I'd hung over the back of my chair. He got up too, his chair squawking against the floorboards. 'I'm sorry.'

I ignored him, gathered up my bag. He said again, 'I'm sorry,' and stretched out a hand towards my arm before thinking better of it. I waited. 'I do want an explanation. I mean, I'm not sure what you mean. But if you've got something to say, I want to hear it.'

Out of the corner of my eye I could see the students looking at us with interest; perhaps they thought it was a lovers' tiff. I stood there for a few moments as if considering, then sat back down with a sigh. 'OK, let's start this again.'

It was better after that: I was the one in control. I told him I wanted to explain why we'd taken so long to reach a verdict. I said I'd worried what he'd think about that, that it had felt hard, unfair almost, to make everyone wait overnight, but that we needed to make sure we'd looked at all the evidence properly.

He nodded. 'Of course. I get that.'

'I just wanted you to know that there weren't any doubts. We weren't arguing about it or anything.' *Except at the end.*

'Thanks. That's good to know.'

I looked down at my beer mat, took a breath to keep my voice steady. 'Were you happy with how it went?'

'What?' The anger was back, as if it had been hiding just beneath the surface all the time. I thought: he can change that quickly. Was that how he was with Chantelle?

'Sorry, that was a bad choice of words.' I took a sip of wine to play for time, rearranging the sentence in my head. 'I mean, were you content with the way your case was presented?'

He shrugged. 'I suppose so. Got the right result, anyway.'

'It must have been difficult to have to listen to all that.'

His hand tightened around his beer glass; I saw his fingertips whiten. 'Yeah, well. It's over now.'

I sighed. 'I know this can't be easy.' I looked at him then let my eyes drop again. I'd done my make-up before leaving and my lashes were heavy with mascara; I hadn't told you that, had I? I'd painted my nails too, Rouge Noir, almost the colour of the wine in my glass. I tapped my fingertips against the stem.

I'd planned to ask him to tell me the truth. That was all. Somehow I'd been sure that if I could just see him again, on neutral ground, I could ask him and he'd answer and I'd know if he was lying. I'd thought if it was necessary, if it looked like things were going to get more difficult, I'd just get him drunk, pretend I was drunk too, wait for him to slide into frankness or slip up when his guard was down. I saw now that I'd been stupid; if things carried on like this, he was going to get up and walk out and I'd never see him again. The chance to find out if he really was innocent would have gone for ever.

He'd finished his beer and was shuffling in his seat, about to make some excuse to leave. I couldn't let that happen.

I reached across the table and took his hand, turned it face up. His palm was warm and dry beneath mine. I could feel his fingers against the smooth, thin skin of my wrist. When I looked at him, I saw the surprise in his eyes, and something else, just a flicker, a question. Because that's all it takes with men, ninety-nine times out of a hundred. You don't have to be beautiful. God knows you don't have to be witty or clever. You just have to be available and prepared to show it.

I met his gaze and held it. I said, 'I feel terrible, almost guilty, you know?'

I want you to know that I – the real me – would never say something like that. The 'you know' bit, I mean, finishing with that irritating upward inflection. I was playing a part, being the kind of woman I thought he'd want. Someone soft and cutesy and in need of reassurance. I think I might have actually batted my lashes.

'It just feels so wrong that we women can put a man, someone like you, through something so awful and just get away with it.'

I held my breath as I watched him. For a moment he just sat there, looking down at my hand holding his. I curled my index finger and ran a burgundy fingernail down the centre of his palm.

When I asked if he wanted another drink, he said yes. I felt his eyes on my arse as I went to the bar.

I stared at the computer screen, trying to concentrate on the words. It was a PQ – a parliamentary question – about error rates on VAT returns. I scrolled up and looked at the header – fuck it. It was an oral question too, one where the peer – I checked the document again; Lord Lynshaw of Everdene, apparently – was going to expect the minister to answer it in person. Except that our minister wasn't a lord, so they'd have to dig out some random peer on the payroll who didn't have a clue about the policy to answer it. I suppressed a groan; we normally got Baroness Cooke, a pleasant but nervous woman, who insisted on a minimum of one meeting and an encyclopedic briefing pack to cover every possible follow-up question. I knew from experience that the preparation would be wasted; she would invariably respond to any probing query by standing like a rabbit in headlights, thumbing through the pack in increasing desperation before promising to write to her noble friend with the answer.

I tapped out a short email and forwarded it to Alan. He'd delegate it too, no doubt, but I was making it clear he'd be providing any necessary backup at the briefing meeting. I'd had more than enough experience of trying to calm Brenda Cooke's nerves. Besides, she responded better to Alan – it was the grey hair and the Home Counties tones, plus the fact that he was a man; she was a Tory peer of a certain age, after all.

I got up and headed for the canteen before Alan could open the email and find something moronic to ask me about it. My phone was heavy in my pocket, pulling at my jacket, ruining the line. I'd carried it with me for days now, something I don't normally do. I don't like being available, having people think they can contact you at any time, ask things of you or unload their boring stories about their boring lives, as if you have nothing better to do with your time than listen to them. There aren't many people who'd do that, of course: my sister occasionally, when she has something she wants to brag about, the latest instalment in Fascinating Stella's Fascinating Life, or my godmother Celia, our mother's sister, who makes a duty call every so often to salve her conscience. I want to tell her she doesn't need to do it – when Mum died of breast cancer I was thirty-one and Stella twenty-six; it's not as if we needed a replacement to make sure we ate our greens. I haven't done it, though; Celia needs to feel important and I'm not a complete bitch.

It's true I can't avoid being contactable for work. For that, I have the BlackBerry, ensuring I am on hand at a moment's notice to respond to the major VAT-related issues of our day. You think that sounds old-fashioned? They tell us they're more secure. It's probably bullshit; more likely some idiot at the Cabinet Office got us tied into a thirty-year contract, but whatever. That's what we've got. I carry mine in my handbag, where it can vibrate away to its heart's content. Most of my communications come from other people in HMRC or the Treasury – VAT policy isn't the kind of thing to quicken the blood of your average Joe, thank God – and civil servants prefer emails to phone calls; it's one of the reasons I can tolerate my colleagues. So if I'm away from my desk I check my messages on the BlackBerry every so often, when I'm stuck in a meeting with people I want to subtly inform aren't worth my time, or when some form of shit is hitting the fan and it's just possible I might need to intervene before Alan does something stupid.

My mobile, on the other hand, I keep mainly for Aidan. I don't carry it everywhere – I don't need that – but now and again I'll get it out, tap out a quick message for old times' sake. For a while he didn't reply and I could almost feel the effort it cost him, but when I didn't stop, he gave in. Now if I drop him a line I can expect the handset to be vibrating within seconds. He's much more reliable than he ever was when we were together.

But it wasn't Aidan I was waiting for that day as I headed to the canteen, the phone knocking lightly against my hip. It was four days after I'd met Ian and I was expecting a text.

His first message had been a surprise. I hadn't wanted to push things when I'd seen him in the pub. I wasn't sure if I could really go through with it, if I could do what it took to convince him he could trust me. So after the hand-stroking, when we'd had a couple more drinks and had established we were both single, when he'd started watching my lips every time I raised my glass and his knees had brushed mine under the table more times than could be attributed to accident, I'd said I had to go, that I'd promised to babysit my niece (ha!). He looked disappointed and I wondered whether he'd really thought he was going to get that lucky, but he rallied when I reminded him we had each other's numbers. Another circuitous journey home didn't appeal and I got up in a hurry, pretending I was already late, leaving him stranded at the table, his pint glass still half full in front of him.

I'd planned to text him when I'd had time to think, when I knew exactly what I was going to do, how it was all going to work. I'd taken my phone to the office that morning, though, just in case, and at half past eleven it gave a little buzz. I felt sick then, I remember, and all at once I was sure that I'd made a terrible mistake. You see, somewhere in the middle of all those plans, the laps of the supermarket, the rehearsed conversations, the situation had somehow become less real. I'd started to treat it as an intellectual exercise, a competition even, to see if I could get Ian to break, or else to tell me something, anything, that would put beyond doubt the question of his innocence. Even when he'd sat across from me in the pub, when I'd felt his skin beneath my fingers, it had all been part of the game. But now he was the one taking the initiative, getting in touch with me at a time of his choosing, and I remembered that I was dealing with a man who might have raped a woman. Someone who might have taken what he wanted without caring whether she wanted it or not; someone who might even have taken it *because* she didn't want it.

I took the phone with me to the loos, my hands trembling as I locked the door and sank onto the seat. I tapped the screen and the message popped up in a blue speech bubble. I read it twice and then let out a little laugh, covering it in the next second with a cough in case there was anyone in the cubicles to hear. It said:

You left your umbrella @ pub. Same place tmrrw & I'll bring it with me.

Of course – it had sat under my chair while we were talking and by the time I'd left I'd forgotten all about it. Ian was just doing the decent thing in returning it to me.

I tapped the phone against my leg. But was that really all this was? He could have asked the barmaid to put it to one side for me, dropped me a line to tell me where it was – but he hadn't. He wanted to see me again.

I sat there for another five minutes trying out different answers, then decided I shouldn't reply right away. I flushed the loo and went to wash my hands. In the mirror above the sink my cheeks were pink and my eyes bright. There was still a knot in my stomach, but something about the message, its very ordinariness, the transparency of its artifice, had chased away my worst fears. I didn't need to be afraid of Ian: I was going into this with my eyes open. I was going to be the one calling the shots.

After I'd kept him waiting for a couple of hours, I replied saying I couldn't make tomorrow evening. It wasn't true, of course – the only thing I had in my diary for weeks was my Tuesday-evening Arabic class, but he didn't need to know that. After a couple more messages, we'd rearranged for the following Thursday, giving me over a week to make yet more plans and rehearse yet more speeches. I hadn't expected him to text me again, but as I'd sat in front of the TV that night, my phone had buzzed: he'd been watching *Question Time*; was the woman on the left the Treasury minister I'd been talking about?

I was surprised on all kinds of levels. Surprised he'd been watching *Question Time* – not because I thought, like me, he wouldn't be able to bear the ill-informed shoutiness of the contributors, but because he struck me as more an *I'm a Celebrity, the Only Way is the X Factor* type – surprised that he'd got as far as identifying a Treasury minister, and surprised he'd been listening when I assumed he'd just been pretending to be interested in my job because it filled in the time before he could reasonably try and invite himself back to my place. I'd tapped back a short reply and we'd been exchanging occasional messages ever since.

The canteen lay in the bowels of the building, a windowless space with food counters orbited by dazed-looking officials. I'd loaded my plate with an omelette and limp salad and was at the till paying when I felt the phone vibrate against my hip. I suppressed a smile as I threaded my way through the mostly empty tables and found a seat at the edge of the room. I made myself wait to open it until I'd finished eating, then tapped the screen and stared down at the words.

It wasn't Ian after all. There was only one person who would send me a message like that. I put the phone back into my pocket. I'd decide what to do about him later.

Chapter 11

I don't hold any animus towards Aidan, truly I don't. The guy's a shit, but I behaved – how can I put it? Not badly, I won't say that. I was provoked, after all. I think most people would agree that what he did fell squarely under the heading of Serious Fucking Bullshit. But I'm prepared to admit I lost my sense of proportion. Yes, that's the way I'd describe it. My behaviour was disproportionate.

That didn't mean, though, that I was going to let him paint me as the villain. I could imagine him shaking his head at some callow police officer who'd barely started to shave, the two of them complicit in their brotherhood of man, telling him, 'She's gone nuts, mate. She just can't accept that it's over.' And then afterwards, sniggering with the bimbo – she's called Kellie, by the way, with an 'ie'; hardly surprising she's roughly as bright as your average bullfrog when her parents couldn't even spell a five-letter name – about how everyone would know, how they'd all be laughing at me, at how I'd 'lost it'.

No. That wasn't going to happen. Aidan deserved it; he had to accept the consequences of what he'd done. Perhaps I should have thought of some other way to make sure he kept his mouth shut, but it was the first thing that came to mind and I was sure it would do the job. And it did, of course. I never had that knock on the door.

I don't know what happened to the car. I like to think he had to drive around in it, at least for a day or two. I imagine him in traffic, trying to ignore people pointing to it and laughing, swivelling their necks to get a look at the guy in the red Audi TT with white paint dripping 'CHEATING CUNT' down its bonnet.

It was a cliché, I suppose, but I hope he had to do that. I really do.

I left work early that Thursday, claiming a non-existent meeting at Blackfriars, from where I'd go straight home. I don't usually do things like that; in normal circumstances I am a follower of rules, the person who does the thing that is expected. I suppose that might surprise you, but it's all about context. People can find they're capable of all kinds of things they'd never imagine under the right conditions. I'm not trying to pretend that anyone would have done what I did; just that it's not hard to find yourself somewhere you'd never anticipated. It can happen to anyone. Maybe one day it will happen to you.

I was home by five and staring at the contents of my wardrobe, trying to decide what to wear. I wanted to get the balance just right: not too obvious, but obvious enough; as if I'd made an effort, but not so much for him as for myself. I didn't know for sure if he was the kind of man to notice what a woman was wearing – he'd said on the witness stand that Chantelle had been wearing black underwear when she'd maintained it had been white, a discrepancy We the Jury had put down to the usual lack of observation skills in men, particularly those about to get laid – but I didn't want to assume otherwise and find I'd got it wrong. In the end I chose a good pair of jeans, snug across what Aidan always said was my best feature, and a black top with cut out patches on the shoulders to show a bit of unexpected yet demure flesh.

Before I left, I went to the kitchen and opened the drawer where I kept the cutlery. I took out two knives – nothing excessive, we're not talking meat cleavers here; just a sharp little blade with a serrated edge perhaps four inches long, my utensil of choice for slicing onions (the serrated blade makes your eyes water less), and a second almost the same but with a smooth edge. I put my onion slicer in the inside pocket of my handbag, then made my way along the hallway to stow the other beneath my pillow. You see: I had used that week wisely.

We'd arranged to meet at seven, and this time I was nearly a quarter of an hour late arriving at the pub. Ian had suggested the time and I wanted to remind him that I was the one in charge, that seeing him wasn't top of my list of priorities. Unlike the last time we'd been there, it was busy; the evening was cool, and warm bodies were steaming up the windows. The area around the bar was packed, and it took me a moment to spot him, hunched at a table on the other side of the room from where we'd sat last time, staring down at his phone with a look of displeasure. He looked up as I approached, and I could see he was irritated at being kept waiting; but he got to his feet anyway, and when I put my hand on his shoulder and leaned in close to air-kiss his cheek, he was smiling as I pulled away again.

He said, 'I'd started to think you weren't going to make it.'

I shrugged off my jacket and saw his eyes wander to my bare shoulders. 'Me too. I was about to leave work when it all went crazy.' I wasn't about to lose my advantage by apologising. 'I've left it with my deputy to sort out, so God knows what I'll get back to tomorrow.'

He laughed. 'She's not up to much then?'

'He.' I took a degree of pleasure in correcting the assumption. 'And no, unfortunately not.'

I insisted on buying him a refill and went to the bar to order. Most of the people there were younger than me, dressed in the effortless way of London twenty-somethings. I had at least a decade on most of them, but I didn't care: I'd never been like them, never relaxed and trivial. Growing older suited me. I glanced back at Ian; he was watching me and smiled when I caught his eye. I suspected he had more in common with these people than I did. I discovered later that I was right, though much good it did him.

You might imagine it's difficult to make small talk with someone you've acquitted of rape, but I think I managed well, all things considered. I kept resolutely away from the subject of the trial, not wanting him to suspect me of ulterior motives, though now and then we bumped up against it all the same: the difficulty of finding somewhere to live after his landlord kicked him out, the brother who hadn't spoken to him since his arrest. It was too large a subject to be avoided with complete success; it exerted its own gravitational pull.

We'd had a few drinks by the time he asked. He'd been steeling himself to do it throughout the previous two pints, avoiding my eyes and looking up at the people at the bar as if they were going to tell him how I'd react. Eventually he put his glass down and leaned forward in his seat.

'Look, Natalie.' Why do people always say that? *Look*. I *was* looking. 'Why are you here?'

It wasn't the phrasing I'd expected. I said, 'You asked me. I wanted my umbrella back.'

He shook his head vigorously, like a dog getting out of a bathtub. 'You could have told me to leave it here for you.'

I shrugged and said again, 'You asked me. It didn't seem like a big deal.'

He stared at me. I could almost hear the cogs whirring in his head. Then he leaned back and rubbed his hands through his hair. The movement left little tufty bits standing up behind his ears, like a barn owl. I almost felt sorry for him.

He said, 'I'm sorry if I sound weird. It's just . . .' A sigh. A self-pitying sigh, if I'm honest. 'It would be a big deal to most people. After what happened.' A pause, then, 'It's not as if my diary is exactly overflowing with invitations these days, you know?'

Something about the way he said it made me angry. I wanted to ask him if he ever stopped to think how it was for Chantelle, how *her* diary was looking now we'd effectively told the world she'd lied about being raped. But that wasn't fair: if he'd done nothing wrong, he had every right to be upset. It was possible, after all.

I've just never been able to stand people whining.

He was looking at me as if he expected a reply. I kept my eyes on my glass when I spoke, so he wouldn't see the irritation. 'It must have been very difficult for you.'

There was an unmistakable whiff of sarcasm in my voice and I could have kicked myself. What was the point in all this planning, all this care, if when it came down to it I couldn't listen to him without giving away the suspicion that he was an evil, lying bastard? I tried again.

'I mean, I can't imagine how hard it's been.' Better. Now look him in the eye. 'I suppose that's what I thought. I thought you might need . . . a friend.'

He looked at me, wanting to believe. 'Thanks.'

'And you must know . . .' Could I say it? I had to say it. 'You must know that I believe you. Absolutely. We all did, *do*. All of us on the jury, I mean. We would never have returned that verdict otherwise.'

He gave one of those smiles where your lips go down instead of up. 'I just wish everyone else felt the same.'

'It must be hard . . .' Christ, couldn't I come up with anything else? 'But surely anyone who doubts you can't be worth . . .' I groped for a way of saying it that didn't sound like I should be on an American chat show, and failed, 'having in your life?'

'Yeah, well, you don't always get to choose that, do you?'

So it was family that was the problem. The brother he'd mentioned before, probably. His parents had been in the gallery during the trial – I hadn't seen them, but Helen had told me; the dad looked like Ian, apparently. Presumably that meant they were being more supportive. And as for his mother: what must it be like to fear you've given birth to a rapist? Did she really have any choice but to believe he was innocent?

I reached across to him then. I told myself I had to do it, I had to do it for all of them. For Chantelle. For Siobhan and Helen. And most of all for me. I couldn't live with the possibility that I'd let a guilty man walk free.

I said, 'It's getting noisy in here. Let's go back to my place.'

Chapter 12

The street lamp outside cast a pale glow across the bedroom, staining the white sheets amber. I crossed to the window and pulled the curtains closed. The amber turned to grey.

Ian had done his best to keep up a conversation on the way to the flat, but my mind was racing and I'd been able only to supply the occasional encouraging murmur. He'd fallen silent as he waited for me to unlock the door, and I'd seen the surprise on his face when I led him straight past the sitting room; but I knew if I gave myself time to think I might not be able to go through with it.

He stood now at the side of the bed, his hands clenched into fists. *He's nervous*, I told myself. *It's just nerves.*

I walked towards him, the carpet making shushing noises against the soles of my feet. One step closer, then another. I watched him uncurl his fists, flex his fingers. His hands were twice as big as mine, powerful. They could hold me down. They could . . .

I reached out, touched his arm. I heard him swallow. My fingertips trembled like butterfly wings, so I moved my hand to his chest, pressing the palm flat against his body to make them stop. I felt the hard planes of his muscles, his ribcage expanding as the breath filled his lungs.

I raised my face to his, but he didn't move. He was staring at me, a spark from the street light reflected in each iris. I thought: *I have to do this. It's the only way.* I touched my lips to his. Then I closed my eyes so I didn't have to see what happened next.

I woke with my hand beneath my pillow, my fingers against something solid. I shifted and felt the blade bite into my skin. The pain was reassuring.

I knew Ian was still there. I could hear his breathing, long and deep. He was asleep. I didn't want to lie next to him any longer. I reached for the handle of the knife and slid it further up the bed, careful not to disturb the duvet, until it was wedged into the gap between the mattress and the bedstead. He wouldn't find it there. I slid my legs out of bed, feeling the tenderness where he'd been as I shifted my weight.

The room carried the stale smell of alcohol and sex. Ian was on his side, turned away, his body a blue-grey lump in the early-morning light. I needed to shower.

The heating hadn't come on yet and I shivered as I padded down the hallway to the bathroom. Inside, I pulled the bolt across and sat on the loo, trying to clear my head. When the seat had left an indentation on the backs of my thighs, I got up and went to the kitchen to make coffee. I'd wait for Ian to leave before I took that shower.

It might sound, I suppose, as though I imagined that having sex with Ian would somehow reveal the truth. That wasn't it; I'm not stupid. I didn't expect him to try to tie me up or slap me around – though apparently women aren't supposed to bat an eyelid at that kind of thing these days. No, I was playing a longer game. I knew if he was ever going to tell me the truth, he'd need to trust me, trust that I'd be on his side no matter what. It was going to take time, but I've always been a patient person. Even Aidan would agree with that – though he might call it something else if only his vocabulary were up to the task.

So no, I wasn't expecting any great revelation. The sex wasn't as bad as you'd expect. At first I was distracted by the voice running through my head, the one comparing every movement to what I'd heard on the witness stand. But after a few minutes of kissing, when I'd realised that if things were ever going to progress, I'd need to move them along myself, I understood: the Ian I thought I'd caught a glimpse of during the trial wasn't going to make an appearance that night.

The smirk that had so disturbed me had gone. And as for those clenched fists, the deep breath before he finally kissed me: I could see them for what they were. He was nervous, though trying to hide it. And was that really so surprising after everything that had happened? Halfway through pushing down my jeans, he'd stopped and, looking up at me, said, 'This is OK, isn't it? You want to do this, right?' It wasn't quite the unambiguous language you hear on those faintly horrific educational ads about consent, but in that moment I knew: this time, at least, I was the one in control.

Now, filling the kettle with water, I reminded myself his reticence didn't mean anything. After all, he was on the radar of the police; he'd know he couldn't afford to put a foot wrong. It didn't mean he'd shown the same consideration to Chantelle. Besides, I wasn't going to be satisfied with trying to extrapolate his character from my own brief experience. The only evidence I was interested in related to what had happened in Chantelle's flat that Saturday in July.

It wasn't long after I'd made my drink that Ian came tiptoeing down the hallway. He stood at the door to the kitchen as though unsure of his welcome, and for a moment we stared at each other with all the awkwardness of two people who've recently seen each other naked for the first time. I raised my hand with the mug in it and asked him if he wanted coffee; I think he accepted to prove to himself how different things were this time.

The conversation was stilted, but as morning-after encounters went – well, I've had worse. When he'd drained his coffee, he said something vague about needing to get back, and I walked him to the front door with my own cup still in my hand. I realised with a sudden panic that he might be ready to treat this as a one-night stand, a necessary milestone in his journey to sexual rehabilitation; *he might not want to see me again.* It had somehow never occurred to me until that moment – my own last casual encounter had been over five years ago, in the pre-Aidan era, and I suppose I'd forgotten how it worked.

I said, 'So . . .' and realised I had no idea what came next.

'I'll call you,' he said, and I nodded and opened the door for him.

He took a step, and then stopped and turned back. He reached for a strand of my hair and tucked it behind my ear. I realised I was holding my breath. He said again, 'I *will* call you,' and this time I smiled at him.

I watched him walk down the hallway, his broad shoulders in that navy coat. I watched him go and tried to tell myself it didn't matter that for a moment I'd forgotten why he was there.

I'd been nervous about ringing her. That doesn't happen to me often. I'm not one of those people who has to work up to making a phone call, who rehearses what they say or picks up the phone

103

and puts it down again before deciding they'll do it later. So I can't explain why every time I'd found Helen's number in my contacts, I'd checked my watch and told myself she'd be in a case conference, or seeing a client, or grabbing a mouthful to eat – something that would make it difficult for her to talk.

Eventually I caught myself staring down at the screen for the umpteenth time and, annoyed with myself, pressed the call button before I could come up with another excuse. I waited as the ringtone echoed down the line, suddenly hoping after all that it would go to voicemail and I could leave a message; but on the fifth ring, she picked up.

'Helen Owens.' She said it as a statement, not a question, and again I thought: just the kind of voice you'd want for a social worker.

'Helen, hi. It's Natalie. From the jury.'

There was a second's pause and I imagined her processing the name. Was she regretting giving me her number? But then she said, 'Natalie! It's good to hear from you,' and it sounded as if she meant it.

'I just thought I'd give you a call and see how you were . . .' I tailed off. I've never been good at chit-chat.

'Oh, you know. Keeping busy.' I wondered if that meant she didn't have time to talk, but she carried on. 'I was thinking of ringing you, actually, but I wasn't sure if you really wanted to keep in touch.'

I was taken aback: I'd told her she could call me, hadn't I? *Any time*, I'd said, I remembered it distinctly. With an effort, I stopped myself from reminding her; I wanted to keep her onside, after all. Instead I said, 'I've been thinking a lot about the case.'

'Me too. It's hard to get it out of your system, isn't it? The weekend after we finished, I couldn't think of anything else. Greg, that's my husband, kept asking—'

'Yes, it's very hard.' I hadn't called to talk about my feelings. And she was busy, she'd said as much: I didn't want her having to rush off to deal with some suicidal Hackney teen before I'd said what I needed to. 'Do you think about what you would have asked him?'

'Who?'

You'd think by now I'd have learned that other people don't follow the same logic I do. I spelled it out. 'Ian Nash, the defendant.' *The man we acquitted.*

She didn't say anything, so I carried on. 'If you could have questioned him yourself, I mean. Instead of having to leave it all to the lawyers.'

'I don't know.' Disappointing: perhaps I'd misjudged her. She'd seemed so sensible in that jury room, but maybe she'd simply benefited from comparison with the others. She said, 'That sounds ridiculous, I expect.'

It was as if she'd heard what I was thinking, and I revised my opinion again. That doesn't happen very often – and in case you're wondering, I mean both parts of that sentence.

She said, 'What I mean is, I still find myself going over it all. And there are things I worry we missed, things that didn't make sense.' She sighed. 'I expect it's just that I don't like the idea of Chantelle thinking we didn't believe her.'

It was what Siobhan had said too. 'People tell lies, you said that yourself . . .'

'Yes, they do. But that goes both ways, doesn't it?'

For a moment there was silence. I said, 'I wish they'd asked him why he went to the gym. It never made sense to me. It's not the kind of thing you do after you've had sex, is it?'

Helen didn't reply; I sensed she was thinking about what I'd said. I balanced the phone on my shoulder as I reached for my notebook and turned to a fresh page. 'So,' I said, 'what things do you worry about?'

I walked back to my desk carrying a plastic pot of salad. Alan was eating in front of his computer too, but in his case it was a polystyrene tray from which some kind of brownish sludge steamed revoltingly. I have tried in vain to role-model appropriate food for an office-based lunch, even from time to time remarking on the pungency of his gastronomic choices. It makes no difference: Alan is oblivious.

He looked up, fork raised halfway to his lips. 'Ciara rang. Asked you to call her back.'

'What's it about?'

'She didn't say.'

And of course you didn't bother to ask. Once, I would have pointed this out; Alan is, lest we forget, nominally my deputy. I have learned my lesson, however. What was it Einstein said? The definition of madness is to repeat the same action and expect a different result.

I took my seat and reached for the phone. By the time the call was finished – Ciara giving me the heads-up on a meeting request the minister should have accepted but didn't want to; best to make sure the advice recommended declining – Alan was on the phone himself.

'Better send it to me here,' he was saying, followed by a recital of the office address. I had my suspicions already, but then he confirmed it. 'Yes, the page just froze. You'll make sure it doesn't go through twice, won't you?'

He'd be ordering another component for one of his model engines. Alan is an enthusiast of the kind you probably imagined had died out twenty years ago. He buys all manner of inexplicable items from sites with names like Engine Room and Loco Connoisseur, and every so often brings in a photo of his newest creation in much the same way other people bring in photos of their offspring. I suppose it's no less interesting.

I toyed with talking to him about using the internet for personal reasons, but it was his lunch hour; besides, I liked the idea that some day a journalist with nothing better to do would submit one of those pointless Freedom of Information requests, find that a civil servant had visited a website called Wonderland Models and get completely the wrong end of the stick.

Alan was spelling out his surname ('No, l-e-o-d, and m-c not m-*a*-c. Yes, let me spell it for you again, m-c-l . . .') and then it was on to his card details. Really, it astonished me how ready people were to give out their personal information in the middle of an open-plan office.

I found myself scribbling on a Post-it note, and by the time Alan had finished his call, it was folded over twice and I was reaching for my handbag.

It's just an idea, I told myself as I tucked it into the inside pocket. I'll probably never do it.

Chapter 13

I'd wondered what I'd do if Ian didn't call me, but it turned out I needn't have worried. Probably he didn't have many other options. I mean, it has to be awkward, doesn't it, working out at what point to slip that little nugget into the conversation? *I think things are going well between us and I'd like to take it further, but there's something I think it's only right to tell you . . .*

Or perhaps he wouldn't say anything at all. It would be a worry, though, surely; waiting for the moment she met the family, asking them not to tell her, the arguments when they said she had a right to know . . .

Ian didn't have any of that with me. I was easy for him, in all senses of the word. At least that was probably what he thought at the beginning.

It was an interested-but-not-desperate week after we'd slept together that we went out again. This time it was dinner, and Ian suggested the venue, an Indian restaurant away from the town centre that in most parts of London you wouldn't give a second glance but which in Lewisham counted as a better class of establishment. There was the initial awkwardness you'd expect

(Ian standing to greet me, almost bumping noses as we both moved to the same side for the kiss on the cheek); but we got through it, and by the time the bill arrived, we were talking easily enough. Ian insisted on paying, waving away my offer to cover half. I doubted he could really afford it, but the look he gave me, a hint of angry pride behind the gallantry, made me decide not to argue.

Afterwards, we walked back to my flat. He'd told me he was staying with a friend, but I got the impression the arrangement wasn't comfortable. I wondered whether he'd outstayed his welcome. On the way, he took my hand. The contact made me jump, and for a second I almost snatched it away; but then I saw his raised eyebrows and got a grip, pretending I hadn't reacted. We were passing some new flats at the time, and to cover my confusion I asked him whether he liked them. If he thought the abruptness of the question odd, he didn't say so – perhaps he thought I was asking him because of his old job, expecting a former estate agent to be interested in such things.

When we got to my flat, I took his coat, noticing how small the hallway felt with him in it, and when I'd hung it up, I offered him a drink. He asked for a beer, but I didn't have any, so instead I opened another bottle of wine while he looked at my bookshelves. I watched him as I cut the foil around the bottle neck, wondering what he was making of the volumes on pion-nucleon scattering and relativistic quantum fields; but the books appeared not to interest him, and instead he hovered in front of the small collection of CDs at the end of one shelf, mostly refugees from Stella's brutally efficient clearance of our parents' home. When he reached out and selected one of them, I had a sudden clear image of him standing at the door to Chantelle's flat, a different CD in his hand. Perhaps I made a noise then, because he looked up and caught me staring.

'You like soul?' he said.

He held up the CD case. A photo of an old-fashioned micro-phone gleamed next to the legend *Original Soul Classics*. It had been a gift from Aidan's brother the Christmas after we'd got engaged; it hadn't even had a cellophane wrapper, and I assumed he'd wrapped up one of his parents' CDs in panic on Boxing Day when he'd found out I'd be joining Clan McCarthy for lunch. I'd listened to it once, but it wasn't really my kind of thing.

I found myself nodding anyway. Ian smiled. 'Me too. I'll put it on, shall I?'

I watched as the ancient CD tray creaked open, Ian's finger hooked through the hole in the centre of the disc as he placed it inside.

I thought: did he do that in Chantelle's flat too? Or could it really have been Chantelle who put on the music, the way he said it happened?

I poured the wine, noting with surprise that the tremor had returned to my hands; but then the music was playing, a woman's voice singing about California soul, and I took a gulp from one glass and took the other to Ian.

He stayed with me again that night, and over the next few weeks we got into a routine: Wednesdays and Fridays a few drinks in the pub and then back to my place for dinner, more often than not a takeaway. We'd eat at the table tucked into the corner of the living room, a candle flickering between us, then sometimes we'd watch a film and sometimes we'd go straight to bed.

We always had sex.

I expect you're wondering how I went through with it. How I slept with a man I thought might be a rapist. Or then again, perhaps you think there's something wrong with me, some weird kink that meant I enjoyed the danger.

That wasn't how it was. During most of our early encounters I was too anxious to do anything but wait for it to be over, calculating whether I could twist away if he held me down, if I could reach the knife if he put a hand to my throat. The fear was why I made sure of our routine from the start: I made up a Thursday-evening art class to go with Tuesday's Arabic lessons, claimed a regular need to work late on a Monday. I needed to know when I'd see him, to plan what I'd say and do. I needed to lie on the bed and run my fingers along the edge of the mattress to check I could reach the handle of the knife (I'd decided by then there was too much of a risk of him finding it under the pillow); to go to the bathroom, the only room in the flat with a lock on the door, and retrieve the mobile phone I'd taped to the back of the washbasin stand, plug it in and check it was fully charged.

I worry that I'm giving the wrong impression. Most of the time I was with him, I wasn't afraid of him. He wasn't a threatening presence, you'll have to take my word for that. If anything, I'd find my mind wandering as he sat across from me at dinner complaining about Sean – that was the friend he was staying with – or the latest job he'd applied for and about which he'd heard nothing back. I'd have to remind myself I was with him for a reason, that at any moment he might let slip something that would give me a clue to the man he really was, something that might help me uncover the truth about what had happened that day in Chantelle's flat. But then, as the evening drew on, I'd feel the tension creeping up my spine, noticing his hand resting on his knee, how much bigger it was than mine, the tendons in his forearms. Sometimes I'd go to the bathroom, sit there deep-breathing until I was ready to go back in, feeling behind the sink pedestal one last time for the crinkled skin of the duct tape.

So no, I didn't enjoy the sex at first. I did what women do in such circumstances, writhing around and making a noise.

It seemed to do the trick for Ian – at least, after that first time, he never asked again whether what he was doing was OK. I got used to it after a while. All things considered, that didn't seem like such a bad result.

I didn't ask him about Chantelle, not for ages. It was obvious he wanted to pretend it was all over, that any questions might make him suspicious about what was really going on. I knew I had to bide my time, wait until he trusted me. It was difficult, but I was patient – I can be a very patient person.

I've had practice.

It was six months into our engagement, another four to go until the wedding, when I first suspected something was going on. There were none of the classic signs: Aidan had always been a vain man, so there was no sudden change in his standard of personal grooming to put me on the scent. He went out with his friends as often as he had before, stayed out just as late. I didn't feel the need to ask for details, so I suppose he never had to lie directly; not until the end, at least.

No, it was more subtle than that. I remember clearly the first time I realised something was wrong. It was the weekend and we'd been to the Tate Modern – there was a new installation in the Turbine Hall I'd wanted to see, a mesh of wooden walkways with patches of soil from London's parks between them. Afterwards I sat across from Aidan in the café.

'He said in an interview that he wanted to ask, "Who am I?"' I said, meaning the artist. He was Mexican, with an unpronounceable surname.

Aidan said, 'Yes. Not original, perhaps.'

'But the title is interesting in that context, don't you think? That he's describing himself as "An Empty Lot".' I looked across at Aidan, noting with affection the stubble that clung to the hollows of his cheeks. It was just at the point when people were questioning whether the Shoreditch beard had had its day, and I knew he'd been prevaricating over whether to start shaving again.

'Hmm . . .' he replied.

'And the notion of gardening that isn't really gardening. It's more about letting whatever is there in the soil just grow.'

He didn't say anything – he was considering what I'd said.

'He's saying you don't need to design the garden, plant some things and pull out others. You can just let it be. That if you give it light and water, that's enough.'

Aidan looked up then and our eyes locked across the table. I knew he'd understood what I was saying. I was telling him how much it meant to have someone who nurtured me, someone who knew I wasn't really empty.

He said, 'To be honest, Natalie, I've never really liked this conceptual stuff.' He stood up. 'Where are the loos in this place?'

He didn't come back to my flat that afternoon. He said he had work to do, and I tried not to mind. I called into the supermarket on my way home to get something for dinner. They had a display of pot plants near the door; perhaps it was the earlier talk of gardening that made me notice them. I bought the dragon tree and took it home with me instead.

I told you I was patient, but that doesn't mean I stopped waiting for the opportunity to ask my questions. Eventually, about a month into what I suppose I must call my relationship with Ian, I thought it had arrived.

I'd been at my desk when my phone chirruped from my hand-bag, earning me an indulgent smile from Alan. I don't talk about my private life at work; before all the shit with Aidan I'd been less careful, but I'd learned my lesson. Besides, I could hardly tell people the truth, and saying nothing at all is a far better way of covering your tracks than trying to invent things. Needless to say, my tight-lipped-ness hadn't put off Alan, who'd somehow sniffed out the arrival of a significant other – or 'someone special', as he put it. I'd taken the path of least resistance when he'd asked, hoping to deter him from further questions by saying yes, I'd met someone, but it was early days. He'd nodded sagely then, happy in his role of kindly uncle. For a moment I thought he might be about to offer advice on my love life; but the horror must have shown in my face, because he let it drop. Now and again, though, he asked how things were going, the enquiry always accompanied by a furrowed brow and a half-smile, as if it were only a matter of time before I broke down and confessed I'd been dumped and was doomed to a life of celibate spinsterhood.

Now I tried to ignore him watching me as I fished the phone from my bag. It was a text from Ian. *Can you call me?*

Just that. Ian wasn't one to end his texts with declarations of affection or pointless rows of xs, but even by his standards it was abrupt.

'Everything all right?'

Alan had swivelled his chair around and was trying to peer at the screen of my phone. I turned it over and stuffed it back in my bag.

'Fine. How are you getting on with that submission?'

He turned back to his keyboard. 'Just waiting for comments from Finance—'

'Do they know it needs to be with private office by twelve?' I didn't wait for him to answer. 'Give them a ring and make sure they're looking at it.'

He grumbled something under his breath but reached for his phone. That would teach him to mind his own business.

I stared at my computer while my mind raced. Why was Ian asking to speak to me when I was at work? Why give no clue to what it was about? Something had happened, that was clear – but what?

I clicked mindlessly at the PowerPoint presentation sent around by the strategy team. 'Horizon Scanning', apparently. A slide covered with circles and arrows stared back at me from the monitor. A schoolboy tactic, using an overcomplicated diagram to disguise the fact that they had nothing to say.

What did Ian want to talk about?

I clicked forward to the next slide. Beside me, Alan was still on the phone, by the sound of it attempting to placate whoever was on the other end of the line. If I left now and took my bag, he'd know it had to do with the text. I chewed at the skin at the edge of my thumb.

Sod Alan. I needed to know what was going on.

I got to my feet and grabbed my bag, feeling his eyes on me as I strode towards the lifts.

The first one to arrive was empty, and I was already pulling the phone from my bag as I stepped inside. There was the message, giving nothing away. Perhaps I should send a text in reply, try to elicit a clue as to what it was about before calling. Make sure he couldn't catch me off my guard.

But would that be possible? I knew what the worst was, after all; it was the reason I wanted to get out into the open air, to try to clear my head before I responded.

I'd left Ian in bed that morning, his face turned into the pillow and one arm hanging over the edge. What if he'd decided to be useful for once, to change the sheets? What if he was the kind of person who turned the mattress? He'd have been bound to see the knife there. Or perhaps it was the phone he'd found. Maybe he'd been in the bathroom and dropped something, caught sight of something taped to the back of the sink as he bent to pick it up?

I should never have left him in the flat alone. I'd grown careless.

The doors of the lift opened and I strode across the lobby, out through the double doors and onto the white glare of Parliament Street. It was hot and the tourists were out in force, big groups led by women with frizzy hair and sunglasses. I kept up my pace as I wove around them, the phone still in my hand, turning the corner into the sudden quiet of King Charles Street.

I walked to the end, then crossed the road and entered St James's Park. The grass was scattered with sunbathers, different shades of flesh stretched out to bake. I kept walking until I found an empty bench, then sat squarely in the middle to deter anyone from joining me.

What would I say if Ian had found something? The knife, though dramatic, could be more easily explained. I was a woman living alone, after all. I could say I kept it there in case of intruders. Perhaps I could even distract him by telling him I felt safer when he was there – men liked that kind of thing, in my experience. I'd have to be careful, though, not to overdo it. I didn't want him offering to come over more often, telling me it wouldn't matter if I was out in the evening, he could just wait in and get himself something to eat, I'd feel better knowing he was there . . . It was all too likely, especially given the fragility of his tenure at Sean's. I'd have to watch my step.

And what if it was the phone that he'd found? What would I say about that?

Could I deny all knowledge, pretend I didn't even know it was there? The model was the cheapest I'd been able to find – probably I was the only person under sixty ever to have bought one. Perhaps I could act surprised, claim the previous tenant must have put it there for some unknown reason and forgot about it.

No, I was being stupid again. The phone would still have power – I'd made sure the battery was fully charged before I left to meet

Ian at the pub, the way I always did, and a side effect of the design being as ancient as the ark was that it lasted for days.

Maybe I should stick to the same story, the fear of intruders. I could say I wanted my own panic room, just in case. I'd sound a bit paranoid, perhaps, but there were worse crimes. Ian wouldn't be able to argue with that.

I tapped the screen of the phone: eighteen minutes since he'd sent the text. I tapped it twice more and put it to my ear.

A small boy in a T-shirt with tractors on it ran across my field of vision, scuffing his feet against the path in a bid to scare away a pigeon. Little shit, I thought. A woman – the mother? No, too young and untroubled to be anything but the nanny – followed, nonchalantly pushing a buggy that probably cost as much as a small car.

The phone began to ring and my stomach clenched.

'Natalie.' I tried to analyse the tone of his voice. He didn't sound hurt or angry. He didn't sound . . .

'Natalie, are you there?'

'Yes, sorry. Just – um . . . Everything OK?'

'Yes, fine. Great, actually!' The knot in my stomach loosened. 'I've got some news.'

'Really? That sounds intriguing.'

'Yeah, I don't want to tell you on the phone. I know you've got your art thing tonight, but could I come over later?'

I hesitated. Was there any chance he'd found something after all, that he wanted to confront me about it? But no, he was brimming with good cheer; even if his acting skills were Oscar-worthy, why bother expending the energy on all that enthusiasm?

I said, 'Actually, the class has been cancelled. I had a text earlier to say the tutor's come down with food poisoning.' I glanced at my watch. 'I can be finished by six-ish if you want to meet then?'

117

'To be honest, later would be better – but no!' He laughed, then stopped himself. He sounded manic – had he been drinking? 'No, wait. Let's meet at the Phoenix.'

'I won't be able to get there until seven . . .'

'That's OK. Better, in fact!' Another laugh.

I said, 'Are you sure you're OK?'

'I'll see you later. At the Phoenix, right? Got to go.'

I stared down at the silent phone. I don't believe in premonitions and I won't pretend I knew what he was talking about; but all the same, I think I knew then that something would change when I saw Ian again.

Chapter 14

The train was steamy and stale, rank with sweating commuters pressed against each other and counting down the seconds to their station. At Lewisham I stepped from the carriage feeling like a sardine escaping its can and joined the horde heading for the barriers. I hadn't worn tights that day on account of the temperature – standards of sartorial elegance at HMRC aren't high, and besides, I'd thought it unlikely anyone would notice bare flesh below the hem of my trousers – and as I walked I felt the burn of a blister forming on my little toe.

By the time I got to the bus stop I was limping, but there was no sign of a bus and the idea of waiting to share another metal compartment with more damp, cross people was too much to bear. I considered going back to the station and getting a cab before deciding against it. The walk wasn't far, and by the time I'd returned and found there were no cabs waiting anyway, I'd have been halfway there. I set off, trying to ignore the pain in my toe.

The Phoenix sat on the brow of a hill and I was sweating by the time I got there, my anxiety about what Ian had to say mostly replaced by irritation: whatever it was, if there was nothing to worry about, surely he could have told me over the phone.

It was dark inside and my eyes took a moment to adjust. The doors at the back were open onto the beer garden and sounds of laughter and clinking glasses carried on the air. Evidently few people fancied sitting inside on a day like today, and apart from a group of women with notepads that suggested some kind of organising committee, the tables were empty.

I made my way to the bar, rummaging in my bag for my purse as someone approached to serve me. I wasn't about to navigate the scrum in the beer garden without at least a glass of wine to ease the pain in my foot. If Ian was out there, I thought crossly, he'd have to call or text to let me know.

'What'll it be?'

I peered around the bulk of the man on the other side of the bar, trying to make out the labels of the bottles in the fridge.

'Something dry and very cold.' The man started to say something, but I'd seen what I wanted. 'Sauvignon Blanc, please.'

I was vaguely aware of him standing there as I opened my purse. 'Large,' I added, assuming that was what he was waiting for.

I should have gone to the cashpoint – I'd have to use my card. At some point I'd need to point out to Ian the folly of continuing to meet for drinks in a pub where a single glass of something half decent cost as much as one of the bottles sitting in my wine rack a five-minute walk away. It wasn't that I minded paying bar prices, not in itself – it was just that if I was going to spend the money, I'd have preferred to do it somewhere more salubrious.

A glass was placed on the bar in front of me, a pleasing mist clouding the sides: at least it had been chilled. I held out my card.

'I think we can say this one's on the house.'

I looked up in shock. 'Ian!' He grinned back, pleased at having surprised me. *How could I have not realised it was him?* I struggled to damp down the horror that he'd caught me off guard. 'You've got a job – congratulations!'

He smiled, but I could see he was disappointed. I was supposed to have strung out the reveal, probably, asked him what he was doing behind the bar. This is one of the reasons I like to have time to rehearse – my spontaneous reactions often don't have the effect I intend.

'That's brilliant!' I gushed, overcompensating. 'How did all this happen?'

All this – as if I were congratulating Alexander on having conquered half the globe. But this was a big deal to him, the first time he'd worked since his arrest. I remembered how happy he'd sounded on the phone. I didn't want to burst his bubble.

He shrugged. 'I got talking to Caitlin and she told me they were looking for bar staff.'

'Caitlin?'

'You know.' He looked surprised. '*Caitlin*. The woman who usually serves us. Black hair.'

The Australian woman who was always flirting with the customers. Had she been flirting with Ian too? I found myself looking over his shoulder.

'She's not in tonight. So anyway, I told her I was between things myself and she fixed it for me to have a word with Matt, the manager.'

So there had been a process, then. A series of conversations, not just a spur-of-the-moment hiring as I'd assumed. Ian must have known this was on the cards when I'd seen him the previous night, yet he'd given nothing away. I felt a stirring of unease.

'You are a dark horse,' I said.

'I didn't want to say anything before it was definite.' He lowered his voice. 'I didn't want you to think I was so useless I couldn't even get a job in the local pub.'

121

I felt bad for him then. I don't like whinging, as I've said before; but it didn't feel like that was what he was doing. Then again, maybe I was just flattered that he'd cared what I thought.

I said, 'Let me pay. And can I buy a congratulatory drink for the Phoenix's newest barman?'

I took one of the stools at the bar while Ian pulled himself a pint. A couple of women, one dark and one blonde, came to the bar and he turned to greet them with a smile, already in charge.

'Same again, ladies?'

Ladies. I frowned down at my glass. I dislike that kind of familiarity. And the word too, the patronising edge to it. My preferred style of service is the reserve you get in expensive hotels or private clubs, the kind where the staff call you 'madam', if they call you anything at all. I looked across at the two women – girls really – giggling and showing generous amounts of plump cleavage as they leaned across the bar. They didn't seem to mind being called 'ladies'. Perhaps they found it a pleasant change.

The one with the dark hair paid and they turned to go. 'Thanks, Ian,' she said over her shoulder.

I wrinkled my nose. 'Already on first-name terms with the punters, then?'

He winked at me. 'We get to keep the tips.'

I bought us both another drink, but after that Ian refused any more, telling me with a laugh that he didn't want to be drunk on his first night. He'd have to clear up with Matt after last orders, he told me, so I left having agreed he'd come around to the flat when he'd finished. I wondered if he'd want to do that every night he worked, and what I'd say if he asked.

When I got home, I went straight to the bathroom and got down on my hands and knees as if I'd dropped something, checking the sight lines to the phone taped to the back of the sink. I needn't have worried; unless you got into the space between the sink and the side of the loo and pressed your head almost to the wall, it was invisible.

The knife in the bedroom was a different matter. There was no way it wouldn't be seen by anyone moving the mattress. I could put it somewhere else – the bedside drawer, perhaps – but what was the point of having it there at all if I couldn't get to it if I needed to? In any case, I told myself, the risk was surely low. Ian's text had made me worry, but I was calmer now, my judgement clearer. He might be well trained enough to straighten out the bed on the mornings I left the flat first, but he'd never attempted to change the sheets, let alone turn the mattress. I wasn't dealing with Mrs Beaton.

Writing this now, I can see I look naïve. You're probably thinking how foolish I was to imagine the only place I could ever need that knife was in bed; that a man prepared to force a woman to have sex with him wouldn't dream of doing so anywhere without sheets and pillows. But perhaps it wasn't a failure of imagination after all. Maybe it was simply that I knew I couldn't control every variable, and that if I stopped to think about that, my nerve might fail. So instead I did what I could and refused to believe that might not be enough.

When I'd finished with the knife and the phone, I cooked scrambled eggs on toast and picked at it while I stared at the TV. I couldn't settle. So there hadn't been a problem this time. How long could I expect that to continue? And in the meantime, I was getting nowhere. Something had to change.

I put down the plate with its half-eaten food. Would Ian have eaten already? I didn't know what time his shift had started. Perhaps the staff were able to get something from the kitchen. Or would those couple of pints I'd bought him at the pub have entered an empty stomach? *I don't want to be drunk on my first night . . .*

I didn't know what hours he worked, but it was a fair bet no pub would need him in first thing in the morning. He'd be excited when he got back, relieved to be earning something again; he wouldn't refuse to share a celebratory bottle of wine, perhaps a couple of bottles . . . And then, when the adrenalin of the new job had started to drain away, and he was relaxed and blurry from the drink . . .

Suddenly everything was clear. This was the moment I'd been waiting for. This was my chance to ask him about Chantelle.

When the intercom buzzed, I looked at my watch: 11.51. I committed the time to memory. Details could be important. I imagined myself on the witness stand: *It was eleven fifty-one*, I'd say. *I checked, because when the buzzer went I thought it was a bit earlier than he'd expected to be back . . .*

When I opened the door to him, he looked tired but still on a high. He held out his arms and I walked into them, smelling alcohol and a faint odour of sweat. It was less unpleasant than it sounds.

I smiled up at him. 'I've opened a bottle. I thought we should celebrate.'

'Thanks, babe,' he said. Aidan would never have called me that; I rather liked it. 'I'm starving actually. Have you got anything to eat?'

So he hadn't had anything. He followed me into the kitchen and watched as I put a part-baked baguette in the oven. 'I've got some pâté in the fridge,' I said. 'OK with you?'

'You're a life-saver.'

He didn't notice I hadn't turned on the oven. I poured him a glass of Prosecco, remembering that the bubbles were supposed to get the alcohol more quickly into the bloodstream.

He took the glass from me with a raised eyebrow. 'Enough there? I hope you're not trying to take advantage of me, Miss Wright.'

There was a silence as we both realised what he'd said, and I watched the flush spread up from the neck of his T-shirt and stain his cheeks. Should I say something now, take the opening and raise the subject of Chantelle? But no, one look at the tightness to his jaw told me that if I tried, he'd shut down instantly. Instead I pretended nothing had happened.

'Perhaps I am, Mr Nash,' I said, trying for playfulness. 'Bottoms up.'

We both drank, and when Ian put his glass down, the level was a good inch lower than mine. Perhaps the verbal misstep had been a gift – now he wanted the alcohol to settle his nerves.

I took his hand. 'Let's go and sit down and you can tell me how it went.'

I led the way to the living room. I'd switched on a table lamp and lit some tea lights on the hearth in readiness, hoping that secrets were more likely to venture into a dimly lit room.

I saw Ian taking it in, a faint smirk showing he'd drawn the expected conclusion. 'Very romantic,' he said.

We sat on the sofa and I kept his glass topped up as he told me again how he'd got the job, how things worked in the pub, about learning to use the till and the beer taps. 'I worked at the student union bar when I was at uni,' he said, 'so I suppose it's like riding a bike. Didn't take long for it to come back.' He'd told me the same thing at the pub and I'd managed to suppress my surprise that he hadn't left school at the first opportunity. How little I know about him, I thought.

I drank more than I'd intended. It was nerves, I suppose. In the candlelight his skin had a golden glow and somewhere along the line we'd turned to face each other, our feet on the seat of the sofa, my legs pressed together between his. I could feel the heat of him against my skin. He cradled his glass on his lap and I saw that the tension had gone from his shoulders. Now was the time. All I had to do was formulate the words.

He said, 'I don't know how to say this, Natalie.'

It was like a slap. *Oh Christ, no, he's going to break up with me.*

He reached across and took a strand of my hair between his thumb and forefinger. I sat there, frozen. This couldn't be happening. I couldn't have done all this, taken this man into my home, my bed, only to have him leave again before I'd found out the truth.

I watched him swallow, trying to find the words to tell me. What had I done wrong this time? I'd tried so hard, been so careful not to be patronising or arrogant, not to exhibit any of the litany of faults Aidan had accused me of. I'd been patient and supportive, listened to Ian complain about his brother, about moody Sean and his moany girlfriend, never once telling him to shut up, or that I wasn't interested, or that actually I'd had a pretty shitty day myself and perhaps he might want to hear about *that* for a change. I'd given him sex whenever he wanted it and it had been OK, not earth-shattering perhaps, but he'd seemed to enjoy it well enough. What had gone wrong?

And then it came to me. He'd met someone else.

Caitlin.

Ian was watching me, a blurriness in his eyes. Were those *tears*?

He said, 'I suppose what I'm trying to say is . . .' He took a shuddering breath. I realised dimly that my fists were clenched. '*Thank you.*'

I blinked at him. 'What?'

'It means a lot, you know? That you believe me. And that . . .' He trailed off and I knew I should be encouraging him to keep going, but for the moment the words had died in my throat.

126

He leaned over and put his glass on the floor, then shuffled closer and took my hands in his. 'You know everything and you're still here. I don't think I could have done this without you. Not just the job, I mean . . .'

For once, the running commentary in my head had stopped. Ian's thumb traced a circle on the back of my hand.

'I mean – everything. I didn't know how I was going to carry on. I couldn't see a future. But now . . .' His voice trembled. 'I just want you to know how special you are.'

I sat there for a moment just staring at him. Then I leaned across and pressed my lips to his.

I woke cold and stiff from the draught that slithered between the gap in the ill-fitting sash windows and crept across the living-room floor. Ian was curled around me, his flesh a warm, damp counterpoint to the chill across my stomach and breasts. I could feel his breath against my neck.

Oh fuck, I thought. *Oh fuck.*

Chapter 15

Perhaps Stella will work out for herself what I've done. And if she does, I wonder what will set those mental wheels creaking into motion.

It's always possible, of course, that something will go wrong, there'll be some kind of discovery, an official intervention. Maybe she'll find an officer at her door – or two officers, isn't that the way these things are done? I can see her inviting them in to her pristine sitting room, offering them tea while wondering what the neighbours are making of the panda car parked outside and whether she can reasonably ask them to move it further along the street. The widening eyes and the pursed lips as they tell her some version of what's happened: *No, I'm afraid I can't help you, Officer, my sister and I aren't close.* Then realisation beginning to dawn, the horrible suspicion creeping in.

She'll probably imagine I've done it to get at her. That's the way my sister's brain works: it's all about her, always has been. And sometimes, I'll grant you, she's right. Now and again it's amused me to do whatever small thing I can to make her perfect life just that little bit less perfect, give the scales the slightest of slight tips back towards me. It's not like they're ever going to balance, but I'll admit it: when there's the chance for a minor correction, I take it. It's only fair.

But that wasn't why I did it. This time it was simple expediency: I needed what I took from her, and she made it easy.

I wonder what she'd have done if she'd known any of this was coming the day she turned up on my doorstep. Perhaps she'd have tried to persuade me against it, but I don't think so. I imagine she'd just have looked at me with that expression she has, the one that lies somewhere between horror and constipation, and got out of there as fast as her DKNY pumps would carry her.

It was a Sunday afternoon when Stella dropped by unannounced, and if Ian hadn't been doing a shift at the pub, he'd have been there with me. He was spending most weekends at the flat by then: I told myself it was the best way to hurry things along, that the more time we spent together the more opportunities there would be for me to find the right moment to ask him about Chantelle. Stella knew nothing about him. I hadn't seen or spoken to her since the christening and it wouldn't have mattered if I had; I don't discuss my love life with my sister, even when the relationship isn't with someone I met when they were in the dock. So when I heard her voice on the intercom, my shock was quickly eclipsed by relief at not needing to explain his presence.

She stood in the kitchen as I made coffee, looking around with an expression of mild distaste. I hadn't been honoured with Evie's presence; presumably she was at home with Michael while Stella attended the reiki appointment in neighbouring Blackheath that she had given as the reason for her unexpected visit. I knew, of course, that there was more to it than that. Stella might well have had a reiki appointment in Blackheath – or an acupuncture session, feng shui consultation or crystal healing, for all I knew – but it could have been held in the flat next door and she wouldn't have rung my bell unless she wanted something. She knew it and I knew it, but for now neither of us was saying anything, circling around each other like a couple of boxers at the beginning of the first round, waiting to see who would throw the first punch.

I said, 'Are you taking sugar these days?' knowing that she hadn't taken sugar in a hot drink since she was eleven.

She shook her head with a grimace. 'Actually, Natalie, do you have anything herbal? Camomile ideally. Michael and I are cutting out caffeine. You should try it – you'll find you have far more energy.'

I stared into the cupboard, ignoring the box of camomile tea next to Ian's preferred tea bags. 'Sorry – just builder's tea. Or instant coffee.'

She sighed. 'It had better be the tea then.'

I kept my back to her as the kettle boiled, adding a couple of spoonfuls of sugar to her mug. When I turned around, she was standing at the window looking out onto the park that had been my main reason for buying the flat.

'Tea's ready.'

She nodded to the view outside. 'There's a group of youths down there.' Stella is perhaps the only person I know who would actually use the word 'youths' in conversation. Well, Michael too, of course, but as an extension of my sister he doesn't count.

I said, 'Yes, that's perhaps not surprising given that it's a park.'

'I think they're dealing.'

'I presume you don't mean in stocks and shares?' She turned to me and I could see she was already annoyed. *First blood to me*, I thought. *And just wait till you try the tea.*

She took the mug from my outstretched hand. There's no room in the kitchen for a table and chairs, and with anyone else

I would have suggested we go through to the living room to sit at the small table beneath the window. But Stella didn't deserve that. I kept her standing while I leaned against the counter.

'So,' I said, before she could start on her usual refrain about how rough my part of London was and how she'd be far too scared to live there alone, 'how are you and yours?'

I knew it annoyed her that I hadn't asked specifically about Evie, although if she'd given it a moment's consideration she'd have realised my enquiry was directed solely towards her daughter. Stella, after all, was standing right in front of me in obvious health, and it was hardly as if I was interested in hearing about Michael.

'Fine, fine,' she said, with unnecessary repetition. 'Evie's sleeping through the night now, which is wonderful. We've got her into a routine, that's the key.'

I bet she said the same thing to other new parents. I wondered how much they wanted to hit her in the mouth.

'Congratulations,' I said. I hadn't actually meant it to sound sarcastic, but old habits die hard. Stella stared at me and I could see her struggling not to react.

'Shall we go through?' She nodded at the doorway as if she were the person who lived there, not me. I tried and failed to think of a reason to keep her on her feet, but she hadn't waited for a reply and I followed her into the sitting room, grudgingly acknowledging that she'd won round two.

She didn't sit down, instead walking over to the bookcases with a casual air. I knew then that I'd been right – she was up to something.

'I saw Auntie Celia the other day,' she said.

'Oh yes?' I tried to keep my voice steady. Stella was scanning left to right along the shelves. My dragon tree sat at the end of one of them, the tips of its leaves brown; I'd been neglecting it.

'She said she hadn't spoken to you for months.'

I didn't reply. What business was it of Stella's how often I spoke to my godmother?

She crouched down and peered at the spines of the books on the bottom shelf. 'Do you ever read them?' she asked.

I shrugged. 'Does it matter?'

'You used to, though, didn't you?' Her voice had got softer, dreamy. 'I always wondered if you understood them or if you were just pretending.'

I laughed, and the sound came out like steel and granite, hard-edged, sharp enough to hurt. 'I understood enough.' *Enough so I could talk to her about them. Enough to have one part of our lives where you couldn't follow.*

She straightened up and I could see her hands working together, the fingers of her left twisting and turning something on her right. She must know I could see her doing it; it was her reminder to me of where I stood in the pecking order. I swallowed and willed myself not to show I cared.

She turned back to me. 'Celia told me about the Hawking book.' I noticed she'd dropped the 'Auntie'. She was getting down to business. '*A Brief History of Time*. She said it could be valuable.'

I could feel my heart pounding in my chest. I stared back at her.

'I looked online and there's a copy of the first edition going for nearly six thousand pounds. And that's only signed by . . .' her brow furrowed, 'the person who wrote the introduction.'

Carl Sagan! I wanted to say. *The person whose name you've forgotten is Carl Sagan! One of the twentieth century's foremost astronomers, cosmologists and astrophysicists. The man who won the Pulitzer Prize, and assembled the first physical messages sent into space, and hypothesised that the surface temperature of Venus was a product of the greenhouse effect . . . Carl fucking Sagan!* But if I did that, I would have engaged and there would be no way back.

132

I ground my teeth together to stop myself forming the words.

'You have got it, haven't you? You haven't lost it or anything?' Stella turned back to the shelves again, as if expecting the book to materialise in front of her. 'You haven't poured wine on it?'

I couldn't help myself then. I snapped, 'Of course I fucking haven't!'

She flushed. 'There's no need to swear.'

I bit down a retort that included the words *in my own home.* I mustn't let her get to me. If she got to me, she'd won.

'Look, Natalie.' There it was again. *Look.* Why was I always the one who was supposed to be looking? 'One of Michael's friends works at Sotheby's, and he said if it was the proper first edition and the signature was real . . .'

Don't say it. Don't say it . . .

'. . . it might make five figures.'

Don't let her get to you . . .

'That's a lot of money . . .'

You'll regret it if you say it . . .

'And with Evie's schooling coming down the line, every penny counts.'

'The thing is, though, Stella, that's tough, isn't it? Because it's mine, not yours.'

And I'd said it.

I heard the petulance in my voice, and I was eight years old again, crying because Mum had told me to let Stella play in the den I'd spent hours building in the basement of our house. *But it's mine,* I'd whimpered. *Mine, not hers.*

'Oh, come on, Natalie.' She took a step towards me and then stopped. 'We both know Mum wouldn't have given it to you if she'd realised how valuable it was.'

My hand clenched around the handle of my mug so hard it should have broken. 'Get out,' I said quietly.

Stella looked like she was about to say something more, and when I opened my mouth again, the words came out on a scream. 'Just get out of my flat!'

After she'd gone, I went to collect the mug of tea she'd left on the edge of a shelf. She hadn't touched a single drop.

Looking back on it now, I don't think Stella meant it to come out the way it did. I think she just meant that Mum would have left the book to both of us if she'd known, something to be shared the way she'd always wanted us to share. That's what I try to believe anyway.

That probably doesn't sound unreasonable to you. You're probably on Team Stella. That's usually the way it goes – it did with my parents, anyway. Pretty Stella, innocent little hard-done-by Stella, always being picked on by her plain, galumphing older sister. And what had she done to deserve it? After all, all Stella ever wanted was to *share*.

I was five years old when she was born. I'd been looking forward to having a sister, if you can believe that. I wasn't worried that my parents would have to divide their attention between us. I believed them when they told me how much fun it would be to have someone I could play with at home, someone who'd look up to me and want to be just like me. 'You'll always be special to us,' Mum had said, cuddling me on her lap, 'our clever little Natalie.'

But somehow, after Stella arrived, it had never been like that.

Far from looking up to me, she saw me as an impediment, the other daughter getting in the way and demanding her parents' time. And after a while, I could see that my parents felt the same. I'd become a distraction, a nuisance. It didn't matter if I did better than Stella at school, it didn't matter that I could talk to them about their work in a way Stella never could; she was the pretty child, the charming child, the one they could show off to their friends. They tried to hide it, and for a while I didn't admit it even to myself – but I think I knew almost from the moment she arrived, blonde and long-lashed and dumb as mutton, blinking up at us all with those big blue eyes.

Both of us have names that come from Latin. You probably didn't know that about Natalie. It's derived from *natale domini*, meaning 'Christmas Day'. I was a January baby, but Mum told me she and Dad weren't thinking of the meaning. They both just liked the name.

They were thinking of the meaning with my sister, though. Everyone knows that Stella is Latin for 'star'.

They kept up the pretence until the end, I'll give them that. Neither Mum nor Dad ever said out loud what we all knew was the truth: that Stella was their favourite child. They were always scrupulously fair on the surface – our piles of Christmas presents the same size, the same amount spent at birthdays. Even when they gave Stella and Michael a chunk of money towards their staid little terrace in Ealing, they took into account the house price inflation that had occurred in the years since they'd helped me buy my flat and presented me with a cheque that paid for a shiny new kitchen.

Maybe it would have been enough to convince me, enough to silence the little voice that told me it was all for show, that deep down I knew that when Stella made one of her quiet asides about being their favourite, she might have been being spiteful but she was also right . . . But it turns out that not even my parents, with all their tact and care, could quite pull it off.

When Dad died – a heart attack, banal yet cruelly effective – he didn't, to my knowledge, leave a will. I never asked about it (though I doubt Stella had the same qualms). He was a decade older than Mum and I imagine they always expected he'd be the first to go, that everything would pass automatically to her and that she'd do what she always did: take care of things with quiet decency. But for once her antennae, usually so delicately attuned to the rivalries and petty grudges of her daughters, let her down.

She thought she'd done right by us, I'm sure; that the value of her bequests was as carefully balanced as her gifts to us had been in life. I don't suppose she would have expected for a moment that when Stella and I sat in Celia's front room, her mangy cat rubbing itself against our ankles as she told us the estate would be split equally between us, then shuffling forward in her chair as she said Mum had wanted to leave each of us a personal bequest – I don't suppose she could have imagined that when I heard those words I'd feel the air grow so hot and thick I almost couldn't breathe as I waited for it to be over, the last chance for Stella to prove she'd been right all along.

I remember watching as Celia looked down at the paper again, though I'm sure she'd rehearsed that moment and knew the words by heart. She'd slopped her tea on the table in front of her and I saw that one corner of the will was damp, a small beige triangle that looked as if it was in danger of tearing.

And then she read that final passage and it was my heart that tore instead.

Chapter 16

I cared about Ian in my own way. I can admit that now. It wasn't what I was expecting, but it crept up on me. My defences were down after Aidan, I suppose. I was weakened, susceptible; I caught him like I might have caught a cold.

I even met his parents once. He'd been keen to introduce me – I think he saw me as evidence to be submitted via them to his doubting brother – and when he'd suggested it enough times that I'd run out of excuses, I concluded it was as well to get it over with.

I think his dad recognised me; I caught him staring when he thought I wasn't looking. You could almost hear the thoughts pattering across the surface of his mind, trying to find a way out of the fog and into the bright, clear sunshine of memory. They didn't quite manage it, though. He wasn't the kind of man who'd have put two and two together and been able to keep quiet.

His mum wasn't interested in how we'd met. She was so relieved that he had a girlfriend ('So educated and well-spoken, Ian!' I heard her remarking to him in the kitchen on our one and only visit) that she fussed constantly around us both, checking that we weren't too hot or too cold, bringing us endless cups of tea and offering a steady stream of cheese straws, after-dinner mints and chocolates in coloured foil. The conversation didn't exactly flow, and in other circumstances I don't think they would have liked me – but clearly they were subscribing to the motto of beggars can't be choosers.

On my side, of course, it was all straightforward; there are some advantages to your parents dying young. I told Ian I had a sister and, truthfully, that we didn't get on. He didn't push it – I think he was as relieved as I was not to have to run the gauntlet of family introductions.

As for friends, neither of us had many. Ian's, I gathered, had fallen into two camps after his arrest – those who dropped him like a hot potato and the ones who'd rallied round with useless though well-meant offers of help. He didn't have to elaborate for me to work out that there had been more in the former group than the latter, and as for the rest, he said he'd mainly lost touch in the months leading up to the trial. Too embarrassed to face them, I imagined, or else he'd struck out in his fear and alienated people.

As for me, I'd got lazy when I was with Aidan, falling into the trap of thinking the people we spent time with were our shared property. We were invited to things as couples, got used to assuming that invitations to one of us were invitations to both, and as time passed all our friends seemed to be in relationships too, one after another settling into marriage and parenthood.

By the time I realised they were Aidan's friends after all, it was too late. In truth, I wasn't particularly upset; for the most part they were the kind of people you could meet for the first time or the forty-first and slip into the same conversation – jobs, house prices, holiday plans. One or two made an effort in the months after it ended, but it was soon clear to all concerned that it was hard work. I didn't blame them for deciding I wasn't worth it – I'd reached the same conclusion about them, after all – but I couldn't help being offended that after everything he'd done, Aidan had walked away with the friends part of the balance sheet so decidedly in his favour.

It wasn't that Ian and I didn't see people; we didn't spend all our evenings together in my flat, tucked up with a TV dinner and a bottle of wine. No, it was just that our circle of acquaintances was small. The Phoenix was the focus of our social interactions; with Ian working there, it soon became something I'd never had before, a bona fide local, and its staff and a handful of regulars assumed the mantle of friends. It suited us both; no effort was required to meet them, nothing expected on either side, minimal personal information exchanged. I don't know about Ian, but I don't think I even knew their surnames. I thought that might help if things didn't end well.

On nights when he was working, I'd go there straight from the office. If it wasn't too busy, I'd take one of the stools at the bar and chat with him over a drink (for which, may I add, I always paid; I didn't want to put him in a difficult position); or if it was crowded, I'd just check what time he was finishing and then head home.

The truth is, I'd allowed myself to lose focus.

I'd made a couple of half-hearted attempts to get Ian to talk about Chantelle after the night he'd started work at the Phoenix. I told him it would be good for him to get it off his chest; but each time he'd brushed away my feeble questions, saying he just wanted to put it behind him. I couldn't think of a way to move things forward, and it began to feel easier not to. He'd done nothing to make me wary of him, shown no sign of violence or misogyny. Surely, I told myself, if he really was innocent, that was all the evidence I would ever be able to find.

Maybe, after all, Chantelle simply hadn't been telling the truth. What was it Helen had said to Siobhan? That there were things in people's lives we couldn't know about, reasons to tell lies we'd never imagine anyone could tell. I knew nothing about Chantelle, nothing but what she'd told us in the witness box. How could I know whether there was something in her life to make such a lie, ugly and destructive as it was, seem better than the truth?

And with every day that passed, I found it easier to believe the jury had been right after all; that here, truly, was a man who deserved his freedom.

As for Aidan, whole days would go by when he barely entered my head. When I woke in the morning he was no longer the first thing I thought of. Our contact was dwindling and I began to think that in time it might cease altogether. Perhaps he'd started to think the same thing.

What it boils down to is this: I'd started to let down my guard. I'm still angry with myself about that. I should have known better. I thought I'd learned my lesson after Aidan and yet I allowed myself to be taken in, to believe that perhaps after all not everyone was duplicitous, not everyone would let me down. I suppose I was just too ready to believe the best of people. It's a mistake I won't make again.

I was happy when I left work that night. It had been a good day. I'd made several incisive remarks at the morning's gathering of senior officials, and had observed the new director general, freshly arrived from the Treasury to bring his wisdom to the grateful ranks of HMRC, looking at me with approval. I'd sorted out another emerging spat with Marsden's tree-huggers in DEFRA, earning me a pat on the head from the minister's office – which I had duly forwarded to Fiona to reassure her there was no need for further action (there is no point, I have learned the hard way, expecting your boss to notice your brilliance unless you bring it to her attention). The unexpected flurry on that front had also meant I'd needed to delegate several tedious pieces of corporate nonsense to Alan, not only saving me from updating yet another risk register but bringing the satisfaction of seeing him hunched muttering over his keyboard while glancing for the twentieth time at his watch. For once, he wouldn't be downing tools at five on the dot.

I tell you this so you know that when I pushed open the door of the Phoenix that evening, I was cheerful. I wasn't in the kind of mood where you misinterpret things, imagine slights where none are intended or pick a fight just because it's that kind of day. I was at ease with the world. I would go so far as to say I was happy.

There were a handful of people dotted around the place, but no one behind the bar. Ian must have gone to change a barrel, but it wasn't good to leave it unattended. Matt would not have been impressed and I assumed he wasn't expected that day. I stood there for a minute or so, and then thought I might as well take a seat at one of the tables. There wasn't much food in the flat – perhaps, as it was quiet, I'd see if Ian could take a break and we'd eat together there.

I was examining the menu when I heard them. She was giggling in a throaty way that sounded like the product of too many cigarettes and blow jobs. There was a low rumble as Ian said something, and then she giggled again, closer this time.

Caitlin. Fucking Caitlin.

Something hot and red unwound itself in my chest and I got to my feet, the chair clattering behind me. A woman at the next table glanced up from her phone and looked away again. I crossed the room to the door to the beer garden and stood there, one hand on the push plate as I waited for them to emerge into the bar.

From there they would have their backs to me, buying me time to observe them unseen.

She came first, dressed in black as always, dark hair caught up in a straggly bun on top of her head. For the first time I noticed how young she was: *Chantelle's age*, I thought, and something stabbed at my insides.

She stopped next to one of the beer taps and Ian came into view behind her. He was wearing the jeans I liked, the Diesel pair with the faded patches on the thighs. I watched him move behind her and for a moment I wanted to believe that there was nothing to worry about, that they were just colleagues sharing a joke; and then I saw him rest his hand on the small of her back as he passed and I knew.

I knew.

I pushed open the door and stepped outside, feeling the air cool against my flaming cheeks. The light was fading and there was no one in the garden, but I didn't take a seat – I couldn't stay still. I took my phone from my bag and walked back and forth along the short path between the tables, jabbing at the screen as I composed the message. I can't answer for my spelling or punctuation that day, but in my defence, I'd had a shock; it conveyed the meaning well enough. When I pressed send, it was as if a bubble of something released itself from my chest with a soft pop. I think that must be the way some people feel when they cut themselves.

I stood there breathing deeply, and a minute later felt the buzz of the phone in my hand. As I was reading the first message, it buzzed again, then again. Three replies, which I think was a record. I felt my heart rate slowing as I read them. My finger hovered over the screen, but with an effort I pulled back from the brink and replaced the phone in my bag. It had given me what I needed for now.

The beer garden was enclosed at the back and I had to scramble over a low wall to get out. I was wearing trousers, which was just as well, but the indignity of it all was hard to bear.

How is it that the person who's cheated on is always the one who's humiliated? Shouldn't it be the other way around? Shouldn't it be the cheater who's pitied and laughed at, the man who's such a slave to his libido that he can't act in a civilised manner? But no; instead it's the woman who's been fool enough to trust him.

It didn't matter that I was with Ian for reasons that had nothing to do with his limited personal charms. *He* didn't know that. He should have been down on his knees every bloody day thanking whatever god he believed in that I'd so much as looked his way. Instead he thought he could treat me like an idiot, lying to me, acting as if he was the one doing *me* a favour! Well, I wasn't going to stand for that. Not again.

I was in bed when he got back to the flat. He undressed in the dark and climbed in beside me, naked and hard. Was it for her? I wondered. Had they fucked already, or was he still thinking about it?

I didn't move, pretending to be asleep. I'd never done that before and Ian evidently thought it was worth persisting. He ran his fingertips down my arm and leaned over to whisper in my ear, 'Are you awake?'

I didn't stir and he tried again, louder this time so I had no choice but to pretend to wake. 'I'm tired, Ian,' I mumbled, but he cut me off with a kiss and rolled on top of me.

I'd thought I could lie there and let him get it over with, avoid what would happen next if I told him I didn't want his filthy, lying hands on me, the screaming row, the furious dead-of-night exit. I wasn't going to let it end like that, not before I'd found out the truth. But the moment he kissed me, I felt something snap. I pulled him close, clawing at his back and tugging his hair. He reared back and I saw the surprise in his eyes, but I pushed him to one

143

side and climbed on top of him, my nails digging into the skin at his shoulders. I looked down at him as we moved together, imagining how it would feel to take the knife from beneath the mattress and plunge it into his chest, drenched in the hot spurt of his cheating blood, watching his wandering eyes widen and die.

Afterwards I lay next to him, waiting to find the right voice to speak. I said, 'Tell me what happened with Chantelle.'

I was pleased that I sounded calm. At first he didn't reply, and I thought he was going to take a leaf out of my book and pretend to be asleep; but as I was about to repeat myself, he said, 'Was that what all that was about?'

I blinked into the darkness. 'What do you mean?'

'Come on, Natalie. The alpha female routine.' His voice was almost a whisper and from nowhere I felt a chill. 'Were you trying to get a reaction?'

I lay very still. I said, 'Did you hurt Chantelle?'

I'd expected him to leap up, to shout at me. I'd expected him to demand how I could ask him such a thing, to start pulling on his clothes and protest that he wasn't going to share a bed with someone who thought him capable of rape. Those were the things I expected.

He turned on his side and placed one arm across my body. He didn't press down, he didn't hurt me, but I knew if I tried to move, his arm would be like iron. There was a rushing noise in my ears and sweat prickled on my top lip.

He brought his mouth close to my ear, but he didn't speak. From outside I heard a snatch of conversation, footsteps on the pavement. Then silence deeper than before. I was alone with him. Alone, just like Chantelle had been that day.

A voice inside my head was screaming at me to find a way out, to pretend I'd only been joking; but instead my lips parted and I heard myself say, 'Did you rape her?'

144

The only sound was his breathing, slow and deep. His arm moved over my stomach to my breasts, his fingers light against my skin. And then I felt his hand on my neck, five points of fire against my throat. I could smell him, his sweat and sex, and it filled my brain so that I couldn't think. I waited for him to start to press.

Finally, he spoke. 'What do you think, Natalie?'

I tried to form words, but the feel of his fingers on my throat forced them back down. What came out instead was a whimper. I hadn't known I could make a sound like that.

He edged closer, the length of his body against me. He said again, 'What do you think?'

His breath was hot on my cheek, but there was a coldness in his voice I'd never heard before. I strained to see him in the darkness, tried to hold his gaze as I slid my hand down the mattress; but his arm was heavy across my body. I had no chance of reaching the knife. No chance, unless . . .

His fingers pressed lightly against my neck. I thought: this man might kill me.

I held my breath, gathered my strength. I would push him hard, fast. If he fell to the other side of the bed, I might have time . . .

He exhaled, a long, drawn-out sigh that stirred my hair. He said, 'You're lucky I can take a joke.' His hand fell away and he blinked twice slowly, as if waking from a dream. 'You'd have to be some kind of nutter to shag someone you thought was a rapist.'

He turned away and pulled up the duvet to cover us both. 'That's right, isn't it, Natalie? Some kind of nutter.'

I stared into the darkness and listened to the beating of my heart.

Chapter 17

At first, I was sure of what had happened. All that night as I lay there, my eyes fixed on the ceiling, I was certain of it. I was convinced Ian had interpreted my question about Chantelle as a threat to expose him, that he'd intended to put me in my place, show me who was in charge. I couldn't close my eyes, almost too scared to breathe, my fingers buried under the edge of the mattress, resting on the handle of the knife I'd finally manoeuvred into position – but I didn't draw it out. I didn't use it.

I saw the grey light come creeping around the edges of the curtains and heard the occasional solitary car outside gradually merge into the low rumble of the early rush hour. At some point I must have slept, because I awoke with a start to find Ian standing next to the bed, a steaming cup in his hand. He told me he had to get back, he'd promised to go with Sean to help his sister move house. My hand was hanging over the edge of the bed and I was terrified I'd left the knife sticking out from beneath the mattress; but Ian just bent and kissed my hair and said, 'Come on, sleepyhead, you'll be late for work.' It was the voice of the old Ian, the one I'd started to think I knew. I forced a smile in response.

I went to the shower and stayed there until I heard Ian call goodbye and the front door close behind him. Then I rang Alan and told him I'd come down with something unspecific and wouldn't be in that day. It was the first time I'd ever called in sick and I heard the surprise in his voice, but I put the phone down before he could ask me anything more.

I poured away the coffee Ian had brought me and made myself a cup of tea instead. Then I went into the sitting room and sat at the table with the mug in front of me. Ian would call later. Maybe he'd even come over when he'd finished helping Sean. What would I do when I saw him again? What would I say?

Perhaps I could try to ignore him. Not answer the phone. But he had his own key now. If he came around, I'd have no way of keeping him out. The locks. I'd have to change the locks.

I reached for my phone, brought up the search engine and typed in *locksmiths, Lewisham*. Then I put it down again.

A doubt was scratching at the surface of my brain. Was it possible that I'd misread the situation? Was there a chance that Ian hadn't taken me seriously at all?

I forced myself to remember what had happened, trying to take it step by step. I'd asked him about Chantelle, I'd asked him if he'd raped her. I'd taken everything that had happened next as his answer, his confession – but what if it hadn't been that at all?

He hadn't hurt me. He hadn't behaved afterwards as if he'd done anything wrong. He'd just pulled the duvet over us both and gone to sleep.

And what he'd said: that I'd have to be mad – 'a nutter', those were his words – to take someone I thought might be a rapist into my bed. That was what most people would think, wasn't it? Was it so hard to imagine that Ian hadn't understood it either? That he didn't comprehend the supreme importance of uncovering the truth?

I swallowed down the bile that had risen in my throat. I wasn't a nutter. I was doing what was necessary. But for Ian, perhaps it really was simpler than that: he thought I believed him.

Didn't it all make more sense interpreted that way? That I'd been angry and on edge after seeing him with Caitlin. That I'd misread his reaction to a question he thought was some kind of joke. A joke in poor taste, certainly, but a joke nonetheless. That those fingers on my throat had been nothing more than a casual touch as we lay side by side, the pressure and the chill in his voice simply products of my overheated imagination. And the next morning he'd made me coffee and told me not to be late for work.

I stared at my phone. What came next if I made that call? What happened when I ignored Ian and he came around and found his key no longer worked? What would I say to him when he started banging on the door? If he really was dangerous, I'd be making myself a target. I had nothing to take to the police, nothing real; but would Ian see it that way? An ex-girlfriend who might report him for threatening her? A man with his history? Might he want to make sure I wouldn't make trouble for him?

And suddenly I realised I was looking at it all wrong. I had to stop worrying about Ian, about what he'd say and do. I had to focus on what *I* was doing, remember why I'd started all this in the first place. And if I hadn't made progress up to now, something had to change. I had to up the ante.

It was time to bring in reinforcements.

The café was dimly lit and smelled of coffee. Despite being nothing much to look at, all the tables were taken. It was lunchtime, after all, and this part of Hackney evidently wasn't overburdened with culinary options.

I ordered a tea and clambered onto a stool built for giants next

148

to a strip of wood that ran along one wall. The stool was heavy and too close to the shelf, so I had to get down again and move it further away. Then I scrambled back into position, swivelling around gingerly so I could keep an eye on the door.

It was nearly fifteen minutes after we'd agreed to meet when Helen entered, her eyes already scanning the room. I waved and she smiled and mouthed 'sorry' as she spotted me, giving a complicated hand gesture that I took as meaning she was going to order her lunch before coming over. I raised my cup and shook my head to tell her I didn't want anything.

She returned a few minutes later, placing her tray on the shelf before performing the same awkward manoeuvre to get onto the stool next to me.

I pointed to the mug that was the sole item on the tray. 'Aren't you getting something to eat?'

She shook her head. 'Can't stay long, I'm afraid. It's mental today.' She was looking at me intently. 'Everything OK? Not that it isn't lovely to see you – but you sounded a bit troubled on the phone.'

Troubled. Such a social-worker word. I straightened my shoulders – I didn't want her treating me like a client – and decided to get straight to the point. 'I've just been thinking about the trial. You remember what you asked that woman at the court, the one who was taking the expenses forms?'

She frowned. 'No, I—'

'You asked her if there was any way to give feedback to the police.'

'Did I?' She lifted her mug to her lips as she thought about it. 'Yes, you're right. I remember now. It didn't seem right that there was no way to tell them where they went wrong.' A pause, then, '*If* they went wrong, that is.'

'You think maybe they didn't?'

She sighed. 'I don't know. It's like she said, the woman at the court; maybe they did look for other evidence and it just wasn't there.'

'Do you really believe that?'

She caught something in my tone and it was a moment before she replied. 'Honestly? I don't know. But I think we have to let it go. There's nothing more we can do now.'

I shook my head. 'I don't accept that.' I studied her face, trying to find some clue that would tell me how she would react if I told her what I was going to do. I thought: sometimes in life you just have to take a risk.

I said, 'I need your help.'

It hadn't been difficult to find her, but then I'd had a head start. I'd tried Facebook and pulled up her profile easily enough – Patterson might have been a common name, but Chantelle wasn't – but she'd kept her details hidden. It was a minor setback. All those questions during the trial about who lived where, establishing the logistics of Chantelle, Ian and Eloise's overlapping lives; I remembered the building. I could picture the photos, the orange bricks, the fake-Tudor gabling, the doors to the three flats huddled together on the small landing – numbers 10, 11 and 12. It was Deptford, I knew, but the name of the flats eluded me.

Ian had told me he hadn't set foot there after the arrest; his bail conditions prevented it. His landlord, he commented bitterly, had given him notice soon afterwards and sent in a house clearance firm to bundle up his belongings. There wasn't room at Sean's for more than a few clothes and toiletries, so his parents had taken away the rest and stored it in their garage. You'd think he'd have been grateful, but apparently the garage was damp and his wide-screen TV had suffered the consequences.

I'd toyed with asking him straight out where he used to live but couldn't find a plausible response to the inevitable question of why I wanted to know. In the end, I called his mum and fed her a story about wanting to buy him a cinema membership as a Christmas present, telling her the form required his previous address if he'd lived at his current one for less than three years. It was preposterous, of course, but I gambled on her being too keen to focus on the positives – her son had a nice girlfriend! She was planning his Christmas present five months in advance! – to ask questions. She bustled about on the other end of the line, and I could hear the pages of an address book rustling as she told me what a lovely idea it was, how Ian loved films, how she'd been thinking she should get started on her Christmas shopping too, it was never too early with all the things the grandchildren wanted . . . And at the end of it all, I had it: 12 Fairfield House, Romsey Road, Deptford.

Helen had tried to talk me out of going. I'd expected as much – sometimes, especially when the stakes are high, it takes something special to recognise what's necessary. Not everyone understands there are times when the usual rules don't apply, that sometimes you have to act outside everyday conventions for the greater good. The important thing is identifying when that's the case. That's something I've always been able to do.

So when Helen told me she thought I should leave Chantelle alone, I had my rebuttal ready. I explained that I'd thought long and hard about the trial and there were inconsistencies in the evidence that bothered me. I told her I just wanted to talk to Chantelle about them in case there was something that had been overlooked. If there was no new evidence, no one would ever need to know the conversation had taken place; but if there was? Justice demanded it be brought to the attention of the police.

She took a bit of persuading, but in the end she saw things my way. I told her I wouldn't involve her in anything; I just wanted to run through with her what I was going to ask Chantelle. I said I knew she'd been worried about the verdict too – wouldn't it be best to put our heads together and make sure I covered all the right ground?

We compared notes, but the conversation wasn't what I'd expected. Helen didn't look at things the way I did; she wasn't organised in her thinking. Even when I showed her my table with the two columns headed 'Chantelle's account' and 'Ian's account', I had to prompt her several times to get her to see the significance of some of the differences. Her doubts, it seemed, were based more on intuition: 'It was just a feeling I had about him,' she said. 'Everything he said made sense, but I just thought there was something there that wasn't quite right.'

Even so, it was good to talk it through. Now and again Helen lingered on a detail I'd considered unimportant: Chantelle's claim that she was wearing white underwear not black like Ian had said; that he'd brought the CD around of his own accord, she'd never asked to borrow it. I didn't know whether any of it mattered, but it reminded me I couldn't afford to dismiss anything. Better to press down on every single inconsistency and see if Ian's story started to creak.

And I liked talking to Helen. It was a relief to go through the details of the case with another person. I'd expended so much energy on thinking about it, changed my whole life because of it – but she was the only person I could tell even a small part of what I'd done, what I planned to do. I consider myself self-sufficient, as I think I've said before, but I'm only human.

I didn't tell her everything, of course. If you'd met Helen, you'd know why I didn't. She was – is – a sensible woman. Our conversation that day served a purpose. Telling her I planned to see Chantelle was a calculated risk. I knew it was something she would never have contemplated doing, but she had a flexible enough mind to recognise that people were different – she was a social worker, after all. She could appreciate the logic of what I proposed and, up to a point, she was prepared to help. But I could see from the start that she wouldn't have understood about Ian. She wouldn't have believed that I was behaving as a scientist, simply putting in place the conditions to test my hypothesis. I didn't want to see her get that look, the worried one people get before they suggest that perhaps you ought to go and talk to someone – someone *else* is what they really mean.

Besides, if I'd been going to confide in anyone about Ian, I would have needed to be sure they'd do more than understand. I would have needed to trust them.

That simply isn't something I do any more.

I'd decided not to wait. Ian wasn't scheduled to work that Thursday and I had my fictitious art class in the evening so he wouldn't come around.

I hadn't seen him since the night it happened, but I'd spoken to him on the phone. I told him I was ill and just wanted to be left to sleep. He sounded offended so I backtracked and said I thought it might be infectious. There were no more offers to keep me company after that. Neither of us mentioned that night.

I hadn't gone back to work since then, reasoning it was a distraction I couldn't afford. Instead, I'd been to the doctor and complained of debilitating fatigue and vague aches and pains, angling for some kind of syndrome. She'd signed me off for a week with a half-hearted injunction to make another appointment if I felt no better.

I heard from Aidan too. I hadn't been able to resist responding to him for long. I'd tapped out a few messages, even more creative than usual, if I say so myself, and been rewarded with the expected replies. I realised he must send them when she wasn't there. I liked to picture that: Aidan making some kind of excuse to leave the room, Kellie's pencil-darkened eyebrows raised in a quizzical little arch as he went to the bathroom, or to put the bins out, or whatever story he'd come up with that time. Perhaps she thought he was having an affair. That would be ironic.

I was careful not to let him take up too much of my time. I knew how I could get if I let myself enjoy our back-and-forth too much. So I contented myself with one or two texts a day. Sometimes I'd reply as soon as I received his message, sometimes I'd wait an hour; sometimes I'd leave it almost the whole day. I liked to mix things up, keep him on his toes.

The rest of the time was mine to prepare for my meeting with Chantelle. I'd looked for Fairfield House on Street View, electronically prowling Romsey Road until I spotted the familiar orange bricks. There wasn't much to see from the street: a narrow strip of housing either side of a brick archway with a sign above reading 'Fairfield Court'. Presumably Fairfield House lay on the other side, but the cameras hadn't ventured that way. It didn't matter. I remembered the patch of grass from the photos, the buildings at right angles to each other forming a squared-off U. Somewhere inside lay the staircase where Eloise had found Chantelle crying, the landing with the blue carpet and its three doors. Somewhere inside was the room where Ian might have raped Chantelle.

I'd made notes of my conversation with Helen and I ran through them one by one, typing them up into a series of bullet points. Then I grouped them under three simple headings: before, during and after. After I'd done that, I started a new page and typed in 'Outline Interview Structure' in bold, underlined text. I wrote myself a script (three more headings: introductions and offer, questions, thanks and next steps), typing and deleting and typing again until I was sure I had the wording right and I'd covered everything I needed to.

Afterwards, I made myself a coffee and mixed up some liquid feed for the dragon tree. I'd cut off the leaves that had gone brown but it was still looking rather sorry for itself. I misted the foliage and topped up the soil level with compost from a small bag I kept under the sink, specially formulated to provide a slow release of nutrients for healthy leaves and roots.

I sipped the coffee while I memorised every part of my notes; I would take them with me, but I didn't want to be reading instead of concentrating on what Chantelle was saying. When I'd finished, I saved the file as 'Meter Readings 2017'. There were other files for 2013 to 2016, the year I'd had a smart meter installed. If Ian got suspicious, he'd be looking a long time before he found anything to alarm him.

I'd decided to call on Chantelle in the early evening, judging that to be the best time to catch her in. I had a dim recollection that she'd worked at a hairdresser's, perhaps still did. In any case, she presumably must work somewhere; Deptford was an unlikely location for a trust-fund princess. I'd checked travel options and had discovered with satisfaction that I could take a bus from the main road near my flat almost all the way. It would take me no more than half an hour, door to door.

The day of the visit dragged. I ran through the questions in my head, but I was already word-perfect. Helen had suggested Chantelle might not want to talk to me, which I thought was a reasonable point – I would be asking a lot of her, and after that verdict she had every reason to mistrust me – so I walked to Lewisham High Street and withdrew four hundred pounds from a cashpoint. I knew any offer of money risked offending her; but if she turned me down flat, I'd have nothing to lose. And perhaps, after all, she'd see it as some form of reparation.

After the cashpoint, I went to the supermarket and bought some groceries. I thought I'd kill time by making a casserole. I could reheat it when I got back from Chantelle's. Casserole is one of those meals that improves with reheating.

I was in the middle of chopping carrots when I heard the knock at the door. The intercom hadn't buzzed so I assumed it was a neighbour, probably Vanessa from 3b coming to tell me she was having one of her parties at the weekend. I could hear her now: *I hope you don't mind? I promise everyone will be out by two a.m.* Two a.m.! As if having to leave your own home or have your entire evening ruined by Gloria Gaynor/Kylie Minogue/ABBA (yes, that's the kind of party Vanessa hosts) is somehow entirely reasonable, beyond reproach, as long as you're told about it two days in advance. I'd rather she just came around and said, 'I'm having a party, the floors are going to vibrate and you're not going to be able to hear yourself think, but hey, I'll be having a good time, so fuck you.' At least it would be honest.

So when I opened the door, fake smile at the ready, I didn't for one moment expect the person who was standing there.

Chapter 18

I told you, didn't I, that Aidan and I had been engaged? What I haven't told you is how it ended.

I'd known since that day at the Tate Modern that something was wrong. He was distant, snappy. We still spoke on the phone on the days we didn't see each other, but the calls were getting shorter and it was always Aidan who ended them. He'd left the bulk of the wedding arrangements to me, an approach that according to our married friends was typical of the prospective groom, and I tried to pretend that nothing was wrong as I ordered flowers and selected wedding favours (miniature bottles of whisky, in honour of Aidan's Scottish heritage) and harangued recalcitrant guests into giving me their menu choices for the wedding breakfast. If Mum had still been alive, I expect she would have helped with it all, but she wasn't, and Stella wasn't interested. It kept me busy and at the time that felt like a good thing. Now I think it stopped me seeing what was right in front of my face.

I wonder if he would have gone through with it if things hadn't come to a head the way they did. Sometimes I think he would have done. It would have taken guts to call it off; explanations would have had to be made. Aidan would have been the instigator, the villain. It wouldn't have suited his image of himself. More than that, it would have required him to take action, to get off his useless, idle arse and make something happen – or rather, not happen. It wouldn't surprise me if he'd decided it was all too much effort.

But that's not how it went.

I'd spoken on the phone to the car hire firm the morning it happened. I'd hired a vintage Rolls to take me to the church – silver not white, much classier – and had let the florist talk me into getting a posy that would fix to the grille at the front. There was therefore the logistical problem of how to attach the flowers to the car, and while the hire people were willing enough, they hadn't done it before and wanted a trial run.

It's hard to believe, looking back on it now, the energy I wasted on stuff like that. I wanted everything to be perfect, you see; to have just one day where everybody was looking at me, one day where people would think everything was beautiful.

So anyway, the car hire place was near Aidan's brother's house, and I thought if we went over there with the fixings from the florist we could drop in and see him at the same time (and his wife, whom Aidan had insisted on asking to read at the ceremony; I wanted to check she knew what she was doing). I rang Aidan to see when he'd be free, but his phone went straight to voicemail so I assumed he was busy at work. I tried him a few more times through the afternoon, but every time it would ring once and there'd be a click and that electronic voice enjoining me to leave me a message.

It was annoying, not being able to sort things out, so I decided to head over to Aidan's flat so I'd be there when he got back from work and could pin him down on dates. I popped in at an off-licence on the way and bought a bottle of red. It was from the same vineyard as one he had raved about on a previous holiday to Italy. I thought it would be a nice treat, something to help him unwind if he'd had a tough day.

You know what's coming next, don't you? It's so obvious it hardly needs spelling out. I didn't bother knocking because I thought he was at work, just let myself in with my key. I didn't catch them in bed – ten minutes either way and it would probably have been a different story – but when I went into the kitchen, I saw them.

She was doing something at the sink and he was behind her, his hands on her waist and nuzzling at her neck. He was naked.

I'd kicked my shoes off at the door as I always did, so they didn't hear me at first. I remember standing there, wine bottle in hand, staring at his milk-white arse and thinking how ridiculous he looked. She – *Kellie* – was wearing a T-shirt at least. So I suppose it could have been worse.

At some point I must have made a noise, because he swung around, his face a pantomime expression of shock and his pathetic erection fading almost instantly. For a moment no one said anything. Then Kellie looked from one to the other of us and said, 'Oh God, is that . . . ?' and I had time to think, *she knows, she fucking knows*, before I turned on my heel and left.

I hadn't said a single word.

Aidan didn't try to follow me. I went home and cried myself hoarse and didn't see or hear from him until the next day. Can you believe that? His fiancée had just walked in on him as good as shagging another woman and what did he do? Fuck all. Gutless bastard was probably scared of how I was going to react. He should have been.

Presumably he thought that waiting until the next day would mean I'd have a chance to calm down. I pretended he was right. I didn't scream or shout. I asked him how long it had been going on (he claimed it was only a few weeks, but I didn't believe him) and if he loved her (he said, 'Love isn't a simple thing, Natalie,' in a way that made me want to gouge out his eyes). Somewhere along the line I realised I truly hated him. It was that look he had; the faux contrition. He thought he was going to get away with it, that he could humiliate me and just walk away, carry on with T-Shirt Bitch as if nothing had happened.

I wasn't going to allow that.

I let him sigh his way through his excuses and platitudes. 'Deep down we both know we want different things,' he said, and, 'We don't bring out the best in each other,' and, 'This isn't the way I wanted it to end, but isn't it better that it happens now than that we make a mistake we'll regret for the rest of our lives?'

You can imagine how hard it was to listen to all his bullshit. How much I wanted to take one of Mum's biggest, heaviest books and smash it down on his head with every ounce of my strength. What it took for me instead to sit there, barely speaking, pretending to think about what he was saying.

I was crying at the end. Aidan, of course, thought I was sad it was over, devastated at losing the great prize in life that was Aidan Fucking McCarthy. He didn't realise that every one of those tears was distilled from pure white-hot rage.

He took me in his arms and I sat there rigid as a board as he stroked my hair and told me it was better this way. I bet he couldn't believe his luck when I finally closed the door behind him with a wan smile.

Anyone would think he didn't know me at all.

I left it a week or so before I went over there again. I needed to think through the logistics, run through the chain of cause and effect. There was never any risk I wasn't going to do it – I just needed to make sure I wouldn't be caught.

I phoned him beforehand, wanting to give him plenty of notice

– I didn't need his girlfriend there for what I had in mind. His flat sat in a block in Bermondsey with ideas above its station. There was a big metal gate to get to the car park in front of it, and next to it a smaller gate for pedestrians. Both had a keypad to enter a code; happily, I knew what it was.

I got there twenty minutes early and set to work. Aidan had told me once that the cameras were there just for show, but I tied up my hair and wore a hat and dark glasses to be on the safe side. It was getting dark by then, which I thought would help if anyone came in or out of the flats – but I was in luck. No one did.

I'd had to bring a large bag, for obvious reasons, so when I'd finished, I stuffed the hat and glasses inside with the empty can and went and rang Aidan's doorbell.

He buzzed me in straight away and was standing at the door when I entered the lobby. I gave him a weak smile, and when I reached up to peck him chastely on the cheek, I saw the surprise quickly replaced by calculation in his eyes.

I repeated what I'd told him on the phone – that things between us felt unfinished, that I'd still been in shock the last time I'd seen him and that I wanted one last chance to talk about what had happened. 'I'm not going to make a scene,' I'd promised. 'This is just something I need so I can move on.'

We sat on the sofa in his tiny living-cum-dining room, my bag carefully positioned at my feet. I told him I understood why he felt the way he did, that I knew it was over, but I wished he'd told me before he'd started to see someone else. He looked a little shamefaced at that point, and I thought *just you wait* . . . but I wasn't interested in his half-baked apologies and moved things on, looking up at him teary-eyed, one hand resting beseechingly on his arm. 'We did have some good times together, didn't we, Aidan?'

'Of course we did.' He sighed, pretending he was remembering them fondly. 'I'll always remember them fondly.'

'And me? Will you remember me too?'

Yes, that's what I said. He should have been on to me right there, but there wasn't a flicker. Just goes to show, doesn't it? When a man's blood flows to other parts, his brain is the first to suffer.

He took my hand from his arm and pressed it to his lips. 'You know I will. You've always been special to me.'

'But – that girl.' I dropped my eyes. 'She's more special.'

'It's not that.' Another sigh.

'What then?' I reached up and touched a finger to his cheek. 'Tell me, Aidan. I need to know.'

He didn't reply. I moved my fingers to his lips. 'Is she prettier than me?'

It was a risk, starting with that question, but he wasn't going to admit it in the circumstances. 'No . . .' he said, and I slipped my fingers inside his mouth.

I kept my eyes on his as he sucked them, then I removed them. I needed his answers nice and clear.

'Is she more intelligent than I am?'

He snorted then. Actually snorted. I mean, it's not as if I have any time for Kellie, but really. What a *shit*.

'Hardly,' he said.

I kissed him then. It took some time, and by the time we broke apart, I'd eased myself onto his lap. I needed to make sure he was in the right frame of mind for what came next.

'Is it the sex?' I rubbed myself against the hardness in his jeans. 'Is it better with her?'

I'd expected he might have some qualms about that one; after all, it had hardly been fireworks between us for a while. But Aidan is, above all, an opportunist. And I was the one sitting on his lap.

'No,' he said, and when I moved against him again, 'it's not like this with her.'

Good, but I was confident he could do better. I reached down and unbuttoned his jeans. The fastenings were awkward and I felt a nail snap in the process, but I reminded myself it was all in a good cause.

'Does she make you feel as good as I do?' I took him in my hands and stroked, firm and smooth, the way I knew he liked it. He groaned but didn't answer. I stopped. 'Does she, Aidan?'

Obediently, he panted, 'No.' His hands moved to my hips, trying to manoeuvre me into position.

I leaned forward and nuzzled his neck. 'You still love me, don't you?' I positioned myself over him so he could feel my heat, congratulating myself on my foresight in wearing a skirt. 'It's me you want, isn't it? Me, not her.'

Something twitched in his jaw. 'Jesus, Natalie . . .'

'Tell me.' I pulled aside my underwear and began to lower myself, then stopped. 'Tell me who you want.'

His eyes were screwed up tight. 'I want you. Christ, Natalie, just . . .'

Honestly, it was almost painful to watch. I swivelled my hips.

'I want you, not Kellie!'

And there it was. We had sex on the sofa and then on the floor, and to my surprise I enjoyed it. I think it was the pleasure of knowing he had completely the wrong idea about who was getting fucked. Afterwards he started to collect his clothes, pretending to look ashamed of himself.

'I shouldn't have done that,' he said.

I propped myself up on one elbow, watching as he tried to put his pants on inside out. I sniggered and he stopped, surprised, pants up to his knees. I looked at his semi-hard cock and sniggered again.

'Erm, Natalie,' he said, 'you know this doesn't change anything, right?'

I stared at him. 'Actually, you might be surprised to find that it does.' He looked at me blankly. I said, 'Be a love and pass me my phone from my bag.'

I actually saw the colour drain from his face. I hadn't known that really happened. He said, 'Don't tell me you've ... you've ...'

I waited. I'll be honest, I took a certain enjoyment from the moment. Eventually he spat it out. 'You fucking videoed us?'

I laughed then, I couldn't help myself. I mean, *really*. As if I'd want the sight of Aidan's bouncing buttocks preserved for posterity! I held up my hand to stop him saying anything more as I collected myself. For once he did as he was told.

'No, Aidan,' I said, 'I did not *video* anything. Though I have to say the irony of being afraid your bit on the side is going to find out you've been shagging your fiancée is pretty fucking hilarious.'

He grimaced but looked too relieved to argue. He'd gone back to struggling with his pants, so I got up myself and took my phone from my bag.

He looked up then. 'So what do you mean, things have changed?'

I didn't answer; I was busy scrolling through to find the best photo.

'Natalie? What are you playing at?'

I smiled at him and held out the phone. He took it automatically and turned it around so the photo filled the screen. For a second he didn't make sense of what he was seeing; but then the penny dropped and he looked up at me with his mouth open.

'You fucking *bitch*!'

I laughed again. And that's when he dropped the phone and launched himself at me.

Aidan isn't a violent man by nature, which just goes to show that if you press the right buttons, anyone can snap. It hadn't taken much to work out what the right button was for Aidan: his almost-new flame-red Audi TT with the leather upholstery and black gloss alloy wheels. He loved that car; evidently my customisation of the paintwork hadn't gone down well.

He didn't hit me, but I can't bring myself to give him any credit for that. What kind of world do we live in, after all, where a man gets points for resisting smacking a woman half his size? He grabbed me, though, hard around the upper arms.

'You fucking bitch!' he said again. Aidan has never been the most creative verbal opponent. His face was close to mine and I could feel flecks of spittle on my cheek. 'I'm calling the police.'

He pushed me away and I watched him grab at his jeans, pulling them on and reaching into the pocket for his phone. I waited until he had it in his hand before I spoke.

'I don't think you want to do that.'

'Really?' he shouted, spit flying. 'You know what, I think I do.'

'Suit yourself,' I said. That was what made him pause. The old reverse psychology – works every time.

He looked at me, suspicion belatedly beginning to dawn that his car wasn't all he had to worry about. 'What the fuck . . . ?' he said eloquently. 'What the fuck are you up to?'

'I think that's pretty rich, in the circumstances,' I said. 'It wasn't me who was fucking someone else two weeks before our wedding.'

'I get it,' he said, though he didn't. 'You're punishing me. I knew you didn't have it in you to deal with this like a grown-up.'

'Yes, Aidan,' I replied sweetly. 'I realise it is very *immature* of me to expect my fiancé, the man who asked me to marry him, to keep it in his pants at least until we were married. It was very *childish* of me to take the view that you ought to pay for what you've done. I suppose that's just the kind of woman I am.'

'You're fucking crazy.' He pointed at me with a trembling finger. 'And if you think I'm not shopping you to the cops, you can dream on.'

I reached into my bag and lifted out the little device that had been sitting in the inside pocket.

'What the fuck?' he said. I told you he wasn't very inventive.

'I told you I hadn't videoed us, Aidan. Starring in some sub-standard sex tape isn't really my thing.'

The hand with the phone in it dropped to his side. He looked as if I'd hit him with a brickbat.

'But I think a sound recording will do the trick just as well. What was it you said again? It wasn't this hot with that new girlfriend of yours?'

He looked like he was about to lunge for me again, presumably to grab the recorder. I held out a hand. 'There's no point, Aidan. It uploads directly to the Cloud. Do you think I'd have told you about it now if it didn't? And don't worry, the sound quality is excellent. Far better than a phone.'

I started to dress, taking my time. Aidan had apparently lost the power of speech. When I'd finished, I picked up my bag and gathered my phone from its resting place on the floor. I turned it over, inspecting the screen. 'Just as well you have carpet,' I said, 'or I'd have had to ask you to pay for the repair.'

I turned to go, but I didn't like the look on his face. 'You've brought this on yourself, Aidan,' I said.

'You patronising fucking psycho bitch,' he replied.

Chapter 19

I'd only seen Kellie once, but as you can imagine, it was in the kind of circumstances that tend to leave an impression. I recognised her as soon as I opened the door.

I almost shut it again straight away, but she pushed out an arm to stop me. Yes, that's right – an arm, not a foot. I told you she wasn't that bright.

'Natalie, we need to talk,' she said.

It occurred to me that someone must have let her in through the front door. Probably they thought she didn't look like a threat, standing there in her cigarette pants and expensive-looking jacket. I could have told them, *Don't judge a book by its cover.*

'No,' I replied, 'I don't think we do.'

She was nervous, chewing on her bottom lip, but she stood her ground. 'I think it would be better if we did this inside.'

I thought about closing the door in her face, but in the end my curiosity won out and I showed her through to the kitchen. I leaned against the counter with my arms folded. I'd like to say I had to fight my ingrained courtesy not to offer her a drink, but really it wasn't that hard.

'So,' I said, 'what do you want?'

Even leaning against the counter, she had to tilt her chin to look at me. She made me feel huge, ungainly. I tried to ignore the voice that said perhaps that was why Aidan preferred her to me. She said, 'I know you've been texting Aidan.'

I'd expected something of the sort, but I wasn't about to give anything away until I found out what she knew. 'Really,' I said non-committally.

She nodded. 'I know . . .' She tailed off and cleared her throat, tried again. 'I know it must have been terrible for you, what happened—'

'What happened?' I cut her off. 'What you *did*, you mean, the pair of you.'

She raised a hand as if to run it through her hair, but it was pulled back in a ponytail. I surmised she didn't wear it that way often; perhaps she'd been afraid things might get physical and wanted to keep it out of the way of grabbing hands.

She sighed and looked up at me with her Bambi eyes. 'We fell in love, Natalie,' she said.

I didn't know whether to laugh or cry. A sudden horrible suspicion made me dart a glance at her left hand – but the fourth finger was bare.

'How lovely for you,' I said, my voice dripping sarcasm. 'Is that why you came here? To tell me how in love you are with the man I was supposed to be married to by now?'

She flinched and a flush rose up her cheeks. For someone who was here to confront me, she was pretty defensive. What were the odds that Aidan hadn't come clean about what had happened?

'I came to tell you it has to stop,' she said. Her voice was surprisingly firm. 'I understand that you still care about him . . .'

I didn't hear the rest of the sentence. So he hadn't shown

her the texts. She didn't know what kind of messages had been winging his way. She thought I was still in love with him!

I turned my back to her and cut into a half-chopped carrot, trying to drown her out while I thought about what this meant. Aidan had lied to Kellie – or at least he hadn't told her the full truth. Of course he hadn't. He knew me well enough to know that if she confronted me, she'd be treated to the sound recording of us having sex after she thought we'd broken up, complete with his less-than-flattering commentary on their relationship.

Kellie was still droning on in the background. '. . . trying to make a new life . . . need to do the same . . . put the past behind you . . .'

I sliced into another carrot. 'Have you seen these texts I've apparently been sending?' I swivelled back to her. Her face said it all. 'I thought not. Has it occurred to you that Aidan might be lying to you?'

Her mouth set in a line. 'Please don't try that, Natalie. I trust him.'

I laughed. 'Just like I did.'

'I don't want to upset you,' she stretched out a placating palm, 'but my relationship with Aidan isn't the same as yours was.'

I stared at her. 'And you know that how?'

'He told me you . . . He told me you were very different people.' *I bet he did.* 'And let's face it, if everything had been perfect between the two of you, he wouldn't be with me.'

I think it was the look she gave me that did it. Not anger or triumph – I could have dealt with that. It was pity. She pitied me.

'You don't have the first idea what you're talking about,' I said. She tried to interrupt, but I carried on. 'Do you know how it actually ended between Aidan and me?' She opened her mouth again, but I wasn't going to stop. 'The real story, I mean, not whatever bullshit line he's been feeding you?'

For the first time I saw a shadow of uncertainty cross her face. 'I don't know what you mean . . .'

'No, I bet you don't.' I took a step towards her; I had her attention now. 'Maybe you should try asking Aidan what happened the last time we were together.'

She didn't like that construction, I could see. The little bullfrog cogs were starting to turn.

I lowered my voice. 'Perhaps you don't know Aidan as well as you think. I know I didn't.' I paused to let my words sink in. 'He isn't the kind of man you can trust.'

Somewhere along the line I'd taken another step, and she was close enough now that if I reached out a hand I'd be able to touch her face. Was it her face that had made Aidan want her? If I looked like that, the delicate features and the big brown eyes, would he be with me now instead of her?

She was looking at me with an expression that at first I couldn't make sense of, and then something shifted and I realised it was fear. She turned and ran; in another second the door of the flat slammed behind her.

I realised with surprise that my hand was raised. I lowered it and opened my palm around the thing I had been clutching. The handle of the vegetable knife had left a groove across my skin.

I didn't go to see Chantelle that night. Kellie's visit had knocked my concentration and I knew I might have only one chance to speak to her. I couldn't afford to be distracted, to risk missing some detail we'd all overlooked.

The next day I went back to work. I'd started to worry that being home alone wasn't good for me, that perhaps I was becoming a little . . . intense. I needed to be surrounded by the everyday sound and fury of the office to pretend that things were normal, to put all the thoughts about Ian and Aidan and Kellie and Chantelle into a box, just for a short while. I thought it would help to take a step back – remove myself from the detail and look again at the bigger picture.

Alan was pleased to see me. He almost sighed with relief when he looked up and spotted me walking across the open-plan. It irritated me, his desperation to offload any responsibility, but I have to admit to finding it gratifying how incapable they all were of operating without me.

It was busy, work backed up as I'd known it would be. I buried myself in activity, and by the time I stepped onto the Tube that night, I'd barely had time to worry that it was an evening when Ian would be at the Phoenix; that he'd be turning up on my doorstep for the first time since he'd placed his hand on my throat.

When I got home, I went straight to the bedroom. The duvet was pulled neatly across the bed but I tugged it out from beneath the pillows and lay on my back on the sheet. Reaching down, I slipped my hand beneath the edge of the mattress and almost immediately felt the handle of the knife; deceptively easy. But it hadn't been like that at all, not with Ian's hand against my throat, the fear coursing through my veins. Perhaps it was just as well: if I'd reached for the knife that night, I might have found myself in a cell by now.

I sat up, considering other hiding places. Beneath the pillow was still too easy to find; besides, it might be even more difficult to reach lying on my back. Perhaps I could get some Velcro, stick it to the edge of the bedside table; but the risk of Ian spotting it was too high unless I placed it low down, and then it would be just as difficult to get at as it was under the mattress.

In the end I contented myself with moving it an inch or two further up the bed. If there was a next time, I told myself, I would be prepared. I wouldn't freeze like I had before.

In the bathroom, the phone was in its usual place. I took it out and plugged it in, watching the green rectangle that showed it was charging grow and shrink again. It was a comfort, but I knew there was only one thing that would make me feel safe again. I had to find out the truth about Ian.

The phone was back in its hiding place and the previous day's uneaten casserole was reheating in the oven – I found I'd lost my appetite after the encounter with Kellie – when the intercom buzzed. Something turned over in my stomach.

Ian. I shut down the laptop with its bogus meter readings file and buzzed him in. He was earlier than I'd expected – he must have swapped a shift and started at lunchtime. I stood in the doorway listening to the footsteps coming up the stairs. There was something unexpected about the sound, an echo of itself. Two pairs of shoes.

I was just processing what this might mean when a figure rounded the corner in the stairwell. The breath caught in my throat at the sight of the uniforms.

It was the police.

Chapter 20

There's something very wrong about having a person wearing Kevlar in your sitting room.

I'd thought about not letting them in, wondering if, like vampires, they couldn't enter if I didn't invite them; but it's the staging of it all that's hard to resist – the uniforms, the aura of authority. One of them said 'Natalie Wright' in a tone of voice I wasn't used to being addressed in, and all of a sudden I was simpering and offering them tea.

They sat awkwardly on my sofa, too big for the space. The thoughts were screaming through my head so loud I half expected the officers to start transcribing them in their notebooks: had Helen got cold feet about helping me? Had she told them I planned to visit Chantelle? And were there actually laws against that kind of thing, something in the rules for jurors? I couldn't remember.

Or perhaps it was Aidan. Perhaps Kellie had confronted him about what I'd said. I should never have asked her if she'd seen those text messages. Maybe he'd found it impossible to resist her demands to see them. Did it count as blackmail, what I'd done? Or had he finally reported me for damaging his precious car?

Stay calm, I told myself. Don't give yourself away before you find out what they know. It was the same advice I'd given myself about Kellie. Somehow it had been easier with her.

I said, 'Are you sure I can't offer you something to—'

It was the shorter of the two officers who interrupted me, an Asian man with a south London accent. 'I'll come straight to the point, Miss Wright.'

'Ms,' I corrected him automatically. At least I had enough sense to avoid my usual adjunct: *My marital status is not your concern.* Something told me this wasn't the time for a lecture on gender politics.

'We've received a complaint of threatening behaviour.' *What the hell?* I stared at him in incomprehension. 'From Miss Kellie Carson.'

'Kellie?' I parroted. They blinked back at me, unmoved as a pair of bookends. 'What has she said?'

'Have you seen Miss Carson recently?' It was the white one who spoke this time. I caught a subtle emphasis on the 'Miss', as if he were deliberately trying to antagonise me. I refused to rise to it.

'Yes, she came here yesterday.'

'I understand that Miss Carson is in a relationship with a former boyfriend of yours—'

'Fiancé,' I snapped. 'Aidan was my fiancé.'

The Asian one scribbled something in his notebook. Had Kellie really skipped the fact that we'd been engaged? *Bitch.*

The white one looked bored. 'Miss Carson alleges that you threatened her with a knife.'

'I what?' I didn't like the way I sounded, spluttery and insincere. Hardly fair when for once I *was* sincere. I tried again. 'That's not what happened. She interrupted me when I was making dinner. I had a knife because I was chopping vegetables . . .'

'Miss Carson alleges that you waved it in her face.'

I felt the anger rising like a tide and took a breath to push it back down again. I had enough on my plate without Kellie, of all people, bringing the police to my door.

'Officer,' I said, deliberately calm, 'I realise you must hear this kind of thing all the time, one person saying this, the other person saying that. All I can tell you is that what Kellie has said happened is not the truth.'

The way I'd said 'Kellie', without rancour, was particularly good. I thought the Asian one looked impressed.

'So tell us your version.' It was the white one. Clearly he was going to be the harder nut to crack.

I sighed. 'Kellie came here unannounced. I was very surprised to see her, but she said she wanted to talk to me about Aidan. She seemed to be under the impression I'd been sending him text messages. She was very exercised about it.'

I wondered how often they came across people who said 'exercised' in relation to something other than the gym. I hoped it was having the right effect. *Don't be patronising*, I reminded myself. Perhaps I'd add in another 'Officer' to make sure I was being suitably respectful.

'I hadn't been in touch with Aidan since we split up, Officer, and that's what I told her.' They didn't flicker, and I took that as a good sign. Should I go into the details, make them see just how much of a shit Aidan was? But that might strengthen my apparent motive. It was a tough call.

'And what happened then?'

An idea formed like a shaft of light right into the centre of my skull. I suddenly knew exactly how to play it. *Oh Aidan, if only you weren't such a deceitful bastard.*

I gave a rueful smile. 'I asked her if she'd seen any of these supposed texts. Of course she hadn't.'

I watched them for a reaction, but I knew already I was right; Aidan hadn't wanted to take the risk of showing them to the police. He'd be worried about how I'd retaliate. He'd probably told them he'd deleted them. Perhaps he had. It would be the wisest course of action for someone who just wanted the problem to go away. Except that, unfortunately for Aidan, his problem was me, and I wasn't planning on going anywhere.

'So why did Miss Carson think you'd been texting her boyfriend?'

'Well, only Kellie can answer that for sure. But if you're asking me what I think . . .' I smiled again, regretful. 'I suspect she's in the same position I was in. You see, we were still together when Aidan started seeing Kellie.' I waited for the penny to drop, but their expressions told me I needed to help them along. 'I imagine she'd heard one too many text alerts on his phone and asked him what was going on. Aidan probably thought he could blame me, claim I was obsessed with him or something. I don't imagine he thought for a moment she would try and talk to me about it.'

The Asian one looked up from his notepad. 'So why is she saying that you waved a knife in her face?'

I studied the carpet at my feet, bit my lip. 'When I asked her if she'd seen the messages, she got quite upset. I think she must have realised then that Aidan had been lying to her. And of course, to know that I'd realised it too – well, I think she was embarrassed.'

The Asian one gave an infinitesimal nod. One down, one to go.

'We were in the kitchen – like I said, I'd been making dinner. A casserole.' *That's right, casserole, like your mum makes. What kind of knife-wielding lunatic cooks casserole?* 'Kellie looked like she was going to cry, and I went over to comfort her.'

The white officer was as square and impassive as an Easter Island statue. It occurred to me that it didn't really matter whether he believed me or not; it was my word against Kellie's, I wasn't about to be charged with anything. Still, I had my pride.

I sighed and leaned forward in my seat. 'Maybe you think I hate Kellie after what happened, but I don't. I knew what it felt like, to be the person Aidan was lying to. I felt sorry for her. I'd been chopping vegetables, and like I say, I must have still had the knife in my hand when I went over to her. I suppose it's possible she thought I was threatening her.'

'But she was mistaken.' He said it as a statement, not a question. I liked that.

I nodded. 'Yes, let's call it that.' A pause, then, 'I don't want to make trouble for Kellie. She's got enough to deal with . . .'

They left shortly after that, the Asian officer giving me the ghost of a smile as he passed me on his way out, letting me know he understood I was the injured party. I almost tapped out a celebratory text to Aidan as soon as I'd closed the door behind them, but I thought better of it. It was always possible the police would make a return visit to tell Kellie they'd spoken to me – and perhaps (one could always hope) to give her some kind of warning about not wasting their time. It didn't make sense to escalate the situation straight away.

It was a couple of hours later when Ian arrived, and by then the initial euphoria of having got away with it had passed. All the same, the distraction had been helpful: it had reminded me that I was good at thinking on my feet. Good at managing situations. I'd been starting to doubt myself, but there'd be no more of that. If I could handle the police, I could certainly handle Ian. I just had to keep my cool.

He looked tired when he got in, his hair mussed up into little tufts around his ears in that barn owl way of his. 'You want something to eat?' I asked. 'I've got a lamb casserole I can stick in the microwave.'

He looked at me as if I were an oasis in the desert. 'You're a life-saver,' he said, and I tried not to let it make me feel good.

I sat opposite him at the table in the sitting room while he ate. It had been a busy night, apparently; Caitlin had called in sick at the last minute and Matt hadn't been able to find anyone to cover. 'Fair enough if she's ill,' he said, in a way that suggested he didn't believe it for a minute, 'but she could have rung earlier. She knows what it's like on a Thursday night.'

Interesting, I thought. Maybe I'd got it wrong about the two of them after all. 'Perhaps she was hoping to get over it in time to make it in,' I said.

He put down his knife and reached across the table to squeeze my hand. 'You always think the best of people,' he said.

My phone rang three times while I was on the bus. The first time it had stopped by the time I fished it out of my bag and I had to check the call log to see who it was, my stomach doing a strange crampy thing at the possibility that it might be the police. For once I was relieved when I saw Stella's name on the screen. She hadn't left a message, which meant I could ignore her without being subjected to accusations of rudeness.

It rang again a couple of minutes later and I stared at the screen with her name on it. I toyed with selecting 'Ignore' but wasn't sure what would happen. Would it continue to ring innocently at her end, or would it switch abruptly to voicemail? Stella would notice something like that – that was the kind of person she was. On the whole, I didn't care, but was it worth it for the sake of putting up with the noise for another second or two? I let the phone lapse into sulky silence.

She left it seven minutes before trying again. The woman next to me sighed, but I refused to be judged. People ignored phone calls all the time. That was what the button was there for after all; it let you know that doing so was an acceptable option. That, I felt, was the real social impact of the mobile phone: taking calls in the middle of an evening with friends, tapping away in the midst of a meeting, choosing to ignore someone who wanted to talk to you; it had legitimised rudeness.

That was fine with me.

Still no voicemail and no text message. I turned down the volume on the phone in case she tried again, loud enough that the woman next to me would hear and be annoyed, quiet enough that she'd have no basis for complaint. It chirruped as I selected the level, and she sighed again.

Stella, I imagined, was looking to reopen negotiations on the Hawking book. I hadn't heard from her since I'd given her her marching orders, which showed an unusual degree of patience on her part. Probably she'd spent her time bitching about me to Celia; I was half surprised not to have had a call from my godmother, one of those conversations in which she kept telling me she didn't want to take sides whilst taking Stella's. I could imagine it now: 'Your mother wouldn't want to see you at each other's throats like this, Natalie. She always wanted you to *share*.'

But what had Stella ever shared with me? Why was it always my things that were part of the contract? When we were kids, nothing was sacred: my favourite doll, the hobby horse with the red reins, even my Sleeping Beauty duvet cover ('*I'm* Sleeping Beauty, not you, silly!'). Then later my clothes, my make-up. And our parents, of course; Stella was never interested in sharing them.

I wondered what she'd say if I called her back, told her I was happy to sell the Hawking book and split the proceeds. That was what she was after, of course; she wasn't looking for some time-share arrangement. She didn't care what that book had meant to Mum, how excited she'd been the day she came home with it, showing me the signature, telling me about the lecture she'd been to. There was no sentimentality in Stella. All she was interested in was cold, hard cash – that and the chance to deny me anything of my parents' that held any value in her eyes.

I realised I was digging my fingernails into my new bag, the Aspinal one that had cost a small fortune. There were crescent-shaped grooves on the black leather. I tried to smooth them out with the tips of my fingers, but the edges stayed sharp. Maybe they'd fade in time.

Outside the window, shopfronts and run-down-looking offices crawled past. It was dusk and the street lights were on, turning everything a dirty yellow. My phone lay silent; perhaps Stella had given up. The woman next to me stirred as the bus slowed, and on the periphery of my vision I saw her gnarled hand clutch the pole in front of us as she pulled herself to her feet. An electronic voice intoned, 'Deptford High Street'. Not long now.

I stood and made my way to the door as soon as the voice announced my stop. No one else moved. I glanced at the LED sign at the bottom of the stairs to the upper deck: Florence Road. That was definitely right.

No one else got out with me and a look at my surroundings suggested they weren't missing much. Next to the bus stop stood a couple of small shops, a barber's and one of those strange places that promised foreign currency and mobile phone repairs and photocopying. Across the road, though, was a decent-looking coffee shop. Maybe I'd go there afterwards, take a quiet moment to reflect on what I'd heard.

I consulted my phone, although I knew the way already, had memorised it. I headed left at the first junction into a street that was immediately residential, Victorian terraces with bay windows on the ground floor, surprisingly well kept. Then left again and more terraces. Another day I might have amused myself by checking out the front gardens as I passed, spotting the recent owners with their gravel and potted bay trees, the ones greeting each new skip as reassurance that the estate agent had been right when he'd promised them this was an up-and-coming area. Today, though, I kept my eyes straight ahead, looking for something else.

The terraces came to an abrupt end, the grey-brown bricks replaced with orange ones. The street must have been bombed in the war and this was the result: a 1980s block of flats with an arch through the middle.

I passed beneath it and found myself in a courtyard, lined on all sides by walls of the same orange bricks. A lawn had been laid in the middle and the grass had been recently cut: its sweetness filled the air. People always say how much they love that smell, but I doubt many of them know what causes it. It's something called green leaf volatiles. Plants emit them when they're in distress.

A path skirted the edges of the lawn and another two crossed it at right angles, the door to a block of flats at each end. I knew the building I wanted was directly ahead – the photo I'd seen had been taken straight on but had caught part of the blocks on either side, and there'd been no sign of the arch. I hesitated for a second and then took the long way around, sticking close to the walls and walking briskly, a combination of stealth and purposefulness I hoped wouldn't excite the curiosity of anyone watching from the windows that glared down on every side.

I checked the sign above the first door I passed, reassuring myself it wasn't the one, noticing the metal panel with its columns of buttons. They were evidence of the number of flats that had been squeezed in, but out here in the courtyard it was eerily quiet. Maybe people were still at work.

A corner, then, a few steps further on, another doorway. Above it, a black sign with white lettering announced that this was Fairfield House. To one side was a metal plate just like the one on the other block, two columns of buttons under a grille that was presumably a speaker. My finger hovered over the one marked 11.

I thought: I could go away now, just leave and forget all of this, tell Helen she was right, that it's better to let it go. I pressed the button and waited.

Chapter 21

The room was small but tidy and so clean I was half afraid I might contaminate it as I entered, the gritty south London air clinging to my coat and hair. I'd removed my shoes at Chantelle's request and my toes, trapped in the nylon of my tights, looked faintly ridiculous. I tried to hide them beneath the coffee table as I took a seat on the cream sofa.

'Can I get you something?' she said. 'Tea or coffee?'

I shook my head, pulling the notebook from my handbag with a businesslike air. 'Thank you, though.'

She was eyeing my bag, probably trying to work out if it was a present or if market researchers were better paid than she'd thought. 'So how do they select people for this? Does someone give you a list? Or is it . . .' She searched for the right word and settled for rolling her hands in the air.

I took a breath. Best to get straight to business. 'Actually, we've met before.'

I'd thought that would make her wary, but she didn't have a clue. 'Oh?' she said, wrinkling her nose. 'Was it that survey thing outside Homebase?'

The sofa was so soft it felt like it was sucking me in. I shuffled forward in an attempt to sit upright. 'No,' I said, 'I'm afraid I'm not here to do market research.'

I half expected her to order me out on the spot, but she didn't move. Her eyes narrowed. 'Then why are you here? Is this about Gary?'

'What? No, I—'

'Because if it is, you can tell him I'm not interested.' Her voice had gone up a register and I remembered her anger on the stand, the way the flush had risen up her throat.

'I don't know anyone called Gary,' I said.

'Then why are you here?'

She'd got to her feet, so I did the same. There wasn't much room and I smacked my shins against the coffee table, wobbling in the tiny space before the sofa. Remember, I told myself, you're here to get to the truth.

'Like I said, we've met before.' I was surprised at how calm I sounded. 'In Southwark.'

I'd hoped it would be enough without having to say the words, the way it had been for Ian; but then I'd run into him in the street only a few weeks after the trial. Too late, I saw that it had been stupid to expect Chantelle to make the connection after all this time.

'Listen,' she said, 'if you don't tell me what you're here for in the next ten seconds . . .'

I took a breath to steady myself. 'I'm here to talk about Ian Nash.'

She froze and I saw the shock in her eyes. 'Who are you?'

I swallowed, suddenly wondering whether I should have thought of a cover story – a journalist, perhaps, someone research-ing the low conviction rates in rape cases. But no, she deserved my honesty. I said, 'I was on the jury.'

She stared at me. 'Get out.'

I held up my hands, palms outwards. 'Please, Chantelle, it wasn't that we didn't believe you . . .'

'So you believed me and you still didn't put him away?' Oh God, the way she looked at me. I felt sick to my stomach.

'It wasn't about believing anyone.' I tried to keep my voice steady but didn't quite pull it off. 'There just wasn't the evidence.'

Her hands were clenched at her sides and for a moment I thought she might hit me; part of me felt I deserved it. But instead she turned away, as if she couldn't bear to look at me any more.

'I've told you already,' she said in a whisper, 'get out of my flat.'

I picked up my bag and shuffled out from behind the coffee table. But I couldn't just leave, not after everything I'd done. I said, 'I'm so sorry about what happened. That's what I came here to say. I'm so sorry and I want to make it right.'

'It's too late for sorry.' There was a tremor in her voice that sounded like she was holding back tears.

'I don't believe that,' I said. 'I don't think the police did everything they could have. If you help me, I know we can find the evidence to send Ian Nash to prison.'

She didn't move, didn't speak. I stood there, every muscle tensed, waiting for her to tell me to go to hell. I could hear the murmur of a television in the flat upstairs.

Eventually she turned back to face me. 'Why do you think this time will be any different?'

I allowed myself to exhale. 'Because it has to be,' I said.

I took her through the notes I'd made, keeping my promise to Helen not to tell Chantelle I'd spoken to her. I told her I had some questions I wanted to ask. 'There were inconsistencies between what you and Ian said – minor things, I mean,' I said. 'I believe that if we look hard enough at those, we'll find the evidence to show you're the one telling the truth.'

185

She stared at me, and at first I thought she was too upset to process what I was saying; but then I realised she was weighing me up. I said, 'I'm good at analysing things. I do it for a living.' I saw the look on her face and hurried on. 'I know you might not agree after . . . Well. The mistake the police made was focusing on the crime – that's not surprising, that's what they're there for. But it wasn't enough. They needed to look at the bigger picture, what you said and what Ian said about what happened before and after . . .' I tailed off and she looked at me sharply. I'd been going to say 'after you had sex'; I'd never said the alternative out loud.

'After he raped me,' she said, and I nodded.

I went through the list I'd made, checking every detail of her account. Every time she agreed that what she'd said on the stand was the way it had happened. Ian had been flirting with her but she'd barely noticed him; she'd never asked to borrow that CD; her knickers had been white, not black ('He was just saying that to try and make me sound sleazy'). She answered clearly, but she was wary of me. I could see it in the straight line of her back as she sat on the sofa, her hands folded tightly together. Her eyes followed the movement of my pen across the paper as I made notes, checking I'd captured what she said. I supposed I couldn't blame her for that.

When I'd got to the end of my questions, I shut the notebook. 'That's all, I think.' I forced a smile. 'Thank you. I know that can't have been easy.' My eyes felt tired and scratchy. I was aware that I hadn't uncovered anything new.

Chantelle hadn't moved. She was gazing at a spot on the wall opposite, so intent that I turned to see what she was looking at. There was nothing there, only the pattern of the wallpaper – a feature wall, I believe they call it – skeletons of pale blue trees stretching out their branches to each other against a cream background.

'I hadn't noticed his music before,' she said. 'It was just noise coming through the wall. I used to turn my own music on to drown it out.' She blinked and turned to me. 'I remember it now, though. I remember what was playing when he did it.'

She was staring at me as if she thought she could make me hear it too.

'It was some song about boats,' she said. 'Watching boats on the sea.' Her eyes were wide, blue I saw now, with pale lashes darkened by mascara; I could see their natural colour where the brush had missed. 'I heard it again on the radio and I threw up.'

Outside, I leaned on the wall next to the door and breathed deeply, clearing my lungs, absorbing the scent of the wounded grass. This time I took the path straight ahead, the one that cut through the middle of the lawn. My footsteps echoed on the paving and I found myself hurrying. At the arch I turned and scanned the windows of Fairfield House. There was a flash of movement at Chantelle's window, her face as pale as a ghost; but when I looked again, she had gone.

I started to vary the times I'd drop in on Ian at the Phoenix. I'd been used to going there straight from work, which meant, I now realised, that he knew roughly when to expect me. So every so often, instead of crossing the road from the station and turning right, I'd carry on and go back to the flat. I'd get changed and make a sandwich, read for a while or watch something mindless on TV. Then, late enough that he'd expect I wasn't coming, I'd turn up and see what he was doing, who he was talking to. Often he wouldn't spot me straight away, and I'd take a table and watch him, pretending when he saw me that I'd only just got there and hadn't wanted to disturb him. Several times I saw him chatting and laughing with Caitlin, her hand on his arm, his fingers brushing her waist as he moved past her in the narrow space behind the bar. I tried to tell myself I was being paranoid, that it was Aidan's fault I felt like this, that it wasn't fair to Ian. And then I'd catch myself and remember that this wasn't about being fair, that I was with him for a reason; and I'd wonder what Caitlin would think if I told her what he'd been accused of, if she'd be resting those stubby fingers on his forearm if she knew about Chantelle.

I could tell he thought I was checking up on him. At first I think he found it flattering, the implication that I was jealous, but after a while the novelty wore off. I denied it, of course, and when that didn't work I tried to make light of it, telling him it was his own fault for having women falling all over him. I laughed as I said it, but it didn't come out right.

We'd stopped having sex every time he stayed over, and when it happened it had begun to follow a familiar pattern: Ian rolling over, leaning in to kiss me, hands in my hair, pushing me onto my back. He'd never put his hand on my throat after that night, never did anything like that again. I didn't know what that meant. I didn't know if it meant anything at all.

It should have been a relief. Mostly, it was. And yet part of me, I'll admit it, was disappointed on the nights Ian dropped a chaste kiss on my forehead before turning over and switching off the light. Perhaps I'd started to hope he'd do something to give himself away after all, go too far, reveal his true colours. Perhaps there were other reasons. Whatever. Like I say, most of the time it was a relief.

And then, about three weeks after I'd been to visit Chantelle, it happened.

I'd been sound asleep, but for some reason I woke with a start. It was still dark, quiet outside in a way that told me it was nowhere near morning. Ian had stayed over that night, but I felt his absence as soon as I opened my eyes. When I stretched out my hand, the sheet was still warm from his body.

I lay there listening to the murmur of an occasional car in the street below. The minutes passed but he didn't come back.

I swung my legs over the side of the bed, feeling the texture of the carpet beneath my feet. I padded to the door and turned the handle slowly, trying not to make a noise without knowing why. The hallway was in darkness, but I could see a sliver of light beneath the bathroom door. Maybe Ian wasn't feeling well.

I took a few steps down the hallway and then stopped, torn between staying silent and calling out to check he was all right. And then I heard it: a low murmur, someone trying to be quiet. A muffled laugh.

I crept closer, leaning forward to listen. Ian's voice, too soft to make out the words. He was on the phone.

I stood there, the night draughts cold on my arms. Then I turned and went silently back to bed.

Chapter 22

I'd picked up the phone without thinking; it was a Saturday lunch-time, prime time for someone in a call centre to ask me about my utility bill. I've heard of people who use creative tactics to deal with those – pretending they're desperate for someone to talk to, asking the caller if they believe in God. I've always meant to give it a try but I never do. Usually I tell them I'm working from home, which seems to put most of them off. Sometimes they ask when they can call back, but I've learned you can say what you like to that and they never do.

So I was all set to give them the brush-off when I realised I recognised the voice on the end of the phone. It was Stella.

Evidently she'd correctly concluded I'd been ignoring her calls to my mobile and had reverted to the landline. I considered putting the phone down again, but I knew she wouldn't give up and it would only make it worse when I eventually spoke to her. I closed my eyes as her voice trilled down the line; it was like being scrubbed with a Brillo pad.

'I've been trying to get hold of you for days!'

I wouldn't apologise; we both knew I wasn't sorry. Instead I said, 'I'm not giving you that book.'

'What? Oh *that*!' she warbled. 'Oh no, I wasn't calling about that!'

My sister does this sometimes, ends every sentence with an exclamation mark. I've come to learn it means she wants something. Despite her protestations, I was sure it was the book – she'd be trying to play a long game and this, whatever this was, was merely a staging post.

'So, how are you? How's work?'

Like she's interested. Stella doesn't even know what I do, or pretends not to. If you asked her she'd say something like, 'Natalie? Oh, she works in an office.' She herself, of course, doesn't work at all. And lest you misunderstand, this is not some selfless sacrifice on the part of a new mother. Oh no! Stella handed in her notice at the same banking firm at which she met Michael a whole three months into their relationship, confident, no doubt, that he'd be picking up the tab for future expenses. Perhaps by then she considered her time served, nothing less than the prospect of a future spent pissing about at yoga and willow weaving sufficient compensation for having endured twelve weeks of both his company *and* a job.

I digress. Stella was still wittering on and it gradually dawned on me that she was asking me to babysit. Me! Babysit! I, entrusted with the vowel-laden offspring of my sister! You could have knocked me down with a feather.

I said, 'I take it Saskia isn't available.'

'I haven't asked her.' *Liar*. 'I thought it would be nice for the two of you to spend some time together.'

I tried not to snort and just about pulled it off. 'I'm not sure I'm equipped,' I said, truthfully. 'Aren't you still breastfeeding?'

'I'll feed her before we go, but I'll leave you a bottle just in case. You'll be fine, honestly, Natalie. It'll only be for a couple of hours.' A pause. 'Three tops.'

191

My brain was whirring. Clearly Stella had some kind of ulterior motive, but I was struggling to work out what it was. Or perhaps it was simply that she had exhausted all other options and this was the product of desperation. 'Where are you off to, then?' I asked.

'Michael has an awards dinner at work.' She sounded uncertain whether to say more, mindful that she hadn't yet sealed the deal. 'I wouldn't go normally, but they expect wives – partners, I mean . . .'

'Black tie, is it?'

I could almost see her squirming on the end of the phone. 'Oh, I don't know. You know what these things are like – dull, dull, dull.'

I strung it out for a bit but in the end I said I'd do it. I thought it might be interesting to poke around the house while Stella and Michael were out. Not that I expected to find much – my sister isn't the kind of person to be hiding a secret rubber fetish, and Michael, I'm confident, is a man for whom sexual danger means doing it on a work night; but still, it would get me out of my own flat for an evening, and if I got back late enough there was always the chance that Ian would already be asleep.

Stella was off like a shot after that, no doubt worried that given half a chance I'd change my mind. I wasn't sure I'd done the right thing – after all, I really didn't have any experience of looking after children, let alone an eight-month-old baby – but I told myself I'd do a bit of research in advance; look up symptoms of alarming childhood illnesses, ways to stop them crying, that kind of thing. *Let's face it*, I thought, *if Stella can manage it, it can't be that hard.*

It was mid afternoon and the Phoenix was almost empty when I called in. Ian was behind the bar, leaning over a newspaper spread out in front of him – *Metro*, I could tell by the font.

He looked up in surprise. 'What are you doing here?'

'Charming,' I said lightly, but he didn't smile. 'I have a report to finish so I thought I'd work from home this afternoon. Fewer distractions.'

'Right,' he said, 'so are you here for lunch, or what?'

It's a strange thing, the way other people can hurt you. I once heard someone claim that it's a choice, that only you can decide what effect another person has on you. I respectfully submit that that's bollocks. You can't just turn off your feelings. No one tries to tell a bereaved person they're choosing to be sad. It's just another way of making people feel bad about themselves. *Don't allow yourself to be hurt*, they say, meaning, *It's all your fault.*

But Ian? I hadn't expected he could make me feel like that. I hadn't thought his casual rudeness could get under my skin. After all, this wasn't a real relationship, and of the two of us, I was the one who knew that. Maybe that was what made it worse – he believed I was with him because I cared, and he still thought it was all right to speak to me like that. He still thought he could treat me like a fool, running around with some Aussie barmaid while he used my flat like a hotel, taking what he wanted from me, as if I were stupid.

I looked at him, the crumpled T-shirt, the messy hair, and from nowhere a wave of fury almost took my breath away. Was she responsible for that? Caitlin? Was she hiding out somewhere in the back, waiting for me to go? Was that why he was being hateful?

I thought: *I'm not having this.*

Aloud I said, 'Yes, I thought lunch might be nice. Any chance you'd be able to join me?'

He puffed out his cheeks like a hamster. 'I'm on my own again. So no.'

Perhaps he and Caitlin had had a tiff; maybe that explained his mood. I shrugged. 'Fair enough. Maybe I'll head back and get a salad or something instead.' I smoothed my skirt over the flat of my stomach. 'I need to shift a few pounds.'

He inspected me, his head to one side. 'You look fine to me.'

How long had we been sleeping together then? Eight weeks? Ten? And that was what it had come to: *You look fine to me.*

'I was thinking I might join a gym.'

'Yeah?' He was only half listening, hadn't worked out yet where this was going.

'Hmm. I'm not sure where to try, though.' I paused, waited for him to volunteer the information; but he had picked up a cloth and was wiping the rim of a pint glass. Apparently it demanded all his concentration. 'Didn't you used to be a member somewhere?'

'Deptford. You'd be better off finding somewhere closer.'

I laughed. 'You mean I won't stick with it if it's not on my doorstep.'

'No, I—'

'They say you need a routine. Did you go after work?'

He was looking at me now, trying to decide if the question was innocent. 'Sometimes.'

'Maybe I should look for somewhere near the office. Drop in on my way home. Was that what you did?'

'Yeah, that's probably easiest.' I heard the door swing open behind me, a snatch of traffic noise from the road outside. Was I imagining the look of relief on Ian's face? He turned to the two men surveying the beer taps. 'What can I get you?'

I mouthed, 'See you later,' as they were ordering, and at the door I looked back and waved; but Ian was pulling a pint and didn't see me.

I stood on the pavement outside. I was going in, of course I was – I hadn't made the journey for nothing – I just needed one last mental rehearsal.

I didn't like the look of the place. The walls were mostly glass, but the lower half was obscured by shiny posters of bright-eyed women with swinging ponytails and men with barbells. They were the same kind of faces you see in computer-generated images of what new flats are supposed to look like when they're finished, all glowing with health and just *thrilled* to be there. I found them vaguely threatening.

A blonde woman wearing trainers and Lycra leggings marched past, one hand on her mobile phone, barely breaking stride as she pushed open the door and was gone. I caught a glimpse of magnolia walls and laminate flooring as the door closed behind her, a water cooler in the corner. Was this the place?

I caught the door before it swung shut and followed.

The space in front of me was small, a reception desk off to one side and opposite it a long wall with a series of doors. The one nearest had the pointy-skirted sign for women on it – the changing rooms, presumably.

The blonde woman was standing next to the desk, still talking on the phone as she wrote something in a book. 'They've been there for almost three months,' she was saying. 'I've told them, if they don't . . .'

'Hello! Welcome to Pure Fit!' The woman behind the desk was young, barely out of school by the look of her. I couldn't decide whether that was a good thing or not. 'Can I help you?'

'I'd like to enquire about membership.' It came out sounding severe; I must have been more nervous than I'd thought.

The child-woman behind the desk was undeterred. 'That's great!' she said, veritably brimming with enthusiasm. 'So have you been here before?'

'Actually, no. I was hoping to take a look around.'

I'd thought she'd call someone to cover the desk, but instead she sprang to her feet and gestured for me to follow. We passed the changing rooms and rounded a corner to where a glass wall stretched in front of us. This time there were no posters to obscure the view, and beyond it I could see a line of machines against a wall, a man in a green T-shirt raising and lowering his arms at one of them.

The girl – Millie, she'd told me she was called – held open a door, and I was hit by the smell: air freshener and disinfectant and an undertow of sweat.

I followed her around as she pointed to machines, giving them names she obviously thought should mean something to me. I nodded wisely.

'And do you need to book?'

Her look suggested this wasn't a question she'd heard before. I feared I was giving away my ignorance.

'Oh no! Members can use the facilities whenever they want! Twenty-four seven. And as you can see,' she swept her arm around the space, 'there's plenty of equipment to go round.'

'Very good,' I said, hoping I sounded sufficiently impressed. 'So does that mean there's always someone at reception? Or is there some way of signing in and out?' Was that the book I'd seen the blonde woman writing in? Would there be a record of who visited and when?

'Reception is open from seven in the morning until eight at night. Outside those times you can get in with your membership card.' She smiled at me brightly. 'There's a swipe system on the front door. All very secure.'

Of course, it would all be recorded electronically. Where would I even start to get access to those records? It was hopeless, another dead end. 'Great,' I said.

'Everything is unlocked during the day, of course, so you don't need your pass except for the lockers. We just ask that you sign in at reception so we know who's in the building in case of a fire alarm.'

I'm not a tactile person or I might have hugged her then and there. Millie beamed at me in return, confident she'd hooked a new member; maybe that meant some kind of bonus. 'So would you like to take a look at the changing rooms?'

I shook my head. 'No, you've convinced me. Sign me up!'

On the way out, I stopped in Millie's wake and adjusted my shoe, gripping the edge of a treadmill for balance. 'Sorry,' I said, 'I think I've got a stone . . . Ah, that's better.'

Back at reception, there were the expected forms to fill in, and Millie tried to tell me I needed some kind of health check before I could use the machines. It involved running on the treadmill, apparently, the logic of which seemed somewhat circular. I was relieved I was still wearing my work clothes; I don't relish purposeless physical exercise at any time, but even Millie could see that a pencil skirt and a treadmill were not natural bedfellows. 'I'll call in tomorrow and do it then,' I lied.

Apparently Millie had time on her hands, because she watched from the other side of the desk, attempting to ask me about what she called my 'fitness goals', as I filled in the form. It was just as well I'd had the foresight to prepare for such an eventuality. Halfway through writing my fake address (I was using Alan's; after all those engine-related phone calls, it tripped off the end of my pen as easily as my own), I stopped and gasped, staring down at my hand.

Millie picked up her cue like a trained Labrador. 'What is it?'

I held up my hand in mock horror. 'My ring!' I cried. 'It's gone!'

'Oh dear!' She seemed genuinely dismayed. 'Was it valuable?'

'Only to me,' I said, blinking rapidly in a bid to summon some moisture to my eyes. 'It's just a plain gold band, but it was my mother's . . .'

'Not her wedding ring?' She put her hand to her mouth. Bless her – she was going to be thrilled when she eventually found it.

I nodded tearfully. 'I thought I felt something drop when we were in the gym. Would you mind if . . . ?'

She was already on her feet. 'Let's go and take a look now.'

'Er, right . . . But I've already taken up so much of your time . . .' I smiled weakly. 'Would you mind seeing if you can find it while I finish this form?'

She thought it was odd, I could tell, but she wasn't a suspicious sort of person. Most people aren't; it's amazing what you can get away with once you've realised that. I watched her go, and in the next moment I was at the other end of the desk, reaching for the signing-in book. I flipped straight to the front, using both hands to hold the weight of the pages so they wouldn't tear, hoping against hope it went back far enough.

My eyes scanned the columns – no address or membership number was required, apparently, just the date, name and time of arrival and departure. The first entry was for someone called Kate Williams, 3 May 2018. Thank God – over two months before Ian had turned up at Chantelle's flat. I checked the time automatically – 7.01 a.m. I bet whoever was on reception that morning loved Kate.

I glanced down the corridor, but there was no sign of Millie. I realised my palms were sweating.

I turned the pages, scanning the dates at the bottom – May, May, May, then on to June. I flipped forward a handful of pages, then realised I'd gone too far. I glanced up again, this time to the front door.

The breath caught in my throat. A couple of women in shorts and trainers were walking towards it. Any minute now and they'd be in, wanting to sign the book, asking what I was doing . . .

Hurry up!

I rifled through the pages – 22 August, 8 August, 24 July . . .

The women had paused outside, talking. One stood with her hand on the door handle.

I turned back to the book, scanning the dates so fast they barely made sense. There – 21 July, the day Ian had claimed he'd left Chantelle's bed and come here. Mark Hayward had been the first person to sign in that morning. My eyes ran down the list of names: Alicia, Phoebe, Geoff, Cherron . . . On to the next page; I could hear the women laughing.

Cameron Taylor – but the date was the 22nd. I read it again, to be sure. Cameron was the first person to sign into the gym the day after Ian had gone to Chantelle's flat.

The voices were growing louder, the door opening, but I had to be sure. I ran my finger down the column of dates. Yes, Mark Hayward was the first name on 21 July. There was no sign of Ian's name.

I fumbled in my handbag for my phone, almost dropping it as I jabbed at the camera icon. I held it in front of the book and snapped a photo, then let the pages fall with a thud.

The two women were inside now, taking cardboard cones from a tube at the side of the water dispenser. I scrabbled at the paper, trying to find the page for today.

'I've told her it's not a competition . . .' Water gurgled into a cup.

Yes.

I was back in front of my form, pen in hand, by the time they reached the desk. They were still talking, something about losing weight, a dress for a wedding.

'Excuse me?'

I jumped. One of them was standing over the book; had I left behind some clue as to what I'd been doing? Had she seen me leafing through the pages?

'Can I borrow your pen?' She gestured towards the desk. 'They need to attach it to a cord or something. Someone's always running off with it.'

I looked down at the pen in my hand; another just like it sat next to the form on the desk. I must have picked it up without realising. I handed it over to the woman, forcing a smile to detract her from the tremor in my fingertips.

I dragged my attention back to the form. Millie could return at any minute, and if I hadn't made more progress, she'd wonder what I'd been doing. I took up the second pen, but my hand was trembling too much – the characters overshot the edges of the boxes, lines jumbling together, illegible. I took a breath, tried again.

Next to me the women had finished signing in and were moving away, heading for the changing room. Down the corridor I heard a door swing shut and footsteps approach. I rummaged in my bag for my phone.

Millie was holding out her hand in front of her, something small and gold pinched between her fingers.

'You've found it!'

She dropped it into my palm. 'Sorry I took so long. It had rolled under one of the treadmills.' Or something like that. I'd nudged it under there, of course, when I stopped to extract the non-existent stone from my shoe. She'd done well to spot it.

'I'm so grateful!' I took it from her and pushed it onto my finger, trying to imagine what it would have felt like if it really had been Mum's ring instead of one plucked from a grubby dish on a stall at Lewisham market; but there was no chance of that. 'I have to head off now, I'm afraid.' I waved the phone at her. 'Family emergency.'

I caught Millie's look of concern as I pushed the application form at her and made for the door. *Poor girl*, I thought, *to be so easily affected by what was happening in someone else's life.* She'd have to toughen up at some point, but I hoped she wouldn't worry when I didn't come back for my health check the next day.

I stood unseeing at the bus stop. *What next?* I kept thinking. *What happens now?*

At first I couldn't think about Ian. I couldn't think about what it meant that his name wasn't in that book. I'd expected that the moment I found something real, some hard evidence that the story he had told the police hadn't been true, I would be elated, all my efforts vindicated. But I suppose it was the shock. Suddenly I knew for sure that he had lied, and I couldn't process what that meant.

Instead my mind wandered in loops, worrying away at what would happen with the gym when I didn't go back. Would the management insist on writing, chasing Stella Wainwright for her membership fee? That would cause some confusion when the letter arrived at Alan's. Maybe I should give them a call in a day or two, tell them . . . what? That I'd been posted abroad with work, or broken my foot, or discovered a heart murmur and been advised against exercise by my doctor?

Or then again, maybe it didn't matter. Let them write! Let Alan's wife ask him why some gym was writing to a woman she'd never heard of at their address! Perhaps she'd suspect marital infidelity . . .

I snorted out loud at that, and a woman in a leather jacket looked around and quickly looked away again. No, not leather, it was fake. Leatherette. Was that what they called it? Add a few letters and turn the real thing into something else, a simulacrum.

Simulacrum. It was a good word, melodic. That was a good word too.

It had seemed right to use Stella's name for the application. She was bound to be a member of a gym already, somewhere glossier, with a juice bar where she'd call in for a goji berry smoothie after yoga. She'd added a few letters to her name when she married Michael, the *Wain* joining the *Wright*. There'd been lots of jokes about it at the wedding: 'Two Wrights can't make a wrong', that kind of thing. Stella hadn't even had to change her initials. Maybe that was why she'd married him.

Simulacrum. Sim-u-la-crum.

The bus arrived, mostly empty, and I took a seat on the same side as the driver, next to the window. Did that count as the left or the right? I'd read once that people always selected the same side if the seats were free. They had a bus-side preference. Was mine left or right?

Right. Wright. Wainwright. Did adding letters to her name make Stella a simulacrum?

Ian hadn't gone to the gym that day.

I tried to grasp it as fact, hold on to it. Here was something that had really happened: Ian had said he'd gone to the gym but he hadn't.

He had lied about it. He'd left Chantelle because he'd taken what he wanted from her. Maybe he was afraid afterwards, realising what he'd done. Had he walked the streets, scared to go back to his flat because he knew it was only a matter of time before the police knocked on his door? Had he used that time to concoct his story?

I'd let this man touch me. I'd let him into my home.

He'd lied to the police and now he was lying to me, hiding out in my bathroom to make secret calls to another woman.

Ian Nash, liar.

Ian Nash, simulacrum.

I'm on to you, I thought. *Your time is running out.*

Chapter 23

Ian kept his phone locked. There was a PIN to open it. I know, because when he left it on the kitchen counter I tried to check it and couldn't.

Keeping your phone locked isn't the behaviour of an innocent man.

I didn't try to guess the PIN. I wouldn't have known where to start. Besides, for all I knew, he had some kind of app that would tell him about failed attempts. There are apps for everything these days. The world is app-happy.

'Is everything OK, Natalie?'

Alan sat opposite me in the airless cupboard that served as a meeting room. He was wearing a pale blue tie and silver cufflinks. I must commend him on that score; he was always well turned out. He'd been saying something about pesticides but I hadn't been listening.

'So what are the next steps?' I said, and he looked down at his notepad and then back at me again.

'Well, I think . . .'

People probably forgot their PINs all the time. There must be some way around it; I should google. Would it matter if there was a record of my search? Perhaps I should use my work computer instead of my laptop. But I'd still have to log in; presumably they could find out what I'd been looking at if they were interested. Whoever 'they' were.

'Alan,' I said, and he stopped talking. Judging by the look on his face, I'd cut him off mid sentence. 'Do you know how to unlock a mobile phone?'

He wrinkled his nose as if he'd smelled something bad. It's what he does when he doesn't know the answer to something.

'A mobile phone,' I said again, hoping I was wrong. 'Do you know how to unlock one? If you've forgotten your PIN, I mean.'

He smiled; no, he smirked. 'Oh dear,' he said happily. 'Didn't you set up a link to your email account?'

'Of course,' I bluffed. Linking to an email account? It sounded like the kind of thing Ian would do. 'But I can't remember how it's supposed to work.'

His nose was wrinkling again. 'No, I'm not sure either. I'd search online if I were you. But if you've linked it to your email, you should be fine.'

I pretended to look at my watch. 'Great. Right, so I need to head out . . .'

Alan was saying something else about pesticides, something about the minister. I heard enough to know I should have been paying attention, but for once I couldn't bring myself to care. 'Just handle it, please, Alan,' I said firmly.

I'd put a non-existent meeting with Treasury officials in my diary so returned to my desk for just long enough to collect my bag. Alan was peering miserably at his screen as I left. It couldn't have been easy for him – all those years of relying on me, then suddenly being told to think for himself. I almost felt sorry for him.

I pressed my building pass against the reader and waited for the beep. Outside, Whitehall was crawling with tourists peering up at the stone edifices and talking to each other in foreign languages. I caught a snatch of Italian, French, then a little further on something that might have been German or Dutch.

I kept walking, turning off into King Charles Street and heading for St James's Park. I hadn't invented the Treasury meeting for any specific reason; I didn't have an errand. I just yearned for space. Space to think about what I'd learned, about what I should do next.

It was getting harder and harder to do that in the flat. It felt full of Ian: his jacket slung over the arm of the sofa, a flyer he'd brought back from the pub on the coffee table, coins from his pockets scattered on the kitchen counter. Even the hallway had mysteriously gained an extra pair of shoes, though I couldn't remember him ever having brought over a spare pair.

And the bedroom. The place where he'd shown me a glimpse of his true self, his hand on my neck. His presence filled the space there most of all.

I crossed the road and entered the park, looking around for an empty bench. They were all occupied, but as I got closer to the lake, a man in a suit stood and picked up a rucksack from the seat next to him. Two women with buggies saw him at the same time and quickened their pace; but I refused to catch their eye and power-walked over there, staking my claim by planting myself dead centre. The women carried on past, tutting as they went.

I'd thought about taking the photo of the signing-in book at the gym straight to the police. I'd almost been ready to get off the bus at Lewisham station and walk the five minutes to the huge steel and concrete edifice that's the local home of the thin blue line. But the closer I got, the clearer it had become that the photo might not be enough. All it proved was that Ian hadn't gone to the gym. Would it be enough to reopen an investigation into a man who'd already been acquitted once?

I didn't know, and I wasn't prepared to take the risk. If I didn't have enough for the police to take me seriously, I'd have wasted my chance. Even worse, they might turn their attention to me. They might think I was some kind of oddball with a vendetta – especially if they found out I'd been on the jury at Ian's trial. Especially if they found out we were together and he was playing around with some other woman . . . And that complaint from Kellie, that might be on file somewhere. It was all too easy to see them putting two and two together and making five.

No, they'd already failed Chantelle once. I wasn't going to give them the opportunity to do it again.

So instead I made a plan. I needed more evidence, and the obvious next step was to check Ian's phone. Let me be clear: it was nothing to do with that clandestine phone call. I knew everything I needed to know about that already. I was certain it was Caitlin he'd been talking to. I didn't need to check the log to know that. I didn't need to find the texts that proved they were fucking. Why waste my energy?

No. I simply hoped that he'd been careless, that he'd left something on his phone to implicate himself. He was the kind of person who carried his mobile with him everywhere, who acted like it was an extension of his body. The police would have checked it after his arrest, of course; but what about later? What if in the months that followed he'd let something slip? An unguarded comment, perhaps, in a message to a friend? A celebratory text that had revealed more than he'd intended?

Or if not that, then yes – evidence of his deceit. Not for its own sake, but because of what it proved: that he was a liar, a sexual predator, always wanting something more, some element of risk. However remote the possibility, I had to try. One way or another, I was going to unlock that phone.

It's true what they say about fresh air clearing the mind. By the time I got back to the office, I knew exactly what to do.

I yawned and stretched, waggling my hands above my head to trigger the sensors that turned the lights back on. They went out automatically after 7.30, an energy-saving policy of which I imagined the DEFRA tree-huggers would approve. In half an hour I'd be plunged into semi-darkness again; unless I'd finished by then.

Alan had looked relieved when I'd told him to go home, and now that I'd finished reading the papers, I could understand why. Thwarted in the first round, DEFRA were down but not out, and had returned to the issue of raising VAT on imports from bee-haters in the time-honoured tradition: they were proposing a public consultation. When I'd returned to my desk, Alan had been grappling with the draft document they'd sent over, huffing and puffing and muttering under his breath. He'd been only too glad to pass it on to me; and when I asked him to leave it onscreen on his computer to save me searching through my emails, he didn't appear to find anything odd in the request. Perhaps he was just remembering that saying about gift horses.

I'd been disciplined, though. I'd worked through the whole document and its four annexes. Now I used Alan's computer to tap out a terse little message to my opposite number in DEFRA explaining why the draft was unacceptable. Then it was back to my own desk to cut and paste it into an email from my own account and press send – the work of moments, no time for Alan's computer to go into sleep mode and require his password to wake it up again.

Then it was back to Alan's machine; I hadn't finished with it yet.

The Google search was disappointing. Every article I found said the same thing: 'unlocking' Ian's phone actually meant using his email account to set a new PIN. I supposed I could unlock it, check it, then reset the PIN before he noticed; but what if something went wrong? What if I was interrupted and didn't have time to reset it? Or if there was still no way of finding whatever the PIN had been originally? What if his email account froze halfway through, or ... any one of a hundred variables. It was complicated, and that made it risky.

But that wasn't the main problem. Even before I got to the stage of setting a new PIN, I needed to access Ian's email. It was web-based and there was another thing all the articles agreed on: I would need his password.

Working out a way to find a password in order to reset a PIN ... Somewhere along that convoluted chain the logic gave way. There had to be a better approach.

I sat there staring at the screen. Alan's keyboard was cleaner than mine, I noticed – none of those tiny breadcrumbs that wouldn't come out no matter how hard you banged it over the waste bin. There were apparently some advantages to those smelly lunchtime curries.

Perhaps I'd been looking at this the wrong way, making it more complicated than it needed to be. Perhaps the answer wasn't to unlock the phone; perhaps it was to separate it from Ian when it was already unlocked.

My fingers were moving over the keyboard again, typing a new item into the search box. The words looked ominous there, disconcerting. But I'm only looking, I told myself. I'm only interested in whether it's possible. It doesn't mean I'd ever do it.

Some time later, I reached for my handbag. The yellow Post-it was still there, one half of the glued edge pressed against the other. I looked at the numbers written there. And then I tapped Alan's credit card details into the form and pressed 'confirm'.

Chapter 24

Stella's house, Friday night, 6.45. I'd changed my clothes twice before I left the flat, standing in front of the mirror and practising my expression. I wanted to get it right: *I am a sophisticated and fulfilled person*, I wanted my appearance to say. *I am here at your request to do you a favour, despite having a million better things to do with my time, because that's what I've chosen to do. I don't want anything from you. I don't need anything.*

I heard the doorbell ring and footsteps coming down the hallway. Thud-thud, not click-clack. Michael.

'Natalie.' He smiled warily. 'Come in. I'll just . . .' He looked over his shoulder as if hoping to escape. 'Stella's just putting Evie down.'

I took off my coat and held it out to him. 'Sounds rather drastic. Should I go and find her?'

He looked panicked. 'No, no, she'll be out any minute.' Another glance over his shoulder.

He was wearing a dinner jacket – a black-tie do then, as I'd suspected. He smelled of some kind of aftershave; no discernible elements, just the overall flavour of expensive. I suppose some women – women like my sister, presumably – would consider him attractive, but he's never done anything for me. He's got one of those blonde posh-boy faces, smooth cheeks and lips like a puffer fish.

He still hadn't taken my coat, so I pushed it towards him. 'I'll go and wait in the kitchen then.'

I haven't been in Stella's home more than a handful of times, but I've always found her kitchen fascinating. The whole house is a shrine to conformity, but it's in the kitchen that it reaches its apex, the very zenith of Stella's desire to appear just like everyone else; or at least, not everyone, but a particular *kind* of Everywoman. The kind who waits at the gates of the type of school Stella imagines Evie attending when she's older (what am I talking about, imagining? She's probably had the kid on some sort of list since she was three months pregnant): shiny hair and Ugg boots, clutching a chai latte in one hand and the keys to a brand-new leather-upholstered four-by-four in the other.

Everywhere is flat and gleaming. The worktops sparkle under invisible spotlights but there is *nothing at all on them*. No jars with tea and coffee, no plant pots or spice racks or toasters or kettles or any of the things that cluttered up the kitchen of the home we grew up in. There are no handles on the cupboards. No tea towel. No waste bin.

Presumably these things exist. Stella cooks, I know. She has told me about the wholesome-yet-gourmet meals she makes from scratch for herself and Michael. At the christening, I heard her waxing lyrical to some unfortunate bystander about pureed-this and mashed-that for Evie. The only conclusion I can draw is that she chooses to *hide them away*. As if the fact that the Family Wainwright eat and drink is somehow shameful.

Michael stood in the doorway. 'Stella will be here in a minute,' he said again, seemingly more to reassure himself than me. 'She can show you where – ah – everything is.' He waved his arm vaguely at the kitchen cupboards.

He hadn't offered me a drink, I noticed. I thought about picking him up on it, asking for something that might risk splashing the cuff of his pristine shirt; but if I did that, I'd have to watch him bumbling around the kitchen, driven in the end despite myself to attempt conversation. It felt too much like hard work.

I expected him to disappear, off to hiss at Stella that I was in the kitchen and she needed to come and deal with me; but instead he hovered in the doorway. 'Evie, ah, Evie should be fine,' he said. 'We've left her with my parents before and she's been no trouble. Not according to them, anyway. Ha!'

'Mm,' I said, conversationally.

'And Stella's friend looks after her now and again. Sasha?'

'Saskia perhaps. The godmother.'

He nodded, choosing to ignore the ice in my tone. 'Saskia, yes.' A pause. A nerve was twitching in his cheek. 'The thing is, Natalie . . .'

'Yes, Michael?'

'The thing is, we know – ah – we understand children aren't your thing . . .'

I stared at him. 'Not my thing?'

'Well, you know. I was the same before Evie. Ha!' He fiddled with his cufflinks. They were curved but pointed at the ends, little silver torpedoes. 'So anyway, if you have any problems, just give us a ring. Stella, I mean. Anything at all.'

'Right,' I said, 'call Stella. Not you, then?'

'Ha!'

'Definitely not you?'

He peered at me as though trying to bring me into focus. I had a dim recollection of seeing him in glasses before; perhaps he was wearing contact lenses. 'Ah well, Stella's the expert. You women have the knack, don't you? Ha!'

211

'I wouldn't know,' I said sweetly. 'Children aren't really my thing.'

He beat a retreat then, mumbling something about checking on the taxi. It was the longest conversation I think we'd ever had.

I'd brought a book and had it propped on the worktop when Stella appeared, dressed in grey silk and with her hair piled on top of her head. Her make-up was immaculate. It was at times like this that I wondered not just if we came from the same parents, but if we were even the same species.

'Has Michael shown you where everything is?' she said. Not so much as a hello, mark you, straight into the logistics. I bet it was the same way she talks to her cleaner.

She showed me the (hidden) fridge and the (hidden) bottle warmer, and took a notepad from a drawer (with hidden handles) and ran a manicured fingernail down the list of emergency telephone numbers. Afterwards I followed her up the stairs to a room at the back of the house, Stella putting a finger to her lips as she opened the door and ushered me into The Presence.

Evie was lying on her back, her little head turned to one side, arms bent as if raising a champion's cup. Already a winner. A mobile dangled over the cot, and in the light from the hallway I could just make out the greyed-out colours of a mural on one wall.

Then it was back downstairs, Stella handing me the baby monitor and giving final instructions, outside an engine, Stella's phone ringing, reminders to call . . . I shut the door behind them and leaned against it, listening to doors slam and the cab pull away. A click, a faint gurgle . . . Evie. I held my breath. Did she know her parents had gone? That she'd been left alone with a woman who didn't have a clue what she was doing?

It had gone quiet again. I tiptoed into the kitchen, clutching the baby monitor to my chest. I would make myself a drink. Tea, not coffee – I was alert enough. Or perhaps a glass of wine, just the one, to calm my nerves. Stella and Michael would have some decent bottles, I was sure.

I put the monitor on the worktop as I investigated the cupboards, tugging gently to work out which side had the hinge. A larder with sliding shelves, a cutlery drawer with a different section for each utensil, a cupboard that appeared to have been built especially for a coffee maker. Everything had its own little space, a compartment designed to fit it.

The baby monitor remained silent. Was that good? But there'd been that noise, that gurgle. A sudden icy terror flooded my veins. What if something was wrong? What if Evie had been choking?

I took the stairs two at a time, only the depth of the carpet stopping the door of the nursery from slamming into the wall as I crashed through. My blood was pounding in my ears as I leaned over the cot, almost too afraid to look inside.

Evie lay there, eyes closed. For a moment I couldn't breathe; but then one tiny fist shook from side to side and she snuffled gently.

She was all right. Everything was all right.

She was dressed in a pink babygro covered in yellow ducklings. It was vile really, but even in the half-light I could see how soft it was, how gentle it would be against her baby skin. Her hair was dark, dark like mine; or perhaps it just appeared that way in the dim light. It clung to the curve of her scalp like down. I had reached out without realising it, the back of my index finger poised above her cheek. It hung there for a second; but no, I mustn't wake her. I drew back and tiptoed from the room.

Back in the kitchen, I settled for a glass of water and prowled the ground floor, the monitor tucked into the pocket of my jeans. I inspected the contents of the larder unit and the fridge, noting the packets of grains and the jars with the distinctive red and white labels of what I knew to be an outrageously expensive delicatessen. Olives and truffles and chutney. Quinoa and bulgur wheat. A packet of bacon lurking on a bottom shelf – Michael's illicit treat, I guessed.

I found the crockery, relentlessly white, and the tea towels, navy and more white and hanging from a stand in a cupboard. Behind one door was a wine rack, mostly full. I selected a bottle and then put it back again.

In the sitting room, I froze as I heard Evie shift and hiccup; but silence followed and I told myself I wouldn't panic again. I discovered a cupboard full of DVDs, but there was nothing of interest. The television stood to one side of the fireplace, staring glassily into the room. Apparently this was one thing it wasn't necessary to hide away. I switched it on and flicked through a few channels, then left it playing to itself while I went to check on Evie.

She was still asleep, her head turned to the other side now. If she opened her eyes, she'd look straight at me.

A shrill ring echoed up the stairs. My phone – thank God I hadn't brought it with me. I rushed back to the kitchen, anxious to cut off the sound.

'Natalie? Everything all right?'

It was Stella. I could hear the anxiety in her voice. I wondered if she felt the need to check on Saskia like this, but I was pretty sure I knew the answer. 'All fine,' I answered breezily. 'Or it was until the phone nearly woke her.'

'You should have put it on silent.' Of course, I should have known it would be my fault. 'She's been OK then? Hasn't woken up?'

I sighed. 'You asked me to call if there was a problem and I told you I would.'

There was a second's silence. Then, 'So everything's all right?'

'Yes.'

'And you've got the baby monitor with you?'

'Stella, if you didn't trust me to look after her, perhaps you shouldn't have asked me.'

'It's not that I don't...' I heard someone mumble in the background; Michael probably. 'You will call, won't you? I don't want you worrying about disturbing us.'

'That's very considerate of you.'

Another pause while she tried to stop herself rising to the bait. 'Right then. I'd better go. We won't be too late, so with any luck she won't want a feed...'

I held the phone away from my ear while she repeated more things she'd already told me. I'd fully intended to hang up first, but something must have been happening at her end because she finished abruptly, telling me she had to go, and before I knew it I was staring at a silent mobile. Typical.

I switched the phone to vibrate but left it on the hall table and turned to climb the stairs. If Stella called again, she'd have to leave a message; I was only following instructions, after all.

There were four doors leading off the landing. Evie's nursery was at the far end on the right, the only one that stood open. Next to it was what I assumed was Stella and Michael's bedroom. The other two doors were opposite, and I started with the one at the back of the house, pushing it open and feeling for the light switch. A cord brushed against my hand: the bathroom then.

The light flickered into life, glaring off white ceramic and stainless steel. Enough room for a stand-alone shower as well as a bath; perhaps they'd taken some space from the room next door. There was a tall cupboard (towels on top, cleaning products and loo roll on the bottom) and another cupboard with a mirrored front above the sink (scented candle in a glass holder, array of expensive-looking beauty products, silver stand with razor and shaving brush, painkillers, mouthwash, sticking plasters, toothpaste). No antidepressants or lubricants or ointment for piles. Not so much as a tube of moustache bleach. Disappointing.

Next door was a double bed and a large, ugly wardrobe that I imagined was living on borrowed time. A desk with a PC was pushed into a corner, too big for the space; perhaps Evie's room had once served as the study. I pressed the standby button and the screen came to life, blinking its request for a password. I typed 'Stella' then 'Evie' then 'Stellaevie'. None of them worked and I turned it off again.

There was a rolled-up duvet and a couple of pillows on the floor of the wardrobe but the rail was bare, presumably kept free for guests. Maybe Saskia and her husband – what would he be called? Ralph? Giles? Hugo? – forsook the joys of Kew now and then to rough it in Ealing. Or more likely it was used by Michael's parents staying over in order to babysit ('She's been no trouble!').

I turned and headed for the final door.

Everything in Stella and Michael's bedroom was cream and white and duck-egg blue, a paean to Laura Ashley. It smelled sweet, the faint echo of Stella's perfume.

How did she do it? I wondered. How did she keep everything like this, so fucking *perfect*, with an eight-month-old baby? Shouldn't there have been an overflowing laundry basket? An unmade bed? A chair covered in discarded garments? I pulled open a drawer three quarters full of neatly folded T-shirts and shut it again, almost too depressed to continue.

Small painted tables flanked the bed, a book on one of them. *Good Strategy/Bad Strategy: The Difference and Why It Matters*. Michael's side then. No book on the other table, not even some chick lit. Mum had got it right for Stella: she'd never felt she'd missed out, not until the Hawking volume and its inflated price tag.

I found the safe in the bottom of the wardrobe. I was prepared to persist with that for longer than the computer, but it turned out there was no need: I guessed right first time. It was, of course, Evie's date of birth. Inside was a man's Rolex – old, an inheritance perhaps – and a couple of jewellery boxes with diamond earrings and a pendant. On top was a shelf for documents. I worked through them one by one.

I suppose it was the recent internet searches that put the idea in my head. I sat on the floor with that little book in my hands for a long time, trying to picture myself holding it out, my heart in my mouth as I waited for the photo to be checked. Thinking back to it now, I wonder whether even then I knew that was what it would come to; whether part of me understood as I replaced it on the shelf and shut the door and pressed the button and heard the beep that confirmed the safe was locked again, whether even then I realised what I was going to do. Or whether I really believed what I told myself: that it was just a theoretical exercise, a game in my head, that I would never really do it. It's impossible to say.

It was in the dressing table that I found the jewellery box, tucked into a corner of the bottom drawer, the old lacquer lid with its scene of a tree and a house tightening my throat. I knelt on the floor and lifted it out gently, cradling it in my lap. Its contents weren't considered worthy of the safe; Stella hadn't even bothered to lock it.

I picked out a string of pearls, rubbing them between my fingers. They were the ones Mum had worn on the rare occasions she and Dad went out without us, leaving us with Mrs Davies from two doors down to go to the annual faculty dinner. Dad always claimed to hate those occasions and Mum went along with his complaints, but I think she enjoyed them really. There was an air of excitement about her when she bent down to kiss us goodbye; it mingled with the mysterious perfume that replaced her usual scent of soap and hand cream, and made her seem different, exotic.

And here was the cross and chain she'd worn every day, the light glinting off the faceted gold. It was a strange choice for a physicist who only entered a church for weddings and funerals, and I'd asked her about it once. She'd told me it had sentimental value, but wouldn't explain why. Maybe Stella knew. Or then again, maybe she'd never given it a moment's thought.

I laid it on the carpet and turned back to the other contents. A watch with a leather strap, gold earrings in the shape of a knot, a silver chain, a pendant with a green stone, an old-fashioned locket, a brooch with two gold hearts that had once belonged to Grandma.

I'd known it had been coming as soon as Celia had said those words: 'Your mother wanted to leave you each a personal bequest.' I'd felt Stella straighten on the sofa next to me and caught from the corner of my eye the glance she shot me, even though I hadn't wanted to see it. I'd shrunk away from her, waiting to hear what came next, trying to focus on the brown triangular coffee stain on the corner of the will. *Breathe in, breathe out.*

She came to me first. Our mother's books; 'her precious books', Celia called them, trying to soften the blow of what came next. I smiled, tried to feel grateful, *was* grateful – for a moment, until the contrast shattered everything else. Because then it was Stella, Stella receiving all her jewellery, no adjective needed to buff *that* to a greater glory, not so much as a string of beads left for me.

It was so obvious, so *glaring*. I got the paper and ink, the dry, dead words that belonged to other people. They were all I deserved. Stella, the beautiful child, got the adornments of beauty. It was she that Mum had imagined wearing them, even as I asked her about her cross and chain, even as I reached out to touch her string of pearls. They were the things Mum wore *next to her skin* and she had given every single one of them to my sister.

Something dropped onto the pendant in my hand, a dome of liquid that rested for a moment on the stone and then rolled away. I dried it on the front of my top and placed the necklace carefully back inside the box.

I'd been half watching a TV programme about police arresting drunk people when I heard the cab draw up outside. By the time Stella and Michael opened the front door I was in the hallway with my jacket on.

'She's been great,' I said, pushing the baby monitor at Michael. 'Like you said, no trouble at all.'

Stella was flushed with relief, or possibly wine. She put her hand on my arm as I headed for the door. 'Thank you, Natalie,' she said (so it must have been the wine). 'I'm so pleased the two of you have had some time together.'

I looked down at where she clutched my arm. The sapphire of Mum's engagement ring sparkled on her fourth finger. 'I'll see you again,' I said and left before she could reply.

You were given everything, I thought. *You have everything.*

You don't get me too.

Chapter 25

I wore the trainers home. They were no more comfortable than the Converse I usually put on for the walk between station and office, but I figured I needed to make it look as if they'd been used. I left them unlaced just inside the front door, next to the sporty-looking rucksack I'd bought at the same store.

By the time Ian arrived, I'd showered and eaten (a drop of plant food for the dragon tree too, now fully recovered) and was curled up on the sofa reading the book that had been delivered to the office that morning. Alan was in the middle of his annual three-week break – he takes it every August, regular as clockwork, regardless of how busy things are. His wife is a teacher, which apparently makes this not only reasonable but sacrosanct – but for once I didn't mind; I knew it would give me a clear run.

I – or rather Alan – had paid extra for named-day delivery, and all morning I'd stuck to my desk like glue. I didn't even venture to the kitchen for a cup of tea until I saw the man from the mail room heading down the open-plan. He stopped at the end of my row of desks and I waited while he inspected his clipboard. 'Alan MacLee-odd?' he snapped.

I didn't correct him. 'He's on leave,' I said, and smiled. 'But I'm his line manager, so if you have something for him, I can take it.'

He grimaced. 'Looks like he's been shopping.' He held out the cardboard parcel with its distinctive logo printed across one end. 'Remind him he's not supposed to get his personal post delivered here. It's a security issue. And a waste of my time.'

I tutted. 'Of course. I'll make sure he's aware.'

Mail Room Man turned away muttering, and I glanced around to check no one was looking before I slipped the parcel into my handbag.

Later I sat in a cubicle in the ladies' loos and ripped a nail tearing into the cardboard. I didn't want to do anything more than scan the contents page, but even that was enough to send a frisson of something – excitement? fear? – up my spine and tingling into my scalp. Did people really do the things it talked about? I wondered. Could *I* do them? Was it even possible in the modern world?

I tore the packaging into small pieces, and later that afternoon I wandered to a different part of the building and dropped them into a recycling bin next to a photocopier. Then I slipped the dust jacket off and shredded it. When I got home, I searched the bookshelves for something to take its place. The answer was obvious as soon as I saw it. The book had been one of Mum's, but it was too basic to have been something she'd bought herself: a gift, then, from someone browsing a bookshelf marked 'Physics'. It had been published in 2012, the year she'd died. The title was perfect: *Hidden in Plain Sight*.

Now I slipped one flap of the jacket inside to mark my place as I heard the front door slam and unwound myself from the sofa. 'In here,' I called.

Ian stuck his head around the door. 'All right?'

I nodded. 'Just reading. There's a pizza in the freezer if you want it.'

I followed him into the kitchen and watched as he clattered about. He did everything noisily, I realised: *thud!* went the freezer drawer; *clang!* went the baking tray; a crash of a glass hitting another as he took it from the cupboard; an oath as the Coke fizzed up and over the rim, forming a sticky pool on the counter. Perhaps when all this was over, I could finally get some peace.

'Busy tonight?' I asked.

He grunted assent.

'But you weren't on your own? Caitlin was there, was she?' Her name dropped into the room like a lead weight, but I'll give Ian his due: he didn't even flinch.

'Yeah,' he said. 'And Matt.'

'I went to the gym on the way home.'

'Yeah?'

'Mm. Thought I should start as I mean to go on.' He was back in the freezer again, pulling out bags. 'There are some chips in the bottom drawer.'

'Right. Thanks.'

'It wore me out and I was in there less than an hour. I'm so unfit.'

'That's the point of the gym, though. To get better.'

'Well, and to stay slim.' I watched him scatter chips around the pizza. *Clatter, clatter, clatter.* 'Is Caitlin a gym-goer? She's got a lovely figure, don't you think?'

'I haven't noticed.' He pushed the baking tray into the oven. *Slam!* went the door. 'Why are you so interested in Caitlin all of a sudden?'

'I'm not. Just making conversation.'

He was shoving the chips back into the freezer, forcing them down with one hand and pushing the drawer with the other. The drawer was squeaking in protest and I knew most of the chips would be broken when I next used the bag.

I'd planned to come at it gently, slip in the question so naturally he wouldn't think twice about answering – but suddenly I was sick of it. Sick of him there, in my flat, crashing about and leaving bits of frozen cheese on the counter and squashing my chips and *lying to me.*

'Why did you go to the gym that day?' I asked.

He had his back to me, so I couldn't see his expression; but I saw the tension that entered his shoulders, the split second when a stillness settled over him as he decided how to reply. He knew exactly what I meant.

'What are you on about?' he said. 'When?'

'After you had sex with Chantelle.'

'Christ, Natalie, not this again—'

I cut across him. 'You said in court you went to the gym afterwards. Why did you do that?'

'Fuck, I don't know! I expect I wanted to let off some steam.'

'After you'd just had sex?'

He pushed past me. 'I'm not doing this again.'

I heard him go into the sitting room and switch on the TV but managed to stop myself from following. I'd messed up. Coming at the question directly wasn't going to help me find the truth. Besides, what good would it do me, even if Ian had decided to stop lying? A confession without evidence was worthless. It would just be my word against his. I already knew how that story ended.

I took a deep breath, then another, forced my fists to uncurl. Then I poured myself a glass of water and made myself drink it down. I had to remember this was a dangerous man. I had to be careful.

Ten minutes and a detour to the bedroom later, I took his pizza and chips from the oven and transferred them to plates. I knew he could hear what I was doing. I knew he'd think he'd won.

I put the plates on a tray with some ketchup and cutlery I knew he wouldn't use and took them into the sitting room. Ian was slumped on the sofa watching some American cartoon he loved. He didn't look up.

'I'm sorry,' I said.

'You should be.'

I placed the tray on the coffee table and took a seat in the armchair across from him, adjusting my position to stop the device in my jeans pocket digging into my hip. I'd paid good money for that recorder, and as I'd told Aidan, the sound quality was excellent. Ian was hunched over his pizza and I took the opportunity to ease it upwards so that the microphone was uncovered.

'I know how hard all this has been for you,' I said.

'Do you?' He looked at me then, his lip curled in a sneer. 'Do you actually have any fucking idea?'

'OK,' I said carefully, 'perhaps I don't know. But you don't talk about it, Ian. How can I understand if you won't talk about what happened?'

'But we have talked about it!'

'No. We haven't. Not really.'

'I've told you about my brother, my job . . .'

You've told me what you wanted me to hear. 'Yes, but you haven't talked about what happened that day. You haven't talked about Chantelle.'

'That bitch!' he spat. 'Why the fuck would I want to talk about her?'

The whining had gone, just like that, replaced with a hatred that was almost physical. I shrank back in my chair, but when I

224

opened my mouth again the voice that came out sounded calm. It's a skill I have, I've discovered; I can be good at acting when I put my mind to it.

'But *I* need to talk about it, Ian,' I said. 'I try not to think about it and then something happens, like today, just going to the gym, feeling tired afterwards, and my brain starts picking away at it. I don't want to, but I can't help it. If you could just tell me, just once . . .'

He stood and crossed the room to where I sat, towering over me in the small space. 'I have told you. I told everyone in that courtroom.'

I wanted to get up too, but he was standing too close to the chair. Instead I reached for his wrist. I could feel the blood pulsing through his veins.

I said, 'But it wasn't real, was it?'

I saw something then, a flicker behind his eyes. He tried to pull away, but I held on to his wrist. 'I mean, the court didn't feel real,' I said, watching for his reaction. 'It was like a stage. We all had to put on a show – even me, even just reading out the verdict that's what it felt like. Knowing everyone was watching you, judging you.'

I let him go then, watched him half stumble backwards onto the sofa. He rested his head in his hands, his fingertips pushed up into his hair. He was trying to hide, to buy himself time while he worked out what lie to tell me next. I felt the anger crawling beneath the surface of my skin.

'It doesn't have to be like that here.' My voice was almost a whisper. 'You don't need to put on a show. You can tell me all of it, everything you did, and I'll understand. I promise you that. I promise you I'll understand.'

I was good – the soft voice, the damp eyes. I almost believed it myself.

I watched as Ian sat there rubbing his hands through his hair. Then his shoulders heaved and he let out a great shuddering sigh, as if he were finally letting go of something he'd held on to for too long. His hands fell from his face and he looked at me.

'I've told you everything that happened,' he said. 'There's nothing more to tell. So if you don't believe me, perhaps it's time for us to call it a day.'

We both lay awake for a long time that night. The tension emanated from Ian's body in waves, his breathing kept deep and even by force of will, trying to fool me into believing he was asleep. I did the same thing, lying unnaturally still, listening for the moment when the quality of silence would change and I'd know he'd given in at last.

It had taken some persuasion to get him into bed at all, but I'd offered up my dignity on an altar inscribed with words about ends and means, and apologised repeatedly until he'd deigned to stay. I didn't imagine I was forgiven, but it was a bus ride and a walk back to Sean's and he'd have been waiting a long time at that time of night.

Lying there in the dark, I tried to analyse how I felt. Would I really be sorry if this were finally over? If Ian woke up in the morning and decided he'd had enough after all? Would it really be so bad to finish with all the plotting and the half-truths, to tell myself I'd given it my best shot but it was time to let it go? Perhaps to reassure myself that if, after all this time and effort, I'd still learned nothing real, nothing concrete that could have changed the verdict, nothing that could make me sure of his guilt – perhaps it was true after all what that woman at the court had told Helen? Perhaps the police had looked for other evidence and they'd drawn a blank because there really was nothing to find.

I tried out those lines, running them through my head, trying to believe them. I couldn't do it. I'd seen what Ian was. That night when he'd put his hand on my throat, the way he lied to me without blinking, the fury when I'd said Chantelle's name . . . And he hadn't gone to the gym. I knew now he'd lied on the witness stand. I knew he was guilty.

That wasn't something I could just let go. Ian wasn't as clever as I was. He wasn't as determined. There was no way I was going to let him beat me.

Somewhere along the line I realised he'd fallen asleep. I eased my legs slowly out of bed, feeling the chill of the night air against my skin. I sat there motionless for a moment, listening to his breathing, then I got to my feet and crept around the bed to the puddle of clothes he'd left on the floor.

Even in the dark it was easy to identify his jeans, the denim rough beneath my fingers. His belt was still threaded through the loops and the metal clinked as I lifted them. I stopped, crouched there on the floor, waiting for Ian to turn over and demand to know what I was doing, but the pattern of his breathing didn't change. I stayed peering into the dark as the seconds ticked by. *What are you doing?* I asked myself. *What do you expect to find?*

I felt along the leather for the buckle, wrapping my fingers around it to muffle the sound as with my other hand I searched for his pocket. Another clink, softer this time; but now Ian snuffled and shifted in his sleep. I stopped breathing. My calves were aching from holding the position and the corners of the buckle were digging into my hand, but I didn't move. I waited until he was still again then counted to thirty before reaching once more for his pocket.

I knew from the weight that I'd found it. I drew out the phone as carefully as I could, but my fingertips must have brushed the screen, because blue-green light suddenly illuminated a patch of the floor. In panic I tried to cover it with my hand, seeing the flesh lit orange. I swivelled towards the bed.

I could see Ian now, his face turned towards me. His lips were slightly parted but his forehead was creased in a frown. His eyes were closed.

I turned back to the phone, cupping my hand over the screen to shield as much of the light as I could. *Enter PIN to unlock*, it instructed. A number pad appeared beneath.

My finger hovered over the screen. What if the phone really did record a failed attempt? But the stakes were higher than ever now; I had to take the risk.

I tapped in 111086, Ian's date of birth. The reply came immediately: *Wrong PIN*.

There was nothing to indicate how many digits were required – perhaps it needed the year in full. I added in the 1 and the 9 and pressed 'OK'. Up it flashed again: *Wrong PIN*.

I glanced towards the bed again. Ian's eyes were still closed.

Perhaps he used the PIN for one of his credit cards. Shame I didn't know what any of them were. Or then again . . . I tapped out my own date of birth.

Wrong PIN. No surprises there.

A noise from the bed. I stuffed the phone back into his pocket, forgetting about the belt. The metal jangled, but when I turned back to the bed, the light from the screen left a blue-grey afterimage that obscured Ian's face. I couldn't see whether his eyes were open or not.

I straightened up and slipped quietly back to my side of the bed, swinging my feet back under the duvet in a single movement.

'What are you doing?'

I'd woken him; or had he just been pretending? Had he been watching me the whole time? But no, his voice was thick with sleep. No one was that good an actor.

'Just went to the bathroom,' I said. 'Go back to sleep.'

I lay with my eyes open and listened to him breathe.

Chapter 26

You might imagine that with so much to think about, so much to plan, I lost sight of Aidan. It's true that from time to time I let my attention waver. The visit from Kellie, difficult though it was, had put that right. Seeing her there in my kitchen, listening to her tell me she and Aidan couldn't be blamed for anything because they were 'in love' – well, I think most people would agree that's the kind of thing that's going to get under the skin. And then the police turning up on my doorstep . . .

You're playing with fire, Aidan, I thought. *You should know better than to try that with me.*

But I knew I had to wait. Tempting as it was, I couldn't risk firing off texts when emotions were running high. Aidan, as the history of our split illustrates only too clearly, can sometimes get carried away. He doesn't always act in his own best interests. So whilst it would have been obvious to any rational person that he was in no better position than he'd ever been to deal with any counter-measures on my part, I couldn't trust him not to throw caution to the wind and turn up in some grubby little police station clutching his mobile phone and spouting words like 'harassment'.

So I waited. It wasn't that hard. I knew that if I kept silent he might think the visit from the police had scared me off. He might start to relax. It would make the moment I pressed send on another message to him all the sweeter.

Perhaps this makes me sound vindictive. Aidan has accused me of that, and more besides, on many occasions. I know I'd never be able to make him understand that's not what this is about; the truth is, it's simply necessary. Enjoyment doesn't come into it. What I'm doing is about *justice*. It isn't fair for Aidan to think he can do what he likes, humiliate me in front of our family and friends, discard me like a pair of worn-out shoes and just walk away without consequences. There *have* to be consequences. What's to stop people from behaving badly if they think they can just get away with it? What's to stop Aidan from doing this to someone else – poor, bullfrog-brained Kellie or whoever comes after her? I have to put a stop to that. It's my responsibility.

It's the same with Ian. I knew what he was capable of, the depths he'd sunk to. What's that quote? All that's necessary for evil to triumph is for good men to stand by and do nothing. We'll set aside the gender-biased language – it was the nineteenth century, one can't expect any better – but the point is this: I'm the one who knows what they've done. I couldn't stand by and do nothing.

I remember the moment I realised how similar they were, Aidan and Ian. I'd been reading that book – *In Plain Sight*, I'll call it, though in my head I referred to it as 'the manual'. I'd been evaluating the advice it contained, not seriously imagining I'd ever follow it. Simply disappearing, leaving all the shit behind and starting over somewhere else, a new name, a blank slate – well, it had its attractions, of course. And it wasn't as if I had anyone to miss – Stella and Michael would hardly have inspired tears on my pillow, and the less said about Ian the better. But I had my career. A certain status I'd worked hard to achieve.

So I was reading it more as a thought experiment, testing its ideas, imagining how they could work. It was talking about setting what it called false trails, how to lead anyone trying to follow you in the wrong direction. And that was when I saw it.

It was what Ian and Aidan had done to me, in their different ways. They'd tried to set their own false trails. They'd pretended they were people they weren't, attempted to blind me to the truth.

I think that's when the idea started to form, though I maintain it was still just a theory at that stage. It was the neatness of it that appealed. Out of the lies, the turmoil, the *wrongness* of it all I could create something new, something that tidied away all the loose ends.

I could reset the balance.

The last time I saw Helen, it was in a pub; not a wine bar full of suits and people trying to decide between the mac-and-cheese and the 'ironic' pork scratchings, but an actual Hackney boozer. It was the right setting for her. Not that I mean to imply there was anything scruffy about Helen, but she was authentic, one of the few people I've ever met who was. It might seem strange, but even though we didn't know each other for long, I'm going to miss her.

She'd warned me that she might be late, so I'd ordered us both a white wine and taken them to a table to wait for her. I'd felt eyes on me at the bar – even in London there are places where new faces stand out – but by the time I'd sat down, they'd lost interest. For want of anything else to do, I composed a couple of text messages to Aidan, trying out a different tone. They looked strange, uneasy. I deleted them without sending.

When the door swung open, I had a second or two to observe Helen before she spotted me. She was wearing a navy trouser suit, one side of the jacket pulled low by the weight of the scuffed leather handbag over her shoulder, the padding there bunched up around the strap. Even from a distance I thought she looked tired. I waved and she smiled when she saw me, pushing her way past the tables.

'I got you a drink,' I said, holding out the glass to forestall the hug I feared might be coming. 'Hope you like white.'

She sank into the chair opposite with a sigh. 'Just what the doctor ordered. After the day I've had . . .'

I listened to her talk about her cases – not the details, I noticed, she was careful about that, not telling me anything that would have breached client confidentiality; just blurry outlines, enough to form a backdrop on which she could pin her feelings. She was frustrated, she said, worried that she wasn't doing as much as she should, anxious about getting too involved or sometimes that she'd stopped caring enough. It was the opposite of the way I talked.

'I'm sorry,' she said, 'you didn't want to hear all that.'

I shook my head. 'I don't know how you do it.'

'Somehow it's stopped feeling like I have a choice.' She gave a humourless laugh. 'Let's talk about something else.'

'Actually,' I said, keeping my eyes on the table, 'there was something I wanted to tell you.'

She leaned closer. 'About Chantelle? Did you go to see her?'

I nodded. 'I didn't find out anything new.'

'How was she?'

'She was angry.' I remembered the way Chantelle's shoulders had sagged as she stared out of the window. 'And tired, I think. She didn't want to talk to me at first.' Helen looked away, her lips pressed together in a line. 'I did find out something afterwards, though . . .'

I told her about the visit to the gym, about checking the visitors' book. She let me talk, not saying anything. 'So,' I said, when I'd finished, 'what do you think? This changes things, doesn't it?'

233

Her brow was puckered. 'I don't get it. Why would he lie about where he went?'

I shrugged. 'Does it matter? He lied about his story. The police can't have checked that, or they'd have told us at the trial. It proves he can't be trusted.'

'Yes, but why say he'd been to the gym if he hadn't? What would he gain from that?'

I suppressed my irritation; this wasn't what was important. 'Maybe it was part of his usual routine so it seemed an easy thing to lie about. Or maybe he'd gone somewhere he didn't want to tell the police, somewhere he thought would make him look bad . . .'

'Like where?'

'I don't know!' I'd raised my voice without meaning to. It must have been getting to me more than I'd thought. I took a breath and tried again. 'It isn't my job to find out, is it? Shouldn't the police be doing that?'

Helen fixed me with a level stare. 'You're right, Natalie, they should. You need to tell them what you've found.'

I felt outmanoeuvred. Was this what Helen did with her clients? I wondered. Asked them questions until they gave her the answers she wanted? I was impressed in spite of myself. But I wasn't going to the police, not unless I could be sure what the result would be.

'Do you think they'd listen?' I said. 'You must come into contact with the police all the time – with your work, I mean. Do you think they'd be interested in reopening the case?'

She frowned. 'Maybe.' A pause, then, 'It's not much . . .'

Like I said, she was honest. We sat there in silence, listening to the hum of the conversations around us. It was Helen who spoke first.

'I hate this too, you know,' she said. 'Having these doubts, worrying we did the wrong thing . . .'

I could feel the 'but' coming so I cut her off. We needed to focus on the facts. 'It never fitted, did it? That story about the gym.'

She rubbed a hand across her eyes. 'I suppose not . . .'

'I mean, why would someone who's just had sex get up and go to the gym? He said he wanted to let off steam—'

'He said what?'

Too late I realised my mistake. 'So do you think the police—'

'When did he say that?'

I felt the blush rising up my neck. 'Say what?'

'About going to the gym to let off steam?' Helen was watching me like a hawk. 'I don't remember him saying that. I don't remember either of the lawyers even asking about it.'

'Yes, they did . . .'

'No, I don't think so. You said as much when you rang me that first time – you said you wished they'd asked him about it.' She studied me, her expression serious. 'Natalie, you haven't been to see him, have you?'

I took a sip of wine to buy myself time. 'I don't know what you mean.'

'Ian. Did you go to see him as well as Chantelle?'

I'd messed up. I could see already she wouldn't believe me if I tried to deny it. Perhaps I should tell her everything. It would be such a relief, after all, to get it off my chest. I could tell her about that night when he'd put his hand on my throat, how afraid I'd been. Maybe I'd even tell her about Caitlin, make her see that he lied all the time . . .

'Natalie.' Helen's voice broke into my thoughts. 'You have to stop this. You have to stop it before someone gets hurt.'

I saw the concern in her eyes. 'You don't need to worry about me,' I said, and smiled, pretending that was what she'd meant.

* * *

235

I asked Ian to move in with me.

It was almost funny to watch him squirm, trying to find a way of saying no that wouldn't sound suspicious.

'I just think it would be more practical,' I said. 'You're here most nights anyway, and while you're working at the Phoenix . . .'

It was the story we told ourselves, that he was only working at the pub as a stopgap, that he'd find something better soon. He'd believed it at first, perhaps I did too; but as time went by, it was clear that the job suited him. He didn't mind the work, enjoyed chatting to the customers. He'd have liked more money, of course, but why worry about that when he was barely paying rent to Sean, when I paid for most of his food and our occasional evenings out? In the early days he'd hated that, insisted on splitting bills or sometimes paying for meals I knew he couldn't afford; but over time it seemed he'd lost his qualms. And of course, there was Caitlin. She must have added a certain something to the prospect of going to work every day.

He screwed up his eyes as if I'd shone a torch into them. 'I'd feel funny about it,' he said. 'This is your place.'

'No reason it can't be yours too,' I said cheerily.

'There's not really room . . .'

'I can make space. I could do with a clear-out anyway.'

His eyes were darting around the room now – I almost expected him to make a run for it. 'The thing is, Natalie,' he said, reaching for my hand and giving it a squeeze, 'it's a lovely offer, but I think Sean would be offended if I told him I was moving out.'

I just about stopped myself from laughing aloud at that. From everything I'd heard, Sean would have set up a shrine to me in his living room if I'd taken Ian off his hands. I was offended that Ian hadn't tried to come up with a better excuse, but it confirmed what I'd already guessed: he was looking for a way out. I was running out of time.

I'd been shadowing him around the flat for weeks, but it was like the Aesop's fable with the wind and the sun; the closer I got, the more he hugged that phone to him as if his life depended on it. It was difficult, too, to avoid alerting him to what I was trying to do. Once or twice I caught him shooting me a quizzical glance as I hung over the kitchen counter attempting small talk while he poured himself a beer, or sat next to him reading *In Plain Sight* while he watched something on TV that would once have had me leaving the room – Formula 1, say, or golf. I knew I had to up my game.

In the end, I think it was desperation that gave me the idea. We'd been sitting in the living room half watching the news on loop when I heard Ian's phone jingle from the pocket of his jeans. He ignored it.

'You've got a text,' I said unnecessarily.

He shrugged. 'Yeah, someone telling me I've been in an accident that wasn't my fault, I expect. I'll check it later.' He stared at the TV as if engrossed in the latest on some government U-turn. A minute later, he stirred, as I'd known he would. 'Just getting a drink,' he said. 'Do you want one?'

'I'll have a water, thanks.'

He left the room, and after a moment I heard the bathroom door shut. I followed and pressed my ear to the door, but there was nothing. He must have been sending a text.

It was a few minutes before he returned empty-handed. 'You forgot the drinks,' I said.

He slapped his head dramatically and headed back to the kitchen. That was the kind of thing he did when he was lying – became more theatrical, apparently more eager to please. It was one of the things I hated about him.

Another delay before he was back with the glasses – another text or two, I assumed. He brought mine over to where I was sitting, then re-installed himself on the sofa. On the television, a politician with hair like a Yorkshire terrier was assuring the nation it wasn't a U-turn after all.

'Twat,' said Ian.

I listened out for his phone, but he'd turned the sound off. I couldn't even hear the dull thrum of it vibrating as another message arrived. I knew it was coming, though: he was still holding on to it. I watched him from the corner of my eye as I pretended to read, saw the screen light up and his quick glance towards me, checking I wasn't looking before he turned back to the phone. The ghost of a smile crossed his face. It turned my stomach.

I watched him tap out a response – another of those sneaky glances in my direction – and his fingers wrapped around the phone again. 'Do you think he'll go?' he said, nodding at the figure on the television. 'Do you reckon he'll resign?'

'One can only hope,' I replied, and he sniggered.

His fingers were illuminated again. Surely not a reply already? Caitlin must find him more interesting than I did. I stood up. 'I'm going to get something to eat. Cheese toastie?'

'Thanks, babe,' he said. I dug my fingernails into the palms of my hands.

In the kitchen, I got out the bread and took a bottle of brown sauce from the cupboard. I didn't like the stuff – it was only there because Ian wanted it.

I knew he'd be tapping away at another text, furtive peeks at the doorway to check I wasn't coming back. What was he saying? Was he talking about me?

The toaster wasn't working so I put the bread on the grill pan, crashing away as I slid it into the oven to let him know I was still out of the way. I was cutting the cheese when I started to smell the toast. An idea formed.

I pulled the grill pan out then slid it back in on the highest shelf. The elements gleamed red hot.

My work BlackBerry was still in my handbag. I retrieved it from the hallway and dialled. A second's pause and the landline trilled through the flat.

'I'll get it!' I called. I picked up the phone from its stand in the kitchen and pressed the button to end the call. 'Hi Stella,' I said, loud enough for Ian to hear, and 'Right, yes,' as I walked back into the hallway and dropped the BlackBerry into my bag.

A pause; I could smell the bread beginning to smoulder. 'No,' I announced, 'I'm afraid I don't see that at all.'

I strolled into the living room, not looking at Ian, and stood at the window with my back to him. 'I'm not sure what more I can say about this,' I said, beginning to enjoy my imaginary conversation. 'I've already explained my position.'

I could smell the toast from here, the acrid tang of charcoal. Surely Ian would have noticed it by now? A trip out to the kitchen to deal with the culinary disaster would give me just enough time to take a look at his phone. I risked a look in his direction but his eyes were on the TV. He must have been waiting for a reply to his last, no doubt scintillating, message.

'I don't want to argue about this,' I said. The smell was stronger now; if I hadn't taken the battery out of the smoke alarm months ago – it kept going off whenever I so much as thought about grilling a slice of bacon – it would have been shrieking in fury. If Ian didn't notice soon, it was possible I was going to have a real problem on my hands.

I turned around and put my hand over the receiver. 'Smell?' I mouthed at him.

He frowned back at me. 'What?'

Oh for fuck's sake. 'I think something's burning!' I hissed.

He raised his eyebrows. 'What?' he said again. 'I can't hear you.'

'No, Stella,' I said, for the sake of form, then, 'Something's burning, Ian!'

Through the doorway I could see wreaths of smoke hanging in the hallway. And still he wasn't moving. I hurried back to the kitchen.

Shit. Thick smoke clogged the air and I hurried to open a window. 'Ian!' I bellowed, flinging the phone onto the worktop.

He appeared in the doorway. 'What the . . . ?'

'The grill!' I snatched at a tea towel and turned the taps on. 'Switch it off!'

The bread was blazing merrily, flames licking around the top of the oven. Ian reached for the handle of the grill pan, then pulled back again.

'For the love of God . . .' I pushed past him and grabbed the handle myself. The pan clattered out, the flames even more alarming now they were no longer contained in the small space. I pivoted on my heel and half threw it into the sink, chucking the wet tea towel after it.

There was a loud hiss as hot metal hit cold water and the flames were replaced by clouds of black smoke. I coughed, my eyes streaming.

Ian stood rooted to the spot. 'Are you OK?' he said. 'Have you burnt yourself?'

I shook my head. 'Take it outside,' I spluttered. 'The smoke . . .'

The taps were still running and the flames had turned to oily black ash on the surface of the water in the pan. Ian looked at it with distaste but opened the drawer where I kept the oven gloves, reaching into the sink and keeping it at arm's length as he lifted it, as if it might bite.

'Just stick it to the side of the gate. No, wait!' Belatedly I realised I could turn this to my advantage. 'You'd better stay there until it cools down. In case there's a child or something . . .'

I followed him to the door and shut it behind him. He wouldn't have his key so he'd have to ring to be let back in – it wouldn't be possible for him to catch me unawares.

I rushed into the living room.

Where was the phone?

I'd assumed Ian would have dropped it on the table in his rush to get to the kitchen, but the only things there were the remote control and his empty glass.

I bent and slammed my fist onto the table, hard enough to make them both skitter on the surface. He must have shoved it in his pocket. My flat was nearly burning to the ground, but he'd taken the time to hide his phone away before coming to help me.

Fucker.

I threw myself onto the sofa, pressing the heels of my hands to my streaming eyes. It was useless. I might as well give up.

I let my hands drop to my sides. But wait – what was this? My fingertips had brushed something smooth and hard, something tucked down between the seat cushions.

I pulled it from its hiding place, hardly daring to breathe. There was Ian's screen saver, the green hill and blue sky – and there were all the icons. There was no password box. For once he'd left his phone unlocked.

I stabbed at the yellow envelope at the bottom of the screen, terrified that at any moment a time limit would be reached and the automatic lock would kick in. Up flashed a list of the people who'd sent him messages – Natalie, Matt, Sean . . . Caitlin.

Something niggled at me, but I tapped her name without stopping to wonder why. *There in 10 mins! Sorry!!!* read the final speech bubble. I scrolled upwards. *Where are you? Need you here NOW.* Then another, in the same blue that denoted a message from Ian. *Where are you?*

I carried on reading. Message from Caitlin: *Washing machine flooded! Need to wait for engineer. Don't know if I'll make it in. Sorry!* Another: *Feeling rough. Can you cover for me tonight?* And another: *Matt in filthy mood today. You've been warned!*

I stared at them in incomprehension. Was this it? Was this really what they'd been exchanging messages over – Caitlin's inability to get to work on time? Had I got it all wrong?

And then at last it occurred to me what was wrong with the picture: Caitlin's name had been halfway down the list. I scrolled back to the most recent message and checked the time and date. It had been sent two days ago. Whoever Ian had been texting that morning, it hadn't been her.

I jabbed at the screen again, trying to return to the list of messages; but nothing happened. The phone had frozen.

No no no. This couldn't be happening! I pressed my finger against the screen, held it there – nothing. I tried again with my thumb – same result. Perhaps I should turn it off and on again – but no, I'd need the password then. Wouldn't I?

I held the phone to my cheek. 'Please,' I croaked, *'please work.'*

Downstairs I heard a door slam. Not Ian, surely? Not already?

I whispered a prayer to the God I didn't believe in and pressed my finger one last time to the screen.

Chapter 27

I'd left work early in the hope of missing rush hour, but I still had to stand on the bus, wedged between a buggy and the knees of a teenage girl who'd got the fold-down seat. I shuffled through a hundred and eighty degrees so I could look out of the window and pretend I was somewhere else.

The voice on the tannoy announced Florence Road and I pushed my way to the doors. Outside the air was crisp, the edge of autumn. I pulled a scarf from my handbag and wrapped it around my neck.

I remembered the route to Chantelle's flat from my last visit, and in a few minutes I was standing outside the door with its metal grille and rows of buttons. I pressed 11 without giving myself time to change my mind.

'Hello?'

'Chantelle, it's Natalie Wright.' There was silence. 'From the jury?'

'I know who you are.' Her voice was weary. 'What do you want?'

I chewed at my lip. 'I've got some news,' I said. 'Evidence.'

It's not much, wasn't that what Helen had said? Maybe Chantelle would feel differently. 'Can I come up?'

She didn't answer, but the door buzzed.

By the time I got to the top of the stairs, she was standing in her doorway, one arm on the frame, the other out of sight behind the half-closed door.

'You've got five minutes,' she said.

I nodded. 'OK, but can I come in?' I glanced around at the other doors. 'I don't want your neighbours hearing this.'

For a moment I thought she was going to refuse, but then she moved to one side. 'All right, but I mean it. Just five minutes. I can't keep doing this.'

I followed her inside, kicking off my shoes before she could ask. She led the way to the sitting room and turned to face me, her arms wrapped around her body. 'So what is it?'

'I know that Ian Nash is a liar,' I said. 'I've got proof.'

I told her about the gym, explaining the lengths I'd gone to to get a look at the visitors' book. I hadn't expected gratitude – of course not; but I'd thought she'd be pleased I'd found something. Instead she looked blank.

'So,' I said, when the pause had become uncomfortable, 'what do you think?'

She examined her fingernails. 'Are you going to take this to the police?'

It was the same question I'd been asking myself. 'I'm not sure. I don't know if it would be enough, not on its own. If there was anything else you could tell me, anything I could check . . .'

She shook her head. 'There *isn't* anything. I've already told the police everything that happened.'

'Yes, but that's just it!' I heard the desperation in my voice. 'Don't you see, Ian told the police he'd been to the gym that day, but they didn't check! They didn't follow it up!'

Chantelle studied me. 'Would it have made any difference?'

'Of course it would have!' But then I stopped myself; how could I say that for sure? I shook my head. 'I'm sorry. The truth is, I don't know. But I think it would have made a difference to me, to know that he'd lied. It would have made it hard to believe the rest of it.'

She shrugged. 'It's not enough. Not now. There are rules, aren't there? He can't go to court again.'

I was surprised that she'd looked into the procedural obstacles. Had she hoped, after all, that I'd find something worth taking to the police?

'I don't think it's that simple,' I said, picking my words with care. I didn't want to mislead her, but in truth, I wasn't sure of the position myself. There hadn't seemed much point in checking before I'd turned up anything new. But surely there had to be a way?

'If there's new evidence,' I continued, 'I believe someone can be retried. We won't know unless we try.' I pulled my notebook from my bag. 'I've brought my notes from last time. Can we go through them once more, see if there's anything we've missed? Please, Chantelle. We can't give up now.'

She turned to the window, as if she might find the answers laid out on the patch of grass below. After a moment, she turned back to me. 'All right. But this is the last time I'm talking to you about this. I can't keep reliving it.'

I nodded. 'The last time. I promise.'

I walked part of the way home, hoping the exercise would clear my mind. The air in the flat had been hot and stuffy and the conversation with Chantelle – I groped for the right word – *enervating*.

245

I hadn't found anything I could use. Chantelle had talked through the sequence of events again, her brow furrowed as she repeated the words she'd already had to say too many times – to the police, in the courtroom. Everything was the same: she'd thought Ian had looked upset when he'd turned up on her doorstep; he'd smelled of drink; he'd told her he needed to unwind. And what happened next – though there she went pale, and I couldn't bring myself to probe the details the way Ian's lawyer had. Instead I moved on: there was something else I needed to ask her.

'You weren't there when we delivered the verdict?' I asked, already knowing the answer.

Chantelle frowned. 'The police told me not to go. They were right, weren't they? I couldn't have stood there and watched you call me a liar.'

I swallowed. 'Did you hear about what happened?'

She gave a bitter laugh. 'The screaming, you mean? Yes, of course I did. I should have expected something like it, but you know, it still surprised me.'

The resentment in her voice almost stopped me in my tracks but I had to ask the question; that scream had haunted me for weeks. 'Was it your mum?'

Chantelle grimaced. 'She can't help herself. Has to make it all about her. I don't think she even realises that's what she's doing. She needs everyone fussing over her. *Poor Kathleen.* As if it was her it happened to, not me. As if she was the one who was raped!'

The shock must have shown on my face. 'You think I'm being unfair.' Chantelle shook her head. 'You don't know what she's like.'

I didn't argue. Who was I to tell her she was wrong? I said, 'I should probably go.'

She didn't reply, so I got to my feet. 'I'm sorry to bring all this back up,' I said. 'I won't come here again unless I've got good news.'

It was the wrong way of putting it, but Chantelle didn't seem to be listening anyway. I was halfway to the door when she spoke again.

'You haven't brought it back up,' she said. 'It never goes away.' I turned back to her, but her eyes were fixed on the carpet. 'I remember it all the time. I can't forget it. That song . . .' Her voice was far away, as if she'd forgotten I was there.

'The song that was playing when he did it?'

'Watching the sails,' she said. 'Watching the sails catch the wind.'

I saw a tear slide off the end of her chin. That was when I left.

Now, walking down the street, I wondered whether after all I was coming to the end of the line. I'd spoken to Chantelle twice now, asking her my own questions in my own way, and still there was no solid evidence to hold on to. Nothing that could prove what had really happened that day, nothing that didn't leave room for doubt. Yes, Ian had lied about at least one part of his story; but was that enough to be sure he'd lied about everything? Would it be enough for another jury?

An old lady walking in the other direction threw me a worried look and I realised I was muttering. 'Yes? Can I help you?' I snapped, and she hurried away. This was no good: I had to get a grip of myself. It was time to stop speculating and stick to the facts. And if there were no more facts to be had – well, at some point I would just have to accept I'd done everything I could. Sometimes, perhaps, it wasn't possible to be sure. Maybe I'd have to try and learn to live with that.

Ian would be back at the flat when I returned; he had an early finish that day. I had to calm down, act normally. I'd barely spoken to him since I'd found that text message, and even he had noticed something was wrong, telling me it wasn't my fault about the grill pan. Ha! Thanks for that, Fireman Sam.

Can't wait to hold you in my arms again, it had read, from someone stored enigmatically as 'R'. It had been like a punch to the stomach, even though I'd known what was going on – even though, apparently, I'd got the wrong person. *Hold you in my arms.* Did people really speak like that?

I'd have to do something about it, one way or another.

But first things first. Ian wouldn't be expecting me back so early – this was allegedly my life-drawing night. Perhaps I'd tell him I was feeling ill and take a long bath. I could lock the door and go over the notes of my conversation with Chantelle.

The last time, that was what I'd told her. Maybe it really would be.

I could hear the muffled music as I turned my key in the lock, the volume increasing as I opened the door and stepped inside. 'I'm home!' I called as I kicked off my shoes, but Ian didn't reply. I hoped he hadn't made himself too comfortable, or making dinner would mean ringing for pizza. I needed something with more substance tonight.

I followed the music to the living room. Ian was slouched on the sofa, the laptop on the table in front of him.

A new song had started playing, a man's voice, smooth and mellow. *Sitting on the harbour wall . . .*

Ian hadn't noticed me. His attention was fixed on the laptop, one hand in his lap jerking back and forth. I followed his line of sight, trying to make sense of what I was seeing.

As purple dusk begins to fall, went the voice.

The screen glowed with orange flesh tones. It was a woman, but there was something wrong with her, something cutting into her naked flesh.

Watching the storm begin . . .

She was tied up, I saw now, the rope wrapped around her arms and legs, wound tight around her chest, squeezing her breasts into an unnatural shape. Her eyes were wide with fear. Ian's hand moved faster.

Watching the sails catch the wind . . .

I felt the sweat prickle on my brow as I backed away into the hallway. I kept my eyes on the entrance to the living room as I grabbed my shoes and my bag. Then I opened the front door again and closed it softly behind me.

Chapter 28

I walked to the station and got on a train, back into central London, wanting the crowds and the lights. My brain was buzzing, trying to analyse what I'd seen and heard. There were only a few people in my carriage and the seat next to me was free, so I took out my notebook and pen. This is evidence, I thought. I should write it down now, create a record while everything is still fresh.

But when I tried to write, my hand was shaking too much to form the letters.

I put the notebook away again and pushed my palms beneath my thighs, trying to warm them up. Outside the window flashed homes and offices, strips of gardens, roads edged with cars.

The sickness rose up from nowhere and I cast desperately around for a sign to a loo. There was nothing, so I had to sit there taking deep breaths – in through the nose, out through the mouth, wasn't that what you were supposed to do? Mum would have known, but she wasn't there to ask. I had no one else.

There was a rapist in my home. I'd invited him into my bed.

My gorge rose again and I swallowed, feeling the burn at the back of my throat.

I had to go to the police, I was sure of that now. I had to tell them what I'd learned. Had Chantelle told them about the music? I wondered. Would they understand the significance of that song? Would they see the connection when I told them how Ian had stared at the screen, at that woman with the rope forming grooves across her body, about how I was sure he wasn't just getting off on the film – he was reliving what he'd done?

This was real. I had seen it with my own eyes.

Would it be enough to make them reopen the case? I didn't know, but I had to try.

The train was coming to a stop. I'd got on without looking at the destination, but I saw now I was at Charing Cross. I stumbled onto the platform and headed for the barriers, relieved I'd had the presence of mind to collect my handbag before I'd left the flat. On the other side, I stopped, unsure where to go next. Suddenly I didn't want to be alone. I knew there was a pizza restaurant just outside, but if I smelled food I might be sick. Instead I bought a bottle of water from a stall on the edge of the concourse and found a metal seat near two women with large pink cases on wheels.

Perhaps I could find a hotel. Send Ian a text, tell him something had come up and I'd needed to go back to work. But what then? I couldn't stay away for ever. What would happen when I told the police? What would they do? Would they arrest him? Or would they just question him? Would they have to tell him why, that I was the one who'd talked to them?

Would they do anything at all?

'Are you all right, love?' It was one of the women with the cases. She had a Yorkshire accent and she and her friend were peering at me in concern. 'You're ever so pale,' she said.

I forced a smile. 'Coming down with a cold.'

The woman looked like she was going to say something else, so I stood. 'Better go, I'm meeting someone.'

'All right, love,' she said. 'You mind how you go now.'

To my horror I felt tears prickling at my eyes. I turned away before she could see them.

I pushed through the crowd of bodies waiting for their trains, out into the cold air. There was a bookshop nearby, I remembered, a large chain-store one. I could head in there and keep warm while I worked out what to do.

Inside it was surprisingly busy, tourists mingling with office workers browsing at the end of a long day. I stood at the bottom of the staircase reading the directory of subjects: psychology, politics, physics, law.

Law. I took the stairs to the second floor, scanning the bookcases for the one I wanted. *There.* A tall man in a suede jacket stood to one side and I gave him as wide a berth as possible as I made my way to the shelves.

Now that I was closer, I could see smaller labels pinned to the front of each section – *Corporate Law, History of Law, Jurisprudence* and, yes, *Criminal Law.* I pulled out one of the thicker volumes and flipped to the index. There it was: double jeopardy.

I took the book into a corner with an uncomfortable-looking wooden chair and stowed my bag on the floor beside me. I started to read.

It wasn't long before I'd devoured everything it had to say on the topic and the nausea was back. The rules had changed, apparently, and at first it seemed the news was good. It was possible for a person to be tried for a second time if the crime was serious enough – like rape. But the more I read, the more despondent I became. The hurdles were daunting. A retrial would have to be approved by the Director of Public Prosecutions on the basis that new evidence had been found. And not just any new evidence – it had to be something that couldn't reasonably have been presented at the first trial. According to the book, it was intended to allow for scientific advances like DNA testing; what it wasn't supposed to do was give the police a second crack of the whip if they'd messed up first time around.

Could my testimony count as new evidence? It wasn't a scientific breakthrough, it didn't have the cold, hard logic of a slide under a microscope – but surely it was convincing enough to put in front of a jury?

I got up, leaving the book on the chair behind me. I should go to the police now, put the problem in someone else's hands. There was an enormous police station at Lewisham – surely it would be open twenty-four hours.

I made my way downstairs and back onto the street outside. I must have been reading for longer than I'd thought – the sky had turned to indigo and the pavements were slick with rainwater. I hurried back to the station, weaving my way around people out for the night for dinner or a play. On the concourse, damp overcoats steamed and umbrellas dripped. The next train to Lewisham was already on the platform, and I boarded and took a seat at the far end of the carriage.

I closed my eyes, but the image of Ian's face flashed before me, the set of his jaw as he watched the woman on the screen. The music must have been his own soundtrack, played alongside the film to take him back to that afternoon with Chantelle. *Watching the sails catch the wind.* She and I had something in common now: I'd never be able to listen to that song again.

The police would ask me how we'd met, why I'd started a relationship with a man I knew had been accused of rape. Perhaps they'd be suspicious. *Of course* they'd be suspicious. And what if I told them what had happened to me, that night when I'd asked him if he'd raped Chantelle? Would they believe me if I told them how scared I'd been? Would they want to know why I hadn't gone to them straight away?

And then there was Ian's lie about going to the gym. I needed to tell them that – it was another piece of evidence, and unlike everything else, it wasn't just a case of my word against his. I could show the police the photo of the signing-in book, tell them to go to the gym and see it for themselves. But how would I explain how I'd found out? Perhaps I should admit I was suspicious of Ian, frightened after that night he'd put his hand on my neck, that I'd decided to investigate for myself. But what would I say when they asked me how I'd got a look at the book? If I lied, they might check with the receptionist and that wouldn't look good; and if I told them about my ruse to get her out of the way, about the missing ring . . . I'd told her it was my mother's. That wasn't the kind of thing that would look good on a witness stand. I could hear her now, the lawyer who'd defended Ian: *You lied, didn't you, Miss Wright? You lied then and you're lying now.*

If it even got that far. Maybe the police would decide I was too unreliable a witness to hang a retrial on my testimony.

The train was pulling out of the station. Through the window I could see the lights of the bridge strung out across the dark ribbon of the river. Would she be at work now, that detective, the one who'd worked on Chantelle's case? I couldn't picture her face but I remembered her all the same – the neat figure in the smart jacket, her hair pulled back from her face, her self-confident briskness, so unlike the craggy-faced men of TV crime shows. What was her name? Emma someone. It was double-barrelled, I remembered. Wilson? Willis? Yes, that was it. Detective Emma Willis-something.

I pulled my phone from my bag and googled 'Chantelle Patterson rape Emma Willis'. The first result was a piece from a local paper, a report from the first day of the trial. There she was: Detective Emma Willis-Jones. No photograph, but a quote: 'Detective Emma Willis-Jones said, "We're confident the jury will reach the right decision."' Her confidence had been misplaced.

Maybe if she'd done her job properly . . .

But no, now wasn't the time to get angry. I had to stay calm. I had to make her believe me.

The train was slowing down; still one more stop before we arrived at Lewisham. I checked my watch – just after 9.30. Ian would be expecting me home soon. There'd be no sign of that film if I arrived now; that song wouldn't be playing. He'd be slouched in front of the TV or watching a film, the way he usually was if he was staying over and I got back late. How many times, I wondered, had he done what he'd been doing that night? How many times had I walked in unaware of what I'd have seen if I'd arrived an hour earlier? When I came through the door, was he still remembering what he'd done? Was he reliving some feeling of power? Was he – and here I had to breathe deeply again, swallowing the saliva that flooded my mouth – imagining doing to me what he'd done to Chantelle?

My hands had gone cold again and I tucked them into my armpits. I had to stop thinking about it. I had to concentrate on what was important: telling the police. Bringing Ian to justice.

There was a small crowd at the door when the train pulled into Lewisham and I allowed myself to be swept along in it, carried onto the platform and out of the station. It dispersed again as quickly as it had formed, and I was alone, heading down the hill towards the high street. There was building work under way, blue-painted hoardings and a maze of traffic lights and crossings. It had changed since I'd last walked that way and I had to concentrate to navigate the new layout. I dodged a group of cackling women and a bus passed across my field of vision – and there it was, a monolith of concrete and glass: Lewisham police station.

I stood on the pavement outside, pretending to talk into my phone as I studied the facade. Despite the size of the building, it wasn't easy to see how to get in. In the middle were a series of blue railings forming a large gate flanked by two smaller ones; but they were firmly closed with a forbidding air. That couldn't be the entrance for the public. I went closer, but there were no signs for a reception – did police stations even have a reception? Perhaps you weren't supposed to drop in at all. Perhaps I should have phoned.

I turned left and walked along the front of the building. Every few steps I passed a long, thin window, a blind down at every one. It was an odd contrast – this huge building advertising its presence yet refusing to reveal its interior to passers-by. I reached the corner and turned back, fighting the urge to give up and leave. But where would I go?

A few metres in the other direction I saw it: one part of the building jutted out further than the rest, and tucked into its side, at right angles to the street, was a small doorway set into a porch with glass bricks. The effect was like a squat Tardis growing out of the wall.

I didn't give myself any more time to think, just pushed open the door and stepped inside. The room was small, painted white. A counter backed by a glass screen took up the whole of one end. There were no posters or leaflets, just a metal bench pushed up against one wall. It didn't look like the kind of place anyone would come by choice.

I stepped up to the counter, assuming my most professional air. The man sitting behind it was dressed in uniform, a shirt with epaulettes. He was staring at a computer screen and didn't look up. I waited, resisting the temptation to drum my fingers on the counter.

Eventually he turned his head. 'Yes?'

'I'd like to see Detective Emma Willis-Jones,' I said. There was a tremor in my voice. I cleared my throat and tried again. 'It's in connection with a former case of hers.'

'A former case?' He raised one doubtful eyebrow. 'Do you have an appointment?'

'No, but she'll want to see me,' I said, sounding more confident than I felt. You always have to remember, eighty per cent of communication is tone of voice.

The second eyebrow rose to join the first. 'Will she indeed?' He tapped away at his keyboard. Did he even know if she was on the premises? I wondered. Maybe she wasn't based there – I'd been acting on the assumption that with Chantelle in Deptford, the detective assigned to the case would be bound to work in this gargantuan building, but too late it occurred to me that she might be somewhere else entirely.

More tapping and a pause while he read something on the screen. He could have been looking at eBay for all I knew. 'And what's the case you want to talk to her about?'

I swallowed. 'I'd rather not say.'

He looked at me then, a long stare of the kind I imagined might have served him well in other encounters. I didn't break the silence. 'Right,' he said, 'well, I'll need your name.'

Behind me, the door crashed open. I swung around, half expecting to see Ian there; but it was a woman, white-faced and furious. I stepped out of her way as she steamed up to the counter.

'I've been mugged,' she announced. 'Some fucker's stolen my phone.'

'If you'll just wait your turn, madam,' the desk sergeant said.

'Did you hear me, mate? I've been mugged!'

It was as if she'd snapped me out of a trance. What was I doing there? What could I tell them? That I'd heard Ian playing music and watching porn and all of a sudden I knew he was guilty? I'd never get to see Emma Willis-Jones; she probably wasn't even in the office. And even if she was, she'd have moved on, be wrapped up in other cases. She wouldn't care about this one any more. She wouldn't have *time* to care.

'What are you lot even *here* for?' the woman was shouting.

'I need to ask you to calm down . . .'

I turned away and made for the door.

I stood on the landing outside the flat for a long time, holding the key in the lock, listening. I couldn't hear anything from the other side – no music, no muffled sound of the television. I'd sent Ian a text when I'd left the police station, telling him I'd had to go back to work, saying I'd be back late. His response had been brusque: *Wish you'd told me earlier. Haven't eaten.*

There'd been another one half an hour later, while I was sitting in a crappy pub on the high street, halfway down my second glass of wine. *Going to bed.*

I made myself respond to that one: it was important he didn't realise anything was wrong. *Home soon*, I typed, *I'll try not to wake you. Xx*

From behind me I could hear the rumble of the television in the flat opposite. For the first time ever it was a comfort; there were other people nearby.

I counted to five to steady my breathing and turned the key.

The flat was in darkness. I reached for the switch, hearing the blood thudding in my ears, and felt the relief as the yellow light flooded the hallway. It's primeval, isn't it, to fear the dark? But that wasn't what I feared most.

I tiptoed towards the living room, knowing as soon as I entered that he wasn't there. The laptop was back in its usual position on the table. Had he wiped the browsing history? I wondered. I should check – I'd do it in the morning.

In the kitchen, a dirty plate and glass sat in the bottom of the sink. It was a silent reproach; Ian usually washed up and put things away. I'd always assumed he was a neat freak, but perhaps he was just conscious of the precariousness of his position, wanting to keep on my good side while I could offer him higher-quality lodging than Sean's sofa. Perhaps R, whoever she was, had started to look like a better deal.

I didn't know anything about him, I thought. *I really didn't have a clue.*

The door to the bedroom was shut tight, and I went to the bathroom to wash and clean my teeth, putting off the moment when I'd have to go in there. I'd considered sleeping on the sofa – the thought of lying next to Ian made the hairs rise on the back of my neck – but that would prompt questions and I wasn't sure I had it in me to be sufficiently convincing. Not yet anyway.

I stared into the mirror above the sink. I didn't look any different – a little tightness around the mouth, perhaps, a certain pallor to my cheeks, but nothing that would be spotted by anyone who didn't know me well. And who, after all, fell into that category?

Later, I lay on the very edge of the bed, my back to Ian, trying to escape the warmth of his body. My eyes were open, and if I'd been looking, I would have been able to make out the grey square of the window, the shadow of the wardrobe, the dark mass of the chair where I'd dropped my clothes as I undressed. But I wasn't looking. I was making a plan.

Chapter 29

'I'm planning to take some holiday.'

'Oh, right. Sounds good.' I watched Alan struggle to look unconcerned. 'You know I'll be away the half-term week, don't you?'

'I'd assumed as much.' I pretended to consult my BlackBerry. 'I thought I might take November.'

Alan's jaw fell open. 'All of it?'

'I have a lot of time owing.' I shot him a sidelong look. 'I'm sure you can cope.'

He cleared his throat. 'Is this anything to do with . . . ?'

'No,' I said. 'It's nothing to do with that at all.'

Kellie drove just the kind of car you'd imagine: a pastel-blue Fiat with cream-coloured upholstery and the clincher – a sticker on the back claiming it was 'powered by fairy dust'. In the early days I'm embarrassed to say I spent more time than I should have in the café across the road from Aidan's flat, watching for the two of them going in and out. Usually they were in Aidan's car – that was before its customisation, of course – but now and again she must have persuaded him to take hers, and I'd see the two of them driving past, Aidan squashed into the passenger seat like one of those clowns in a box.

I found out all kinds of things about Kellie during that period. I won't go into details about how; I fear it doesn't reflect well on me. Let's just say that a combination of persistence and a willingness to spend a bit of money will get you a surprisingly long way. I suppose you might be wondering why I bothered. It was simple: at the time, I believed there had to be a reason for what Aidan had done, that if I knew enough about Kellie I'd be able to make sense of it, understand why he'd chosen her over me. I worked out in the end that there didn't need to be a reason: Aidan was like one of those climbers who talk about Everest; Kellie was just *there*.

But like they say, knowledge is never wasted. Wednesday evenings used to be Kellie's Zumba class, held in what had once been a church hall in Greenwich. She'd always driven there, presumably preferring to sit for twice as long on the clogged roads as suffer the indignity of getting the train. I only hoped she hadn't changed her routine.

I'd spent the previous week prepping for this, taking one last, lingering look at my old exchanges with Aidan before deleting them all. I composed a fresh message and read it back; it looked less strange than the last one I'd tried, the evening I was waiting for Helen in the pub. Perhaps it had just taken time to get used to the idea.

I pressed send.

I added a few more over the coming days. Inevitably, Aidan's replies hadn't been quite right, but I thought they'd do for a quick read – I wasn't going to be letting Kellie take a printout, after all. And I didn't seriously want Aidan to be blamed; not in the end, anyway. Not in a deprivation-of-liberty sort of way. I just wanted him to be made to sweat a little, one last parting gift to remember me by.

The car park was busy and at first I didn't see the Fiat; but I didn't panic. I walked each row methodically and on the third pass I found it, tucked out of sight next to a jeep twice its size. I took the note from my handbag, read it one last time, then folded it twice and slipped it under her windscreen wiper.

Then I walked back to the coffee shop to wait.

'I know things have been difficult lately,' I said.

I felt Ian shift and I pressed my head more tightly to his shoulder so he couldn't see my face.

'What do you mean?' he said. He was always careful like that.

'I know I've been . . . off. I don't mean to be. It's just that things are tricky at work at the moment. I suppose I've been taking it out on you.'

On the television, a yellow cartoon chicken was engaged in a street fight with a fat man in green trousers. It was one of Ian's favourite shows.

'It's OK,' he said. 'I know you've been stressed.'

'I think we should go away. Take a few days together, just you and me.'

I felt the muscles of his neck tighten. 'You don't need to do that. I know how busy you are.'

'I want to,' I said, and before he could formulate more excuses, 'I want to make it up to you.'

The chicken had punched the man and he'd fallen into the middle of the road. A lorry was bearing down on him, blaring its horn.

'It'll be my treat,' I said.

* * *

I could tell Stella had been surprised when I rang – it's not a thing I do, even though we'd had something of a detente since the babysitting episode. She'd phoned me a couple of times since, the first time ostensibly to thank me and check I'd got home OK; the second – hoping, no doubt, to have softened me up – to reprise the subject of the Hawking book. 'I know it's upsetting to think of selling Mum's things, Natalie,' she'd wheedled, 'but we both know she'd have made special provision in her will if she'd realised what it was worth.' I told her I'd think about it.

It was a couple of weeks later that I made a call of my own, offering my babysitting services once again. She seemed pleased and it took only a moment for her to agree that yes, it would be lovely for her and Michael to have a night out. 'Ooh, date night!' she'd trilled in a way that set my teeth on edge.

Michael hadn't, I felt, displayed quite the same enthusiasm when I arrived on their doorstep; he had the air of a man concerned that someone, somewhere was getting one over on him, though he couldn't quite work out how. Maybe he's brighter than he looks. He didn't have a chance to quiz me, however: Stella was bundling him out of the front door and into a cab faster than you could say 'Brief History of Time'.

I went straight up to Evie's room. She was asleep again – she really is the most tranquil child – and I stood and watched her for a while. My previous stint chez Wainwright had given me more confidence in my childminding abilities, and after a few minutes I bent down and stroked her cheek. She snuffled, and one little fist uncurled like a starfish. I placed my finger across her palm and she clutched it, apparently on reflex, surprisingly strong for one so small. I wondered if she'd wake up, but she settled again so I left her and went to Stella and Michael's room.

It wasn't quite as tidy as it had been on my last visit. One of Michael's jackets lay across the arm of a chair, a tie draped over its back. In the corner of the room the sleeve of a shirt dangled from the top of the laundry basket as if signalling for help. Perhaps they'd tidied up before I came last time, expecting me to go snooping. It seemed I'd already got to the stage where familiarity had bred contempt.

A glossy brochure lay on the floor next to Stella's side of the bed – so she did read something after all. I went over and inspected it: *St Ursula's Preparatory School. Outstanding education in a caring environment.*

I flicked through the pages until I found the fees, and winced. This must be what was behind Stella's sudden interest in the value of Mum's books. Looking at those figures, I was surprised she hadn't been back to inventory the lot.

I replaced the brochure and wandered to the other side of the bed. *Good Strategy/Bad Strategy* was still on the bedside table. Maybe it wasn't the roller-coaster read Michael had been hoping for. I picked it up and turned idly to the contents page. *Discovering power,* I read, *Using leverage.* I smiled and put it back, careful to replace it at just the right angle.

I turned to the wardrobe and opened it, kneeling on the carpet so I could see properly to punch in the numbers on the safe. I checked through the contents, but there was nothing new. I took what I needed, tucking it into the back pocket of my jeans, and closed everything up again. When I got to my feet, my heart was thudding and I had to rest my hand on the frame of the wardrobe and take deep breaths. *Calm down,* I told myself. *This is the easy part.*

When I felt better, I checked the wardrobe again, wanting to be sure I'd left no sign of my presence, no stray hair clinging to a shirtsleeve, no accidental failure to re-lock the safe. I knew they'd discover Stella's missing passport eventually, put it all together, but there was no need to make it easy for them.

I needn't have worried. There was nothing out of place. Just one more thing to do.

At the dressing table I stooped to open the bottom drawer. There it was, just as I'd left it; Stella probably didn't open it from one year to the next.

I lifted out the jewellery box and sat cross-legged with it on the floor. My fingertips brushed across the lacquer, feeling the bumps in the surface that were the edge of the house and the little tree. I opened the lid and took out the items one by one, weighing each one in my hand before placing it on the carpet. When they were all spread out around me, I turned the jewellery box upside down and found the tiny metal bar. One twist, two, and half again. 'Clair de Lune'. I'd always loved that music.

I lifted up the pendants and the watch, the earrings and the brooches, savouring the feel of them, half remembering, half imagining when Mum had worn them. When I'd finished with them, I laid them to rest in their silk-lined casket. The cross and chain I left until last. I didn't have the right skin tone for gold; it looked garish against the palm of my hand.

I could take it, I thought. It doesn't mean anything to Stella. And it might be a comfort in the days ahead, surrounded by unfamiliar things. There was nothing to identify who it had belonged to, nothing to tie it to the mother of a woman called Natalie Wright. It wouldn't be dangerous.

I hung the chain around my fingertips and held it to the light. The cross turned slowly from side to side. 'Clair de Lune' tinkled to a close. I folded my other hand around it and placed it gently back in the jewellery box.

Later, after Stella had rung to tell me she was on her way back ('Traffic's been *deadly*, we've been in this cab for *hours*'), I tiptoed back into Evie's room to say goodbye. She looked so peaceful, that feathery hair gently hugging the curve of her scalp. I couldn't help myself: I bent down and lifted her gently, remembering to cradle her head in the palm of my hand the way the books said was important.

She made a faint clucking noise and wriggled in my arms. She was heavier than she looked. I took the seat in the corner of the room; this must be where Stella nursed her if she woke in the night. Her head rested against the crook of my arm, just as it must do against Stella's. Perhaps she'd wake and start to cry, appalled to find it wasn't her mother holding her. I shifted her on my lap, waiting for those translucent eyelids to flicker and reveal her silver-penny eyes. 'It's all right, Evie,' I whispered, 'it's your Auntie Natalie.'

The wriggling stopped and she slept on, a soft, warm bundle in my arms. Trust Stella to have produced a baby that slept soundly through the night. Maybe if things had been different with Aidan . . .

I stopped the thought before it was formed. Enough of this. I got to my feet and carried Evie back to her cot.

I'd just hit the sofa when I heard the cab chug to a stop outside. I'd planned to leave as soon as Stella and Michael returned, but when I went to get my jacket from the hall stand, I found that instead of slipping it from its hook, I was taking Stella's passport from my jeans and tucking it into the inside pocket. Then I headed for the kitchen and took three cups from a cupboard.

From the hallway came the sound of a key turning in the lock. I stuck my head around the door frame. 'Evening, all,' I said in an attempt at jollity. 'Anyone for tea?'

Stella paused in kicking off her shoes. 'Oh! I thought you'd want to be off.'

I shrugged. 'There's always time for tea.'

Over her shoulder I could see her surprise mirrored on Michael's face. 'Smashing,' he said, though his tone suggested it was anything but.

Another time it would have made me smile, watching them trying to hide their disappointment that they wouldn't immediately have their house to themselves. For some reason, that night it didn't have the same effect. 'I can go now if you want,' I said. 'If you're tired.'

'Of course we don't want you to go!' Stella smiled, and I was surprised at the little bubble of warmth that formed in my chest. *She's my sister after all*, I thought. *Despite everything, she's the only one I've got.*

She had turned away and was taking off her coat. 'It's just that Michael has to be up early in the morning . . .'

I pushed past her and grabbed my jacket.

'Natalie, wait – no need to rush off. We'll call you a cab . . .'

I already had the door open. 'Goodbye,' I said.

I didn't turn around, but I could feel them watching me as I walked down the path. It wasn't until I heard the front door shut that I raised my hand and brushed away the moisture on my cheeks.

Chapter 30

The office grapevine had been buzzing with rumours about my boss, Fiona, for a while. Apparently she was leaving the department, taking up some consultancy role. I'd been too busy to spend much time considering what it would mean for me, but when I saw the email from her PA inviting me to an early-morning meeting, I felt a surge of excitement. I was the obvious choice to cover her post, and perhaps if I played my cards right – which of course I would – it would turn into a permanent appointment. The money would be nice, of course, but that wasn't what I wanted. You won't find a more hierarchical system than the civil service – it was part of the reason I liked it – and another rung up the ladder meant more than a pay rise. It meant acknowledgement of my intellect. It meant respect.

I arrived at Fiona's office at 8.30 on the dot. Her PA wasn't in yet, so I went straight to the door and knocked (another of the trappings of power – an actual office, rather than a desk in the middle of the open-plan). She looked up from her screen with a frown. 'Natalie, please take a seat.'

There was something in the way she said it; the excitement I'd felt on my way there was replaced by a vague sense of unease.

'I've called you here because we've had a complaint,' she said.

I stared at her dumbly. Surely Alan hadn't found out about the credit card? Even if he'd spotted the order, realised someone had used his card, there was nothing to trace it to me. I'd been so careful . . .

'From DEFRA,' she said.

I laughed; surely not those godforsaken pesticides? I stopped when I saw the look on her face. 'I see. So what's their problem?'

She picked up a sheet of paper from the desk in front of her. 'Perhaps it would be best if you read it yourself.'

I took it from her. It was a printout of an email. I scanned it, my eyes snagging on particular phrases: *obstructive . . . discourteous . . . lost the confidence of the minister.* That last one caused me a moment's panic until I realised who they meant. Elliot Marsden, of course. It was that stupid pet project of his, the draft consultation document I'd emailed DEFRA officials to say was unacceptable. It should have been Alan delivering that message, of course, but I remembered it now – volunteering to do it for him so I could use his computer to search for information on unlocking Ian's phone. And now here I was having to deal with the aftermath.

'I see,' I said again. 'So Marsden is throwing his toys out of the pram because he hasn't got what he wanted.'

'I wouldn't put it like that.' She fixed me with a stare. 'You do realise who Marsden's spad is?'

I had no idea, but whatever the answer was I was suddenly certain it wasn't good news.

'Tricia Gould,' she said. A pause for it to sink in. '*Gould.*'

As in Daniel Gould, Fiona's boss. How could I have missed that? Still, I wasn't going down without a fight. 'Private office were clear that the minister agreed with our advice,' I said. 'That draft consultation was—'

'Tendentious rubbish?' Fiona broke in, and I flushed. They were the words I'd used in my email. 'I'm afraid Tricia didn't take too kindly to your description.'

She'd asked another deputy director to take over liaising with DEFRA on the consultation, she said, and had the grace to look embarrassed when I asked who. I'd known it would be a man – Tricia Gould was well known to have a problem working with women, even those who weren't *obstructive* or *discourteous* – but Craig Wormington? An official so wet you could wring him out and use him to clean your bathtub? DEFRA were going to walk all over us.

I left the office white-faced and tight-lipped with humiliation. Fiona had suggested I tell people the change was to even out workloads, but I knew there was no point. Alan was on the phone to his opposite number in DEFRA every five minutes these days – he'd know the real story by the time the day was out. And to have to watch him creeping to Wormington . . .

Back in the flat that evening, I turned the pages of *In Plain Sight*, looking up now and again to where Ian lolled on the sofa, the remote control in one outstretched hand. He hadn't commented on my early return from work, hadn't asked if I was all right.

No, I thought, *I won't miss him. And I won't miss that bloody job either.*

Chapter 31

Ian hadn't wanted to take the trip. It was obvious as soon as I mentioned the idea of a holiday that the last thing he felt like doing was being alone with me for days at a stretch. I wondered if he'd talked about it with the mysterious R, reassured her that it would be the last time. It made me nervous not to know, a variable I couldn't control; but it wasn't going to stop me doing what needed to be done.

The drive to the cottage was a long one, the road framed on either side by towering firs, a mountain rising up ahead of us clad in the same dark green. I felt like I was in a film.

'You're too close to the edge!'

'Sorry,' I said, 'I don't think I've got used to the car yet.'

I'd considered renting something glamorous, the kind of car Aidan would have loved, red and shiny and impractical. Ian would probably have loved it too, but this wasn't the trip for that kind of vehicle. Instead I'd hired a grey four-by-four, the kind that no one would give a second glance – especially not up here, where every third car seemed to look the same.

'It's breathtaking, isn't it?' I said. It was part of my reason for choosing Scotland. I wanted us to have something beautiful to look at. Something to set against all the ugliness.

'Watch out for the bend!'

I took my foot off the accelerator and eased into the turn. 'It's fine, Ian,' I said. 'Calm down.' The road opened up again, dark with the shadows of the firs. 'We'll be there soon.'

Aite Sìth was a low, square building on the shore of one of those long spits of land that hang down from the west of Scotland, clinging to the mainland in defiance of their future island status. I'd had to give up on the sat nav and follow the instructions from the website for the last few miles, Ian hunched frowning over the crumpled paper. He'd been sulking since he'd mocked me for being a technophobe who insisted on printing everything out, only to find that his mobile reception had failed before we'd even left the main road.

'It can't really be down here,' he'd said as we'd turned into the narrow rutted lane. Yet two miles on – two miles during which I silently congratulated myself on the choice of the four-by-four – the road came to an abrupt end and there it was.

The drizzle that had blighted the last hour of our journey was gone and the sun glowed on the white paintwork of the tiny cottage overlooking the sea. I got out of the car and breathed the crisp air, sweet with salt and evergreens. I turned to Ian, arms spread out. 'Isn't it beautiful?'

He looked doubtful. 'Bit isolated, isn't it?'

I found the key underneath a stone (Ian: 'No key safe? Seriously?') and walked through the cottage while Ian fetched the bags from the car. It was low-ceilinged, the walls lined with wood – pine, perhaps from the trees covering the slopes of the mountain behind. They cast their shadow across the rooms, keeping them dark in spite of the sunshine outside.

'Can you give me a hand?' Ian stood in the doorway to the kitchen, laden with cases. I took the cool bag from him.

'I'll put the kettle on,' I said.

Later we sat at the window of the small living room and watched a heron pick its delicate way through the shallows. Ian's foot tap-tap-tapped against the floor. 'Christ, it's quiet here,' he said.

'Aite Sìth,' I replied. 'It means place of peace.'

'Sounds like a fucking graveyard,' he said. Then, 'Sorry. I'm just not used to places like this.'

I watched him out of the corner of my eye. 'I thought it would be good for us,' I said. 'Get us away from everything. From everyone else.'

He blinked, bit his lip as if to stop himself replying. *No, I thought, probably not the right time for that. He'll wait until we're ready to go, tell me this break has given him the chance to think things through. Made everything clearer.*

'It's raining again,' he said.

I'd planned to encourage him on a walk. I thought it would be better, more natural somehow. I wasn't sure how I was going to do it even then. Odd, I know, for someone who plans things the way I do, but it's true. I couldn't think about it. I would work up to it, imagining each preparatory step, the things I'd do and say; and then afterwards, the return to London, beginning a new life. But in the middle there was nothing, a great white blank. It didn't matter. I trusted myself. I was sure that when it came to it, I'd know what to do.

The weather kept us inside. Ian laid a fire that sputtered in the grate and coughed black smoke into the room. ('The wood's damp,' I told him. 'Everything's damp,' he said.) I sat at a table facing the wall and worked on a jigsaw I'd found in one of the cupboards. It showed a photograph of the cottage, the water sparkling in front, a blue sky hung above the deep green of the pines. It was more difficult than it looked but I kept picking up the pieces, turning them this way and that until the picture began to form.

That night in bed I felt the warmth of him near me, the weight on what had become his side of the mattress. It was the same side as he slept on at the flat, where sometimes he'd turn, still slumbering, and drape a heavy arm across my body. The same side he'd slithered from in the darkness to shut himself in my bathroom and giggle down the phone at R. The same side he'd laid on when he put his hand on my throat and refused to tell me what he'd done to Chantelle.

I climbed on top of him and kissed him hard, biting his lip. 'What's all this?' he said, amused; so I bit him harder. When I pulled back, I saw his eyes were squeezed shut, probably imagining I was her. I rolled away.

'Are you OK, babe?' he said, sounding confused.

I didn't answer.

It was the week before we went to Scotland and I'd spent all morning wondering if Kellie would answer my summons. I needn't have worried: she couldn't resist. Curiosity is the mother of invention – no, that's not right. Invention is the mother of curiosity; that's how it went that day, anyway.

She was clutching my note in one pink-taloned hand as she stormed into the coffee shop. She'd crumpled it up and then thought better of it; I could see the network of creases across its surface. People looked up from their lattes as she stomped past, following her trajectory in anticipation. She came to a halt in front of my table, quivering in fury.

'What the fuck,' she hissed, holding my note at the level of her nose, 'is *this*?'

'I'm so glad you're here.' I resisted the temptation to stand up and tell the gawpers to mind their own business. 'I was worried you wouldn't come.'

'Like I said,' she waved the paper, 'what the *fuck* is this?'

'Please, Kellie, I'll tell you everything,' I said. 'Just sit down for five minutes and I'll tell you what I should have told you long ago.'

I could see she was torn: sitting down felt like giving in, but she wanted to know what I was talking about. She pulled out a seat.

'Five minutes,' she said. It seemed that was all anyone was prepared to give me these days.

I'd been uncertain whether to play her the recording there and then. I didn't think she was the type to get violent, but I was nevertheless concerned about the possibility of some physical reaction – ripping out the headphones in a frenzy, perhaps, treating the entire coffee shop to the sounds of Aidan and me in flagrante. And though I'd always imagined the moment with a thrill of *Schadenfreude*, now that it was so close, I wasn't entirely sure I wanted to see Kellie's face when she heard those words. I didn't want a reminder of what I'd felt the day I'd walked in on her and Aidan. I couldn't afford to feel sorry for her; she still had work to do.

Instead I said, 'I know Aidan didn't show you my texts.'

I watched her brow crinkle then smooth again, as she realised I was watching for a reaction. 'I didn't need to see them.'

'I realised that when you came around,' I continued. 'You would never have said what you did if you'd known what was really going on.' I handed her the phone. 'Don't read them all. You don't need to do that.'

She snatched it from my hand, and I frowned as I watched her scan the words; she was scrolling down too quickly to be taking anything in.

'All I wanted was for him to leave me alone,' I said. 'You can see that, can't you?'

Of course she could. I'd made sure my messages, at least, were unambiguous: *Please stop threatening me . . . You're making me really scared . . . If you don't stop, I'm going to the police . . .*

She was scrolling back to the top. 'The first of these is dated two weeks ago,' she said and threw the phone back onto the tabletop. 'That doesn't make any sense.'

I nodded. 'I know, I know it looks odd. The truth is, I was deleting them until a couple of weeks ago. They were horrible, Kellie.' I looked down at the table. 'Why would I want to keep things like that? I only changed my mind because I thought they might help you see what he was really like.'

'This is such crap.' She looked around as if about to ask someone else's opinion. 'I don't know why I'm here. You're such a liar. Aidan always said you were a liar.'

I nodded. 'Of course he did. He was trying to make sure you'd never listen to a word I said. I told him he should tell you himself, but he wouldn't. So I said I'd do it, that it was only right. That's when he . . .'

It had taken a moment, but that amphibious brain was beginning to stir into life. She sat up straighter. 'Tell me what?'

I lowered my eyes, bit my lip. I said softly, 'We slept together, Kellie. After you thought we'd broken up.'

She went white, but there wasn't any screaming. She tried to say she didn't believe it, but I could see straight away that was a lie. She'd been the other woman, after all; she knew what Aidan was capable of.

'The thing is,' I said earnestly, 'I'm not sure how it happened. I had a new phone and there are all these functions . . . It was an accident, you have to believe that.' I took a breath and looked her in the eye. 'But there's a recording.'

And that was when she walked out.

I followed her onto the street, pushing past the grey-haired woman at the next table, ignoring her delighted stare. Kellie had taken off at a rate of knots, and I started to run to catch up with her; but then she changed her mind, strode back towards me, her jaw set. I thought she was going to hit me, but instead she stopped an arm's length away.

'You're disgusting,' she spat. 'You disgust me.'

I felt a surge of fury. Lest we forget, *she* was the one who'd been shagging *my* fiancé. But I swallowed it down. I had to focus on what was important.

I said, 'I'm scared of him, Kellie. I'm scared for you.'

She took a step back at that, her mouth twisted. 'What are you talking about?'

'I told him you deserved the truth.' She snorted, but I pressed on. 'I said if he wouldn't tell you, I would. That's when it started.'

She didn't want to hear it, but she couldn't walk away. She said obediently, 'Started what?'

I swallowed. 'He's been stalking me. Sending me texts – threatening me. You saw the kind of thing.' I could see her struggling to recall the words, probably wishing now she'd paid more attention. 'I showed you them, Kellie,' I said. 'Remember that. I'm the one who showed you those texts, not Aidan. What does that tell you?'

She stared at me, her lip curled in a sneer; but I could see in her eyes that I had her. She said, 'If this is all true, why are you telling me now? Why not go straight to the police?'

'It's all right if you don't believe me,' I said. 'I wouldn't blame you. I just couldn't live with myself if I didn't warn you. Aidan and I were together once. He told me he loved me too. And now he's doing – *this.*' I flung out my arm, as if surrounded on every side by Aidan's iniquities. 'He's a dangerous man. That's why I haven't been to the police, Kellie. I'm afraid of what he'd do.'

She snorted again then. I mean, *honestly.* What if I really had been trying to warn her about a violent boyfriend? There's no helping some people.

'We're finished here,' she said.

'I can see that. Just be careful of him, Kellie. I can stay away from him, but you live under the same roof.' I made sure I had eye contact when I delivered my killer line. 'I don't want to wake up one day and find you've just disappeared.'

Chapter 32

'Looks like it's finally stopped raining,' I said.

Ian looked up from his book. It was about lighthouse keepers, stories told by the men who'd done the job in the days before it was automated. He'd found it in the bookcase at the cottage and every so often he'd read a bit to me. He'd never have looked at something like that at home; I took that as a good sign.

'Let's get some air,' I said. 'Get our bearings.'

Outside, Ian walked on ahead, scrunching over the pebbles to the edge of the water, while I stood at the entrance to the porch and tried to do up my walking boots. It seemed to take an age. My fingers were trembling.

When I caught up with him, he pointed into the distance. 'Let's stick to the beach and see how far round it goes.'

There was a different quality to the air there, something old and heavy. It seemed to dampen the noise so that the crunch of the pebbles beneath our feet, the call of a seabird, even the low swoosh of the wavelets breaking on the shore, came to us as if muffled through glass. After a while we stopped talking and just stared at the view, the silver water that merged with the sky, the distant grey smudge that was the isle of Arran.

At one point Ian said, 'You're right, it is beautiful,' and the small part of me that remembered how I'd come close to caring for him felt both happy and sad.

We'd been walking for an hour or so when I told him I needed to stop: the old pebble-in-the-shoe routine. He sat next to me on a low flat rock while I unlaced my boot and pretended to tip it out. 'All set?' he said.

'Shall we stop for a while?' I said. 'Let's just take it all in.'

We sat there looking out to the horizon. The tide was out and the pebbles in front of the rock were small and round, shining with water. Ian picked one up and flung it out to sea. The waves barely disturbed the surface and it bounced once, twice, before disappearing from view.

'There's something I need to tell you,' I said. Something in my voice made Ian pause in his search for another pebble. 'I went to your old gym.'

His eyebrows knitted together. 'What?' he said. 'In Deptford?'

I took a breath, then another; I thought about backing out. 'I know, Ian,' I said.

'What are you talking about?' There was an edge to his voice now. 'What do you know?'

I swallowed. *Say the words*. 'I know you didn't go to the gym after you left Chantelle.' He didn't say anything, so I carried on. 'I checked the signing-in book and I know you didn't go that day.'

'Jesus Christ.'

'Why did you lie about it?'

'Jesus fucking Christ!'

'Just tell me, Ian, tell me where you were . . .' He was on his feet, walking away. 'Ian!' I shouted. 'For once, just tell me the truth!'

I was running after him, but he stopped abruptly and I almost cannoned into his back. He swivelled to face me. 'What do you want me to say, Natalie?' The edges of his lips were white. 'You don't want the truth. I've told you the truth. I've told you again and again, and you won't believe it.'

I shook my head. 'I saw the signing-in book. Your name wasn't there.'

'And that means I'm a liar, does it?' He grabbed my arm and shook it. 'You think I did it, don't you? You think I'm a fucking rapist!'

I forced myself not to pull back. 'Are you?'

He pushed me away in disgust. 'How can you ask that?' He started walking, then turned back again. 'All that bullshit when we met, all that rubbish about how you knew I was innocent, you never doubted me . . . And you have the gall to call *me* a liar!'

'You have to tell me,' I said again. 'I won't go to the police. I just have to know what happened.'

'What kind of a sick bitch are you? What kind of sicko sleeps with a man she thinks is a rapist?'

I flinched. 'I had to know . . .'

'This is never going to stop, is it?' He was pacing now, back and forth along the shoreline. 'You're never going to let it drop.'

'I know you lied!'

'I went to the fucking gym!' He screamed it at me, his hands balled into fists. 'I don't know why my name isn't in the book!'

He was so convincing, stomping around the beach in fury. For a moment I almost believed him.

'Maybe it was in a different book, or maybe someone ripped out the page . . . I probably just forgot. That's it! I probably just forgot to sign in.'

I said quietly, 'I know you're a liar, Ian. You lie all the time.'

'I do *what* now?' He stared back at me, all outraged innocence. And I'd thought I was good at acting.

I said, 'I saw you watching that film. I saw you listening to that song. I know about R.'

He turned away, but he wasn't quick enough; I saw the flash of consciousness in his eyes. For a second he didn't say anything. Then he looked me right in the face and said, 'I think you've got problems, Natalie. I haven't got a fucking clue what you're talking about.'

He started heading back the way we'd come. 'I'm off,' he said.

I watched his back, his broad shoulders as he walked away. He thought he could get away with it, I realised; he thought he could treat me like a fool and just leave.

Not again, I thought. *This isn't happening again.*

I was right about one thing at least: when the moment came, I knew what to do.

There was a lot of blood. It's common with head wounds, apparently. I'd been running when I hit him, and I suppose it multiplied the force of the blow. He'd heard me coming, my shoes sliding on the stony shore. It's possible too that I cried out; I don't remember clearly. He was turning towards me as I reached him, and the rock that was somehow in my hand struck him on the temple.

There was a crack, much louder than you'd expect, and he just sort of crumpled. I could see at once that it was conclusive. Like I said, there was a lot of blood. It was running down the side of his head in rivulets, staining the pebbles. His face was already grey. I didn't want to look at it, but I did. I took off my jacket and folded it over and placed it beneath his head. He was making noises, mumbling something. I bent close to him.

'It's all right, Ian,' I said. 'Stay still. Everything will be all right now.'

He tried to reach up, as if to pull me closer. His lips were still moving, so I put my ear to them. I could just make out the words. 'I'm sorry,' he said. 'Tell Chantelle I'm sorry.'

Chapter 33

Everything is ready.

I've cleaned the flat and emptied the fridge, just as I did in Scotland. There are probably traces of Ian all over the place, but I'm not worried about that. I just want everything neat and tidy. And I don't like the idea of leaving food rotting behind me, turning to stinking brown mush, milk curdling in the fridge. It savours of metaphor.

I've stripped the bed. The sheets – the ones he lay on – have gone. If I could have done it without drawing attention, I'd have burned them. I removed the knife from beneath the mattress and the phone from behind the sink, scrubbed away the sticky remnants of the masking tape.

I've disposed of the few things he left here. It didn't take long; I suppose he was mentally already halfway out of the door. There was nothing among them to give any clue as to who R was. I suppose now I'll never know. She's probably wondering already why he hasn't been in touch, why he hasn't returned her calls. Let her wonder.

Outside it is still light and I look at my watch. Three o'clock. Plenty of time. I look for my jacket. It should be on the hook beside the door; but then I see it draped across the sofa. I must have dropped it there, distracted, when I returned from the last of my errands.

It hadn't gone the way I'd expected.

The walk from the bus stop was familiar by then, the ugliness of the dilapidated shopfronts and the cracked pavements almost welcoming. It wouldn't be like this where I was going, I imagined; the thought pulled at something in my chest.

This time, a woman with a buggy was struggling with the door to Fairfield House. I hurried down the path to help her, and when she smiled and thanked me, my throat closed up and I couldn't reply. She looked as if she might ask if I was all right – I'm not sure what I would have said if she had – but then she seemed to change her mind and disappeared into a flat on the ground floor.

There wasn't a bell on the door of Chantelle's flat, and too late I realised I should have buzzed from the front door. I knocked instead and waited. There was a spyhole in front of me, I saw. Would she open up when she saw who it was or pretend there was no one in?

The door swung open, then stopped, held in place by a chain. Chantelle peered through the gap.

'What are you doing here?' There was an edge to her voice. 'You said you wouldn't come back.'

'No,' I said, with an attempt at a smile. 'I said I wouldn't come back if I didn't have good news.'

I saw her eyes narrow at that.

'Can I come in?' I said. 'It's important.'

She stepped back and let the chain off the door. I followed her inside and started to kick off my shoes before realising what I was doing. 'Stop,' I said. 'I don't need to sit down. This won't take long.'

She turned. There were no windows in the hallway and it was too dim to see her face. 'So what's the good news?' she said. 'Are they going to charge him again?'

I shook my head. 'I'm sorry. That's not going to be possible.'

'Then I don't know what—'

'You don't need to worry about Ian Nash any more.'

'Right.' She made a sound somewhere between a laugh and a sob. 'And you know that how? Got some mates to rough him up, have you?'

I didn't reply, and she said again, quieter this time, 'Have you?'

'Like I said, you don't need to worry about him any more. No one does.'

She raised a hand to her mouth. 'Jesus,' she breathed, 'what's happened?'

'It's better that you don't know. I just wanted you to understand – there's nothing to be afraid of now.' She was staring at me, not moving. I took her by the shoulders and gave her a little shake. 'You understand, don't you, Chantelle?'

She took a step away from me. 'What have you done?'

She was opposite a doorway now and the light from the room beyond fell on her face. 'I was responsible,' I said. 'I was responsible for letting him out, and now I've dealt with him. He can't hurt you again.'

Her eyes were wide. 'He's . . . ?' She trailed off and put her hand to her mouth again. Something cold uncurled in the pit of my stomach. 'Oh Jesus,' she said. 'Oh Jesus, he—'

'Don't!' I held up a trembling finger. 'Don't you say another word.'

I opened the door and left her there, her hand still clasped over her mouth.

My bag is packed, Stella's passport tucked into the front pocket

(I've dyed my hair, but I'm banking on no one looking too closely at a thirty-eight-year-old white woman in sensible shoes). I'm not taking much: a few clothes, some pre-paid mobile phones, Visa and Amex gift cards – bought with cash, invaluable for online purchases – and a couple of books. (You didn't really think I'd leave the Hawking for Stella, did you?)

I've watered the dragon tree. I'm going to leave it outside the downstairs flat, the one where the old lady lives. I've put it in a new, expensive pot and bought a thank-you card to go with it, though of course I didn't write anything inside. I think she'll take care of it – it's a beautiful plant, after all. People love beautiful things.

As for this . . . what to call it? Confession? No, testimony, that's a better word. It's a risk leaving it behind, I know that. I know it would be safer just to go, take my head start and leave them all wondering. Not that many people will waste their time on that – my disappearance may create a passing flutter, no more. I can hear the description now: *out of character.* And then after a while they'll conclude that perhaps they didn't really know my character at all; that there's always been a certain reserve, a degree of guardedness; Alan shaking his head and saying, 'Natalie always played her cards close to her chest.' Never one to pass up an opportunity for a cliché, is our Alan. I won't miss him.

People who advise on this kind of thing – and there are such people, I know that now – would tell me that it's stupid. They'd warn me that a written account is creating a link between my past and my future, a link that doesn't need to be there. They'd tell me I need to let it all go.

I understand that. But this is a calculated risk. Because what was the point of any of it if I leave behind more questions? What if in a year or so another judge fixes his beady gaze on twelve good men and true and tells them what a simple task they have before them? That all they need to do is be sure? Take it from me, it's not as easy as it sounds.

So I'm posting this to my solicitor – I've told him it's to be opened alongside my will, but I expect the police will get there first. A mysterious package delivered a day or two after my disappearance? They won't be able to resist that. The solicitor is an obdurate old boot, though, I've made sure of that – he'll make them work for it. By the time they get their hands on this, I'll be long gone. And if, by any chance, the police are as shoddy in my case as they were in Chantelle's and fail to follow up the proof of postage left on my coffee table, I'm confident Stella will be demanding death certificates and will readings with indecent haste. It won't be easy, but hey – whatever else you can say about my sister, she's persistent if there's something in it for her (and Evie's outrageous school fees, of course). Aidan had just better hope she's successful.

I wonder how long it will be before the police come calling for him – he's my ex-fiancé, after all. Kellie will do the right thing then, I'm sure of it. She'll tell them about the texts now that the seeds have been planted. Aidan will have deleted them from his phone, no doubt, but the police have ways of retrieving these things. They'll have time to look more closely at the wording than Kellie was able to, of course. Time to see that the messages don't quite hang together. But it will be enough to make them ask some questions. Enough to make him sweat for a while until this little missive turns up. And Aidan, I hope, when the dust has settled and he's had time to reflect on what he's learned, will bring himself to be grateful to me in the end.

If you ever read these words, Aidan, remember this: I have been merciful. I could have hung you out to dry, but instead I've left you this gift, this absolution. And if, as I believe and trust, you've found yourself sitting for hours in some dingy interview suite, eyeballed by a hard-nosed, rosy-knuckled detective – a man, of course, someone who scares you, who doesn't believe your protestations of innocence – I want you to remember the lesson. You thought I was weak, but you were wrong. You thought you could hurt me and it wouldn't matter. As I said to you once before: you've brought this on yourself.

Ian's lesson was more painful, more final too. Will they find the body? I expect so, in the end. As he himself discovered, these things have a way of coming out in time. It won't be easy, though. I've made sure of that.

As for you, my unknown reader, you won't be hearing from me again. I've taken the necessary steps to ensure I won't be tracked down. The air tickets were bought online with Alan's credit card, two sets going in different directions, just as *In Plain Sight* advised. One was to Jordan, a little joke on my part; perhaps if anyone gets curious, they'll find out about my Arabic lessons and conclude I've run off to join Daesh. I won't use either of them, though. I'll be paying cash for where I'm going – and I'm sorry, but this is where my candour ends. I've told you all you need to know.

Well, all except one thing. I promised you the truth, and that's what I've given you – almost. There was one part that wasn't strictly accurate. It was the way I wish it had happened, but it didn't. There was no whispered confession, no plea for forgiveness. Ian gurgled and moaned at the end, but he was well past words by the time I'd finished with him. I had to make sure he wasn't getting up, you see; he was so much bigger than me, I wouldn't have had a chance. So after he'd gone down, I hit him again and again until he stopped moving.

I don't regret it. What choice did I have? I knew what he was, the things he'd done. I couldn't let him go unpunished.

That verdict was my responsibility. And now I've put it right.

Acknowledgements

I am very grateful to the many people who have helped bring this book to life.

First of all, to my brilliant editor, Hannah Wann, whose firm yet diplomatic challenges have improved it beyond measure. Also to Jane Selley for her eagle eye, to Sarah Murphy and Krystyna Green, and to everyone at Constable and Little, Brown. I am so thankful for your support and professionalism.

A huge thank you to all the friends, family and colleagues who've read drafts, offered advice and put up with stream-of-consciousness rambling and the occasional rant. Special thanks to my sister, Lisa Oyler. Thank you too to Melanie Sturtevant, Kathryn Thomas, Lisa Goll and Henry Tam. And to my lovely dad, who always remembers to ask how it's going, and knows how to tactfully drop the subject when the answer is 'not well'.

Thanks to everyone at the London Writers' Café, and to the warm and witty community of readers and writers on Twitter. And to Sophie Hannah and all the Dream Authors who've shared their thoughts and experiences. I've learned such a lot from you all.

Thank you to Dr Andrew H. Thomas, who wrote the *Hidden in Plain Sight* series of books on theoretical physics. Natalie couldn't have asked for a better title to conceal her escape manual!

To my beautiful Patsy, who keeps me smiling. And to my special girl, Poppy, who spent many hours curled at my feet while I wrote this book; I miss you very much.

And to my husband, Mark: for his patience, wisdom, love, and fine line in contemporary dance. I know how lucky I am.

Finally, and most importantly, to you, the reader: thank you for letting this story into your imagination. I'm more grateful than I can say.